lives in Norwich, where she teaches English at Norwich School. She is a graduate of the Creative Writing MA at the University of East Anglia. *Foxlowe* is her first novel.

'To read *Foxlowe* is not unlike wandering through Foxlowe itself on some long night: I felt never quite certain where the corridors would take me, nor whom I might meet on turning a corner; and in the final moments I found myself hurtling down a flight of steps into the dark'

SARAH PERRY, *Guardian*

'*Foxlowe* weaves a darkly disturbing Gothic spell in hypnotic and compelling prose' ESSIE FOX

'An engaging, uncomfortable, gripping and pretty darn chilling story of the power of manipulation and desperation to be loved. It is also a deft exploration of the psychology of brainwashing. I cannot recommend this book highly enough; whatever Wasserberg does next I will be rushing to read it' *Savidge Reads*

'Mesmerizing, gripping and beautifully written. It completely sweeps you up from beginning to end. I loved it'

KATE HAMER, author of *The Girl in the Red Coat*

'Wasserberg has a strong and distinctive voice and this is an excellent debut' CLARE MACKINTOSH, author of *I Let You Go*

'An extraordinary, astonishing story of a girl's longing for motherly love. Beautifully harrowing, and powerfully haunting, it is the most heartbreaking tale I have read this year' LIZ NUGENT, author of *Unravelling Oliver*

'I thoroughly enjoyed this vivid and claustrophobic coming-of-age debut' TASHA KAVANAGH, author of *Things We Have in Common*

'Dissonant, haunting and superbly atmospheric. An immensely subtle and profoundly affecting debut'
PARAIC O'DONNELL, author of *The Maker of Swans*

Foxlowe

ELEANOR WASSERBERG

4th ESTATE • *London*

4th Estate
An imprint of HarperCollins*Publishers*
1 London Bridge Street
London SE1 9GF
www.4thEstate.co.uk

First published in Great Britain by 4th Estate
This 4th Estate paperback edition published in 2017

3

Eleanor Wasserberg asserts the moral right to
be identified as the author of this work

A catalogue record for this book is
available from the British Library

ISBN 978-0-00-816410-2

Printed and bound in Great Britain by
Clays Ltd, St Ives plc

For my parents

Prologue

At Foxlowe everyone has two names. One is a secret, meant to be lost. For most, it worked like this: first they had the one they came to Foxlowe with peeled away like sunburnt skin. Then a new name, for a new life.

I used to get jealous of the Family with their secret outside names, while I only had the one, like half a person. Sometimes an old name would slip, strangled at a syllable with a blush. This was a sign to watch for, in case someone might wish to become a Leaver.

Now I am doubled that way, named twice, but for me, it's worked in reverse: my new name came later, on the outside, like putting on that crusty old skin that should be lying on the floor.

My one name was Green, but no one calls me that any more. I had no old name to peel away, because I was born at Foxlowe. Freya named me first, of course. She named all of us, except for one. There's a power in naming. Green was strange even for home — most of the women had flowers, or pretty ideas, like Liberty.

If I could speak to Freya, I'd tell her not to worry, because I hold my new name ever so lightly, ready to shrug it off, if ever Foxlowe could start up again.

Of course I wasn't Green all the time. With Toby, it was *the ungrown*; once Blue came, it was *the girls*, too.

Since this is a story for Blue, first here is the little bit I remember of the world before Blue was in it. I knew that it's not only names that double: time was split in two, between two Solstices. The winter one falls when the year is dying and you have to be careful then, because the Bad is strong in the dark. The summer one is when the sun sets twice at the Standing Stones, and the Bad is weakest. I don't remember when I learned these things, only that I knew them by the time Blue existed. I knew Freya and Richard and Libby were the Founders and that the others were the Family and I even remembered that there was a time when I was the only ungrown, before Toby came. I knew that when I was born, it brought the Time of the Crisis, and that everything Freya did, even the things that hurt, were to keep the Family together and safe ever afterwards.

I am meant to tell Blue's story, but it doesn't flow as it should: there are broken and jagged edges to it, and some pieces are too sharp for the tongue to tell. I could begin with Blue's naming, the first little thing I did to love and to hurt Blue all at once. Or I could tell the moment Foxlowe began crumbling all around us, with the front doorbell ringing. But wherever I begin, it all leads to the same place. To the sweet rotting smells, and the warm, slick blood.

PART ONE

Green

I

Tiny red beads came from the lines on my arm. Those soft scars give way like wet paper. There's a game that helps: footsteps in the dust, twisting to match the old strides without taking the skin away from the Spike Walk. Another: name steps all the way to the yellow room end of the Spike Walk. *Freya, Toby, Green, Egg, Pet, the Bad*. I made it to the final nail and squinted at the arm. Red tears and the lines swollen hot; a crying face. I turned to Freya, her long arms wrapped around herself at the ballroom end of the Walk. She nodded, so I breathed deeper and licked some of the salt and coins taste to make it clean.

Freya spoke. —And back again, Green.

Her voice was low, but even softened there was broken glass in it.

I lifted my other arm to the nails that had once hung pictures on these walls in Foxlowe's old life.

—No, same arm, Freya said, smothering a smile. —Until it bleeds, is the rule.

—It *is* bleeding.

I held up my arm for her to see. Freya gave a slow blink.

—And back again, Green.

I put the torn skin back to the first nail. By the time I stumbled into Freya's embrace there were flames under my skin, and I knew the Bad was burning away. I pleaded silently into the wood smoke scent of Freya's dress. She twined her fingers in my hair, tight at the roots, pulled to search my face. I tried to look pure and good, fixed on her dark eyes and sharp, veined cheeks. Freya nodded, uncurled to her full height, and led me out to the ballroom, where Libby knelt on the huge red rug.

Libby wrapped me in the cardigan with the daisy shaped buttons and left me for the kitchen. The curve of a broken button fitted snug around the tip of my little finger.

It wasn't Freya who returned but Libby with the poultice of lavender and honey.

—Why're *you* doing it? I asked, as Libby wrapped the warm cloth below my elbow. Freya did this for me, while telling the story of the Crisis, then she'd bring her forehead to mine, and pour her thick, black hair around us, making a little world for us away from the rest of the Family. This was her way of forgiving me. A little ritual of our own, an always.

—What did you do for the Spike Walk? Libby asked.

She liked to answer questions with questions. Her full name was Liberty, but only Freya ever called her that. Her hair was greasy with egg yolk, ready to wash out when the water came on after sunset.

I shrugged. It was between Freya and me. That morning I'd tried to pierce my ears with a needle and ice snapped from the attic window frame. It wasn't for that I was punished, but because Freya, who could read all my secrets just by looking at my face or the way I moved my hands, knew it was because I wanted to look like Libby.

Libby's earrings were blue hoops with little gold birds perched on them. They were special. Richard had brought them for her from the outside, and they never went into Jumble. She let me play with them now that my arm was bandaged, pressing one against my ear, while she held up the back of a spoon for me to see the blurry image. My hair didn't move like her curls but like the knotted hair of a wet dog left out in the rain.

After a while the Family came in from the gardens, their arms full of holly, or branches of white and red berries. I looked for Toby, but only the grown had been outside collecting for the Solstice decorations. They were flushed from the cold and the carrying, but it was almost festival time, and they filled the huge room with whistles and snatches of song and bits of stories. I threw my head back to see if the sounds bouncing around the ceiling beams were visible. Richard dragged a crate of wine and raised his eyebrows at Libby as he passed. She gave him a wide smile and shifted her hips on the floor, touched her sticky yolked hair. His eyes slid to my arm, then away, and he left towards the kitchen. The Family started to pull out vine and branch, strangling them into wreaths.

I was finding deeper breaths now, my heart settling.

—That's it, breathe into it, Libby soothed. —Imagine the pain like a ball that's moving to your hands.

I always tried but my pain ran in lines, so I made it into a track to be walked across the moor, leading to my fingers. Libby had me make a fist and release it. She told me I could watch the ball float up and away like a bubble. Instead, behind my eyelids were threads spooling out from the new cuts, unravelling, unpicked bad stitches.

—Have you heard the secret? Libby asked me.

—Secret? Is it new family? New clothes? I said. —Can I have a—

—No. It's something really good, she said, giggling so her snaggle tooth showed.

—New … animals? More dogs, are there going to be puppies?

Libby shook her head, plaiting the tassels at the edge of the ballroom rug.

—I know, I lied.

—You've guessed! And I'm not supposed to tell, Freya wants to!

—Why hasn't Freya come? I said. —Is she to do with it, the secret?

Libby held out her earring. —Try it on your other ear.

But I didn't care about the earrings any more. I tried to think of all the secrets there had ever been, but it wasn't new family or animals and I knew it couldn't be a Leaver, because Libby said something good. I begged Libby to tell me, hung from her shoulders, kissed her then kicked her, and eventually she said, —Green! Enough, go and find Toby and play, and she shoved me away.

He wasn't far, on the middle landing, eating berries from the new wreath that hung there. His woolly blond hair stuck out from his head in untidy curls; a layer of dirt crusted around his knees. I stole some berries and for a while we showed each other our red-stained tongues.

—D'you know there's a secret happening, something good? I asked Toby.

—Like what?

—Something to do with *me*.

He frowned. —You have to clean, is all. We all have to before Solstice.

—Stupid, that's not a good thing.

—Stupid, of course they aren't going to *tell* you it's a bad thing, stupid!

—Libby said something good. Are you calling Libby a liar?

My palm made red shapes on the skin of his back, where the safety pin left his t-shirt gaping. He kicked me away and twisted my arm, right where the fresh blood was. I spat in his face, foam on his cheeks. That settled it. Spit wins. Besides, Toby might be older, taller, but he was still newer than me: I remembered the day he came, in Valentina's arms, and was dumped next to me on the ballroom rug. *Play*, they said. *You can't remember that*, he always said, *you were only a baby. I do*, I said: the strange plastic on his jacket, and the outside smell. He'd been named October; Freya said it was right. She told me that outside Foxlowe it was a name for the time when leaves turned to fire.

Sitting on the step, we picked at things. Toby peeled away a huge scab on his knee I'd given him a day or two before. I plucked at rotten wood, and we drew on the fresh wood underneath with the berry juice. I loved to sit on the middle landing. From there you had a view right down into the main house. You could see the front entrance hall, and the ballroom ceilings stretched out of sight. The hallway leading to the kitchen was below too, so you could watch as people rushed in and out, carrying tea or fruit back to the studios. If you looked up, you could follow the staircase right up to the attic, making your stomach ripple with the height. Best of all, the stained glass window had a panel of clear glass with a view over the back lawns and the moor beyond, so you could peer out, bathing your feet in the blue light. The middle landing was the heart of everything.

Toby looked up from his bleeding knee and tugged at my poultice.

—Spike Walk?

I nodded.

—Valentina won't let Freya take me any more, Toby said.

This was a lie. From Toby or Valentina, I couldn't tell which.

—Freya didn't properly forgive me after, I said. —I might have to do the Walk again.

—What did you do?

—A Libby thing.

Toby nodded. The tides between Freya and Libby were always.

—Where is she then? Toby said. After a pause he said, —Maybe she's a Leaver! and laughed.

I pulled my cardigan closer around my waist. Freya had made it for me. The daisy buttons were from a shop she told me about that had them in jars, like sweets, she said, and I didn't understand her, sweets are in rows from the oven or from chilling in the goat shed, ready to cut into brittle pieces and suck. Freya laughed, pulled me to her and nuzzled my neck, saying *Imagine it*, talking about the outside for a while. Then we'd played All The Ways Home Is Better.

There had been a Leaving that year, just as the Summer Solstice was coming, a strange time to go, when the house was aglow and everyone was happy. She'd been pretty, the Leaver had, and liked to sit on the back steps sewing patchwork quilts. We were already forgetting her. After a Leaving, there was always a slump, and careful watching of each other, lots of Meetings and the reshuffle of chores, and if people were gone for longer than expected, on shop runs or disappearing over the moor, things went quiet until they came back.

I slipped the hard edge of a daisy petal under my thumbnail, and tried to think of Freya as a Leaver, outside, in one of the box-houses she told me about. Foxlowe without her, like a hungry stomach.

—Don't be stupid, I said.

We stared each other out, until my stomach complained, a guttering sound, and we went off to find food.

In the kitchen, bread smell swelled up the room. Toby tripped down the steps and leapt onto the table, upsetting the wine. The Family cheered and slow-clapped. Pooling around my fingers, the red stream was sticky and cool.

The Foxlowe kitchen was a cave, a stone mouth with a cold floor that made an easy game of trying to jump from slab to slab, just as we did out on the moor. There was a long gutter, where blood used to run, Freya said, when they killed animals down there in Foxlowe's old life. Windows along one wall looked out on the back lawns. A table stretched along the centre, sticky with fruit juice and oil. Everywhere paint and brushes, lumps of curdled milk, crusty teabags. Dogs huddled the huge aga stove. The Family had come from the ballroom, following the smell of fresh bread.

When the Family was together like that, grown and ungrown, we got loud, shouting over each other, calling names, throwing arms wide. Libby looped around the table, kissing cheeks, her fresh-washed hair spilling over faces. I looked around for Freya, who liked to complain about the waste and vanity of Libby using the yolks, but she wasn't there. Once, she'd tricked Libby by leaving old eggs out, long after they floated in still water, and Libby's hair reeked for days, Freya laughing so hard I thought she would be sick. Now, Libby looped her arms around Richard's neck, and he breathed in her newly softened curls.

Richard wore different clothes to the rest of us. There were paintings that looked like him in the upper rooms, the same fox faces with narrow noses and narrow eyes, and some of the clothes were the same: waistcoats and long black coats, white shirts full of moth holes. He never hugged us or swept us into a dance or pulled us onto his knee, so I didn't know the smell and feel of him like the other grown, but he was all bone, strong in Freya's way. His beard grew patchy and he was always scratching around his jaw. Sometimes the Family called him *boy* as a joke, but he was, Freya said, not *that* much younger than she was, if you were counting, and anyway older than Libby, who had airs of a grown but could have only just bled to look at her. Richard was one of the Founders, so there was little chance of him being a Leaver. Sometimes I secretly wished he would, didn't like his eyes following me around the house or the way they would flick away from me if I tried to catch them. He eyed the blood on Toby's knee.

—Still fighting, October, he said.

His voice faded at the end of words, like he got bored of them.

—This is supposed to be a place of peace, he said, circling his hands, his roll up making a smoky trail. —But you two … always bring … a kind of endless nasty fight, into our midst.

Toby licked the wine from his hands and pointed to the centre of the table.

—Butter, is that the secret thing? That's shit, he said.

—What secret? Libby said, smiling.

—Is it just cleaning? I said. —Where's Freya?

Richard frowned, and Libby looked away, and the Family chewed and swallowed.

I crawled under the table. Libby lifted Toby down. He nudged me with a fist and I hit him away.

—Try again, Toby said. —Say her name and see what they do.

—She can't be a Leaver, I whispered.

—Ask again, he said.

But I was too afraid to name her to the Family and have them look away. Thing was sometimes Leavers slipped away like that, quick and silent.

Libby passed some cake dipped in honey to us. —An undertable picnic! she said. I glared at her.

The shuffle of feet and laughter faded as the Family moved to the ballroom. The mulled wine steamed on the stove.

—Thought Freya would have taken you, Toby said. —You must have done something really bad. What did you do to make her a *Leaver*?

I lay down on the icy stone.

—What was her name, that last Leaver? I whispered.

Toby scowled at me. Getting each other into trouble was our favourite game.

—Really, I said. —I forgot. I won't tell.

—Brida, he said.

Her Foxlowe name. When she came, it was something long, an E name, I tried to remember.

Toby dug a bogey out of his nose and wiped it on the stone. —Valentina didn't like her, he added.

—Freya neither.

—Maybe Freya went to tell her off.

—Yes, I said.

—Let's get some clothes and food and stuff and go after her! he said.

—Shut up! She'll come back!

Toby pinched me hard. It was to say *Sorry* and *There, because you shouted at me and I was trying to be nice to you*, and *It might be true what I said, so get ready*, all in one red nip of the skin, his favourite place on my wrist, all my scars there not from Freya but from him. We talked that way, when it was something important. I didn't squeal or fight, just watched the blood flow into the skin, grateful for the sharpness of it, then Toby went back to the grown, leaving me lying under the table.

Candles on the table made a ring of light around the wooden curled feet. Freya would say, *Here's a fairy ring*, safe or dangerous, depending on the story.

Freya's fingers, greasy and rough on my cheek, her bitten skin coated in vaseline. Her hair around her shoulders like black straw. Dark eyes narrowed, squinting back at me. In the weak light Freya's crooked teeth were hidden, and she looked pale, almost pretty like Libby. She hunched her tall figure further under the table.

—What have we here? A fairy crawled under my table looking for milk.

She made *look* sound like *luke*.

—And still asleep, she doesn't want to talk.

I shot under her arm, and she held my head against her wool coat. She smelled of the outside: leather and plastic, and petrol from the old car we used for the shop runs.

—You came back, I said.

I tried to burrow further into her but she held her side away from me. In the crook of her elbow was a bundle of clothes. She'd brought new things! I grasped for it, but Freya sucked air through her teeth and cuffed my arm away. The bundle made wet sounds.

Freya knelt next to me and shifted it high onto her chest.

—This is our new baby, she said.

2

Wisps of red hair stuck out from a striped scarf. I reached out to touch the tip of an ear. Pink skin and tiny gold hairs. It was cold.

I thought of the cool flesh of the baby goats we'd found lying stiff in the shed.

—Is it dead? I said.

Freya frowned and ducked from under the table and I followed her, pulling the hem of my dress, wanting at once to wrench the baby out of Freya's arms, where *I* belonged, and to hold it myself, look at it.

—She's ours, Freya said. —She's our new little sister.

—It's family?

—She is, said Freya. —She's going to live with us.

—Oh.

My Freya's hands, the bitten nails and blackened tips, scent of soil and sometimes blood — they were wrapped around this new thing's body, the head cupped in her palm.

—It's staying? I said.

Freya turned her eyes on me. —Something Bad moving? she said.

—No.

—Seems like a nastiness there. Seems like a little Bad there, she said.

—No, I said. —The Family's in the ballroom, I added.

—We'll show them in a while.

This was strange, but I loved when it was me and Freya alone, without all the Family in the way, so I just smiled, until she turned her back to me, shushing as the new thing wriggled and kicked.

I thought of the goats again. —Does it need milk? I asked.

—Well, Freya said.

She brought out a bottle from a new bag, covered in pictures of sheep. She tipped it so I could see it was frozen. She held the new thing higher on her chest, and fetched a lit candle from the table, handed it to me. The gas hissed when Freya turned the dial. I waved the lit candle towards the sound. The ring sparked with a tiny roar.

I loved the blue lights when the gas was on. I breathed on the flames, watching them bow and stretch, while Freya put the bottle into a pan of water. After a while she brought it out with the tongs she used for taking potatoes out of the bonfire.

—Lift your sleeve up, she said. I gave her my good arm. She pressed the bottle to my skin and I yelped, jumping back. She held the bottle in place another long few seconds. I breathed into the pain the way Libby had taught me but just as I was about to thrash Freya released me.

She kissed my hair. —Now your arms are in balance, she said. —Feel how they speak to each other now?

The flashes of fresh burn answered the throbs in my cuts like music. I nodded. Freya put the milk aside to cool. —That's how you test it, she said. —That same place on your arm. If it burns, you leave it a while.

We took new little sister to the Family, and they asked questions, Libby asking lots of times, —Did she say it was all right? Did you ask her? Are you sure she knows she's welcome? As though she didn't know it was only a baby, and couldn't answer. Toby asked, —Is that it, the secret? I realised it was, and he only said, —That's shit.

My hands dangled, lost at my sides as I followed Freya to the back rooms. Usually she held my hand tight in hers and stroked the back of my palm with her thumb, but now New Thing filled her arms, wailing a thin cry that cracked at the edges. It was late, the latest I had ever stayed up without falling asleep in the kitchen or the ballroom, waking up cold and finding my way to an empty mattress.

We took the Spike Walk. The spikes were rows of nails that stuck out of the panelled wood. They used to have paintings hanging on them. The story goes that when Richard first came to Foxlowe he sold them all, to pay for the first meals and clothes. I ran my hands lightly over the nails as we walked, followed my hours-old steps.

The end of the Spike Walk widened into the yellow room. It was smaller than the ballroom, but prettier, I thought. There was still some wallpaper left, turning brown, and a bed with a broken frame and thick pillows that had spat out some of their feathers, drifting across the room. White shapes crouched in the shadows, ghosts of wood and cotton.

Freya kicked a ghost out of her way and it groaned across the floor. She shook a sheet away from something and I went in to see. It was an old chest, carved oak like the table in the kitchen. Freya opened a drawer. There were mouldy towels in there; she shook them out and a stiff mouse dropped, rolled across the floor. She held the drawer up.

—Here's your bed, baby girl, she said.

Freya took off her coat, and patted down the pockets. She took out some sprigs of dry lavender. We lined the drawer with the coat so that New Thing would know her the way pups sleep on the bellies of their mothers. She tucked the lavender around the edges.

—Now it'll smell nice.

Freya corrected me. —Help her sleep. She'll be quieter now.

Freya was wrong: that first night New Thing screamed so high, so endless, that the Family came up to the attic, to help shush and rock, and I whispered to Toby, —New Thing hates us. It hates it here. It should go away again.

—I like it, he said. —It's nice to hold.

It was true it was warm, and though the weight of it pulled at my arms I liked to balance it on my knees on the bed in the attic, blow on its eyelids, see if I could wake it up and make the big cheeks flush with red and the whole face collapse in wailing.

—New Thing'll be bad for us here, I said to Toby. —It'll be bad for you. Valentina might love her.

—Looks like she's Freya's to me, Toby hissed back.

Until New Thing came Freya's love for me was like thc bricks in the walls and the roots of the oaks at the edge of the moor. Now all the Family were circled around New Thing in Freya's arms, stretched towards it like a bonfire, and I tried to make Freya see me, worried at my scars, hung over the back of chairs, but she didn't look up.

It didn't take long for Freya to see how I hated new little sister almost from the beginning. It was in the faces I gave her and the way I held her a little too rough. Then she overheard my name for her. I thought it would be the Spike Walk but instead I was Edged. Freya told the Family this one morning by tossing me the burnt part of the bread and making sure they all saw. They all had to look away when I spoke and no one was allowed to touch me. I was alone, edging around the circles the Family made around New Thing. I snatched eye contact and accidental touch when I could, watching and listening, haunting rooms.

The rest of the Family loved New Thing. The sounds it made they repeated, called to each other like a new language. After that first night, its crying wasn't so frightening. The Family worked out what it liked: the jingle-jangle sounds of Libby's bracelets, shaken above it, Freya's knuckles in its mouth, the powdery milk not too hot. And what it didn't like: the sun streaming through the kitchen windows, the dogs panting over it, and the damp orange blanket made it cry. They spent hours just lying on the kitchen floor, next to the aga, staring at it.

Aside from Freya, Ellen loved New Thing best. Her full name was Ellensia, but we'd all forgotten to use it. Her flesh spilled out of her clothes like filling from a pie, and she liked to wear kaftans she made herself, bad stitching pulling at the seams. She'd take New Thing into her arms and rest her on her vast stomach, singing bits of songs I didn't know, cooing, until Freya took her back. Once, Ellen dared fight Freya on how to make little sister sleep, and she said, —I *have* done this before, you know, and we all looked away, sad for her at the mistake, and Freya only nodded, and said softly, —Yes, and where is that baby now? and Ellen left the kitchen with spilling eyes.

Meeting came. At the bay windows, Dylan and Ellen lay on their backs, drawing pictures in the frosted glass with their nails. Dylan was huge and strong, the bulk of him like an oak tree, and he gave bear hugs and wet kisses. He liked to spin us around, even Freya, even Ellen, who liked him, she said, because he make her feel dinky. Dancing to Richard's guitar were Pet and Egg. Egg, Eglantine, was tall and thin. Through his vest, bones pushed out like they were trying to pierce the skin. He had thick black hair and a moustache he liked to grease with cooking fat and twist into curls. Egg was always with Petal, Pet for short, a boy with a girl's name. Pet wore blusher on his cheekbones, so he looked like the broken dolls in the attic. He and Egg were always snaked around each other, Pet's fingers in Egg's hair.

A burning oil lamp sent jasmine puffs into the air. Candles burned everywhere, in old jars, stuck into wine bottles and cluttered along the mantelpieces. Someone had even put tea lights in the old chandelier, balancing them against the crystal. Toby lay with his head on Valentina's stomach. I pulled at him to come sit with me, for the Naming, but he shook me off. I crouched next to him, Valentina giving me a weak smile. She was Toby's mum; he'd called her that, *Mum*, for a while before he lost the habit, while she never seemed to name him at all. Her long blonde hair was so thin you could see the pink scalp underneath. Freya and Libby called her *Sweetheart*; behind her back, they called her *Bitter Bambi*, and in one of their strange truces they could make each other laugh by widening their eyes and snarling all at once. In the coldest days after Winter Solstice, Libby gave Valentina the down quilt that she'd taken from Jumble so long ago it was considered hers, and on the days Valentina went quiet and sad, Libby took Toby on long walks, or taught him dance steps in the ballroom. So I knew *Bitter Bambi* was something unkind: Libby liked life to be in balance.

—We're naming her now, Valentina whispered to me. —Then she'll be family and you'll *have* to love her, Green, or everything will be very hard for you.

Freya stood up with New Thing in her arms and we all fell silent. She'd chant the new name and we'd watch it soak into new little sister like rainwater into grass. There was no outside name to peel away, not that she'd ever remember. Freya spoke for a while about the Family and Foxlowe and we all recited All The Ways Home Is Better.

—Now, I have a name for new little sister, said Freya.

I thought of the worst things: the rusted nails in the Spike Walk, the hunger of a starve day, the Bad. New Thing was hooked over Freya's shoulder, so when she turned, the little face peered over, still wrapped in that striped scarf. Her eyes caught on the chandelier. The tiny wet mouth twitched into a smile and she made a small sound of joy. The best things came: jewels on cobwebs, Libby's little birds. The flames glowing the night I watched Freya heating the milk.

—Blue, I whispered, too quiet for Freya to hear. —Call her Blue.

—Green has a name for her, Toby called.

Everyone looked at me. I kicked Toby hard and said, —No I don't.

—She does, she just whispered it!

I dug my nails into his arm, and he howled. Valentina sat up and pulled him to her, glaring at me.

Freya bounced the baby in her arms, not looking at me. —Green is Edged, she said.

—It was the first name called, said Libby. —Isn't that the rule?

—Freya always does the naming, said Richard, and Libby rolled her eyes, lay back on the floor like she was sunbathing in the cold air.

—Well, said Dylan. —It might be nice to—

—A nice way to end the Edging, Ellen jumped in.

Libby sat up. —What is the name, Green?

—Nothing, I said.

—*Nothing?* Freya crowed.

—Blue, I croaked. Libby caught it and repeated it louder. It sank into Blue and took her and we all knew that was her name.

—There's a power in naming, Freya said to the Family, continuing to Edge me. —I hope Green knows what she's given her. Blue can be many things.

—It's the lights on the cooker, I said.

—It's cold, Freya said to the Family.

—And she's a colour like Green, Richard said.

—Yes, and you know she's on the tape, said Freya. —With you and Green. Her song is all about sadness.

—Oh, I said.

—I love it, Libby said.

Above us in Freya's arms, Blue squirmed and opened and closed her mouth.

—There's a power in naming, Freya said again.

—She's Green's now, you know. She should do the calling, said Libby.

So I took Blue into my arms, and gave her the name *cold* and *sad*. That was the first little thing I did to hurt her.

3

Life ever after that is full of Blue, and all the trouble she made. It was Blue who made the end of Foxlowe, and Freya and me and all the Family. That wasn't her fault, but mine. When Blue was a baby everything was already ruined, it only took a long time to happen. Let me tell you about the Bad first, so you understand. We had lots of stories about it, so we didn't forget. You need to hear them countless times before you can follow the words in your own head, and then tell your own version. Mine is part Freya's, part Libby's, knotted together voices.

The Bad is everywhere on the outside. There, it is ignored, and because it has been forgotten, it can move in new ways: it does not creep, or skulk around the edges of shadow, but soars in the open. Listen, and believe it: on the outside, the Bad can force a helpless one to do *anything*. Imagine the worst you can. Outside, people will twist knives into flesh, pull off one another's skin. Eat each other.

Now, it is harder for the Bad to take one of us, as it can so easily for outside people, because we have the protection of the Stones and the rituals. And we know the Bad and call it by name.

Never think that safer than the outside means *safe*.

You have to learn for yourself what the Bad feels like; everyone feels it differently. In the Time of the Crisis, when the Bad got into Foxlowe, it crouched on Freya like a giant fly, and made her world dark, so when the sun shone in, it couldn't reach her. It made her limbs weak and everything hollow and hopeless. But others speak of the Bad as a voice, inside their own heads, or pain scratching around from inside the skin. Others perceive the Bad as a ghost, a figure you can glimpse in the corner of the eye; it can move things, and kneels on your chest at night. The Bad can twist your mouth to speech, or curl your hands into fists to strike something weaker than you. The Bad can kill. Once, when the Scattering was not done properly, it found and killed the baby goats. It causes illness and pain, infection and fever.

Listen to the things we know, to protect yourself. The Bad thrives on the dark and the cold; it is a winter force. So be careful when the sun is weak and the air bites you. Stay off the moor, where the Bad is strong. If the Bad catches you there, run to the Standing Stones. Even in the winter the Stones hum with a thousand ancient blessings. If you are closer to Foxlowe, run so you are inside the Scattering Salt.

If, despite all our care, you feel the Bad has taken you, you must tell the Founders. They will take you to the Stones, if the sun is strong enough, and Solstice is close. In winter, you will be given candle flame on the skin to try to force the Bad out. It hates heat. If the infection is deep, you may be bled. Summer Solstice will heal you, if nothing else works, and you may have to wait for the double sunset.

The children are the easiest for the Bad to slip into. They must be watched.

The Scattering is something we learned from the Time of the Crisis. Remember that the Bad had come inside the walls. One of those mornings, Freya felt the Bad in the kitchen, scratching across the floor, and twitching her fingers. On the flagstones lay the baby Green, where the Bad had taken full root. The Bad filled the kitchen until it was as black as night and spread cold through the air. In the gloom, Freya watched the tiny chest rise and fall, rise and fall, and the Bad pressed on her, urged the pillow into her hands. As she took it she knocked the salt jar from the table and it smashed, scattered salt across the floor. The room immediately lightened, the air warmed, and although the Bad was too deep in the baby to force out, the skulking Bad pressing on Freya was gone. This is what we commemorate in the Scattering, that Freya was stronger than the Bad in the end, that we have ways of keeping it out.

4

Only a handful of sunsets after Blue's Naming, it was Winter Solstice, my breath clouding in the attic. I woke to a new dress at the bottom of the bed, and shivered into it under the covers. Freya bounced Blue in her arms. It was still dark. Her face was lit by a torch, gaping shadows around her cheeks and mouth.

She spoke to me. —You'll be cold. Come on then, she said, so soft, and I went to her and sobbed as she stroked my hair and shushed me. —All right, all right, it's over now, you know I hate it too, she said.

I wiped my nose on the new dress. Freya had used the material from an old apron of hers I loved: thick cotton, flower print. It had a full skirt that came down to my feet. On it were new white buttons, that she must have got when she fetched Blue, and hidden. I wished I had a mirror, like the big one in the ballroom, too high to catch my reflection in.

We came out into the colder air of the landing, me clutching Freya's hips, bowing my head into her warm stomach.

—It's good that it's so cold. It means the year's ready to go. Cold and hard like a dead thing, Freya said.

The staircase glowed with candlelight and led down to scented air and an inside forest: ivy curled around the banisters, holly in the doorways, dried herbs scattered on the floors. The rooms smoked with hot wine and the glowing ash from roll ups, and lamps burning oils that we'd saved all year: jasmine and lavender. In the hallway, incense smoke made it hard to see. Ellen and Dylan's voices drifted over tinny sound: one of the tapes, dug out of their box in the yellow room.

As much as anything was anyone's at Foxlowe, the tapes were Freya's: she'd brought them with her from her old life, and they were all one voice, the same woman singing every time. The song I'm named for played all the time before the tape got too wobbly to play, but Freya could remember the words anyway, mine and Richard's song too, on the same tape. She'd sing snatches of her favourite song while she made the bread: *I'm afraid of the devil, I'm drawn to people who ain't afraid* ... We didn't call it the devil, but we knew who she meant, all right. Ellen and Dylan's laughter was the sound of festival days and nights, as they sang along, wishing for rivers, and Freya picked up the tune, changing the words how she pleased.

Freya brushed Blue's head with her fingertips. —This is where you live and belong now, she said to her. —Take her, she said.

I tried to lift my arms, but my hands were stuck to my new dress.

Freya crouched, so the baby was level with me, only a small gap between the red hair, the pink skin, and my arms. —Come on, Green, it's all right. You won't drop her.

Then Blue was in my arms. Freya let the baby's head drop against my chest. I didn't like the sour smell of her, or how her spit bubbled in the corner of her mouth. But I moved how I had seen Freya move, *rock shush rock*.

In the kitchen, there was honey and jam saved from the summer, gritty and thick, and goats' milk, still warm. We were the last to come down, and the Family threw smiles and nods my way when they saw Blue in my arms. The aga roared and torches swung from beams. Libby waved to me as I put Blue into one of her drawers by the food stores. Toby opened his mouth wide to show me the mush inside and I caught him perfect on the back of the head, so his jaw clamped down on his tongue. Freya and Libby laughed, but Libby passed Toby some warm milk. He poured half out for me.

Libby wrapped me in the heavy red coat from Jumble. In the pockets, rotting roll up stubs and soil. Freya pulled my hands out to peel two pairs of gloves over my fingers. Fingers froze quickly during the Scattering.

Outside the animals stirred, the chickens rustling and crowing, the goats beginning to bleat. The Family rushed all the light of Foxlowe to the kitchen door, like blood to a new cut. We held the candles from around the house, some just balancing tea lights on their hands, and the torches swung and flashed, illuminating faces, beams, the glinting eyes of dogs.

Freya wound her dark hair around her neck and opened the door to the black of Winter Solstice morning. We poured out with cheering and snatches of stories of the Bad, *The salt keeps it out, This is why we, You must remember to, This is important*, my feet slipping in too-large boots.

We streamed down the back steps and onto the gravel, across to the fountain, down the ice coated marble steps beyond. The stars were still out, but a weak glow was beginning from the Standing Stones. I collected iced cobwebs that sparkled in our torchlight, and other treasures: frozen leaves, an icicle hanging from a marble finial, a snail shell.

Toby pulled me to the frozen fountain to watch the fish twist and dive together under the ice. We knocked on the sheets, like glass, to bring their white and orange forms ghosting to the surface in the torchlight. If one came, the others would turn and follow, like one giant creature. The grown had a name for them: the shoal. *How is the shoal getting on? Should we eat one of the shoal?*

Pet and Egg did star jumps to keep warm. The dogs panted clouds and snuffled ice onto their muzzles. Richard came over and laid a hand on Blue's forehead.

—Take her back in, he said.

—She's fine, Freya said.

He opened his mouth to say more, but Libby clapped her hands together.

—Richard! Come on, it's bloody freezing!

He bent his face closer to Blue, his face stretched to one side as he bit his cheek. Freya stared over the top of his head, far out to the horizon. He tried to catch her eye when he raised his head but she ignored him. After a few seconds her half smile twitched up one side of her face and she returned the gaze. Behind us, Libby called Richard's name, sing-song, then louder, until she broke off the rhythm and called out hoarsely to all of us.

—Right! Let's go! You know how this works. A whole circle around the house, it must be unbroken. If you run out of salt, make sure someone fills in the line for you. Let's *go*.

Richard grinned apologetically as he loped back to Libby. Freya's hand on my shoulder turned me to the moor.

—Look out there. That's where the Bad is coming from. The salt keeps it out, she said.

It was buried under the dark, but I knew the moor rolled out, cut through with stone wall and the dots of sheep. In daylight the hill called the Cloud would sit stark against the sky, its rocks jutting. The Standing Stones lay just behind the house, hidden by the drop and roll of the moor, and I began to feel the itch of being away too long: we'd stayed off the moor for most of the winter.

White dropped on white and showed it grey: the early frost had lost its glitter under our boots. My bag brought us to the edge of the lawns where Egg took over, wiggling his hips and casting his salt from side to side in a wave. Pet took us up to the house. We carried on like that until Freya's salt met Richard's in a pile outside the front door. She'd passed Blue to me and as the salt piled up I whispered into my arms, *We're safe now. The Bad is strongest today but it doesn't like salt.*

We made Foxlowe full of light and music. Some stories say this is to help keep the Bad away, others to celebrate the new Scattering and it is only the salt that matters. I loved the house full of fire and sound, played chase games with Toby in the usually dark places: the back corridors with the old bells and cobwebs, the cellars full of paint and sacks of flour, our shadows ballooning with the rarely lit torches hanging from every doorway. The grown ups chased each other too, squealing and slamming doors, or danced or lay with their heads on each other's stomachs, drinking and smoking far into the night, their lips and chins red.

It was easy to take Blue.

Someone had tucked her into her drawer on the middle landing, where she lay swaddled and open-eyed. The Family had been carrying her and swinging her over shoulders, rocking her while they danced, but she got heavy, and the Family could get bored of the ungrown on Solstice days when the moonshine flowed, and so here she was, alone. Toby was with Valentina; she'd grabbed him as we ran through the front hall, swept him up and kissed him, and they had gone to the yellow room, where I knew she'd be tearfully clinging to him and telling him stories about their old life that he'd try to retell to me later, but wouldn't quite remember the details. He just liked the way she held him close those nights, and let her words wash over him.

Blue's mouth blew kisses at the air as she gazed at the beams. When I leaned over her, her eyes refocused, the little black dots blooming, and I thought how I might be a strange moon to her, so big. I knelt and pulled my hair around her drawer, in Freya's way, so my face made the world. She started to cry.

I thought about Freya's face turned away from me and how I couldn't get into her arms any more, then scooped Blue out of the drawer. Above me, the grown's footsteps and slamming doors echoed, and the ballroom rang with music.

The night sounds: a sniffing, the air rustling. They smothered the feet on flagstones and voices as I closed the kitchen door behind me, and stepped out. I glanced back to the house where glowing balls of candles and torches bobbed up and down as the grown carried them about. Blue thrashed in the freezing air. My throat was tight. Any moment the Family would catch me outside on Winter Solstice night and I'd be Edged, sent to the yellow room, put on a starve day, or worse.

The lawns were frosty and quiet, the steps and the fountain white against the black sky. The oaks swayed in the distance. The moor rolled out behind them, the Stones waiting for us and for summer. I held Blue to me, suddenly excited. Everyone was inside but us. I could race across the deserted gardens, under the stars, in the strange midnight green laced with ice, as long as I stayed inside the salt line.

Something shifted in the gloom. I held Blue's warmth to my chest, and wobbled towards the salt line. The Bad hung there in the quiet, and a kind of pause, a deeper black in the air behind the line, like spilled ink. Freya had told me how the smallest gap in the salt would let it through. It could flow and squeeze and drip like the tiniest raindrop, then swell into a flood and wash us all away.

Blue began to mewl. Behind me I heard the goats bleating softly. I thought how I would do anything in the world to keep Freya for mine. But perhaps it wasn't that so much. Perhaps I just wanted Blue to be one of us, the ungrown. She would take the Spike Walks with us and we could soothe her afterwards and teach her how we imagined the pain leaving. We'd show her how to hide the Bad if you thought it was bubbling up. And I thought about how now she'd be more like me than like Toby. Freya just didn't like him all that much. But she knew the Bad was in me for sure because of the Crisis. This would put Blue in the same place. Make us more Family.

Whatever the reason, here's the truth: I took that baby and I laid her out in the cold outside the salt line for the Bad to take.

Inside, Toby and Valentina were at the kitchen table. My heart quickened, but Valentina's head was in her arms, and she barely looked up. Toby was sucking on the cloth that had been wrapped around the boiling sugar. He let it drop from his mouth when he saw me.

—You never, he said.

—It was only for a second.

—Not like you weren't safe inside the salt, he said, and shrugged, but I could tell he was impressed.

—Come and look, I said.

I pulled him to the window in the studios, half-finished canvases and sculptures all around us. We cupped our hands to the glass.

Somewhere, Blue's wails carried.

It took Toby a while to see her. I waited, breathing white against the glass.

—Is that new little … is that Blue?

—Yes, I said.

—She's outside the salt line!

—Yes.

I thought he wouldn't want to go outside but he wriggled right out of the studio window, the torch swinging wildly as he kicked it on the way out. I thought he might yell for the grown, but he only glared at me through the glass, and beckoned. I followed him, running to the edge of the safe places. The air had lost its crisp chill from before. I felt dizzy with a heat that roared in my head.

Toby stopped just where he should and I stood silent beside him. I gripped his hand and he didn't shake me off. Blue was screaming now and we watched her, counted in names, clutching hands, not bothering to pretend we weren't afraid. Then Blue's cries moved to a higher pitch and my panic lunged me forward. The Bad let me pass right through it, swirled around in the air and kissed at our skin as I brought her back over. I stood with her in my arms, staring at Toby. A rush of violence came from the Bad and I imagined throwing Blue to the ground, drawing blood, until it ebbed away.

—Sorry, I whispered in a rush of horror. —Sorry Blue, sorry Blue, sorry.

—Maybe it didn't get her, Toby whispered.

—It got her, I saw it.

—Me too, Toby said. —You'll have to ... Green, this is so, I think you'll have to be a Leaver.

I started to cry then and held Blue to me and kissed her and begged Toby and said sorry so many times that he fetched dried long grass from the sheds and bound our hands together. We swore we would never tell the Family what I'd done.

5

See, Blue would understand what I did, because like all of us, once she was old enough she'd learn about the Time of the Crisis. The Time of the Crisis isn't Blue's story, but mine. Freya would tell it to me after a Spike Walk. She'd be lying next to me, stroking my hair, kissing the broken skin. Freya's breath in my ear was just soothing sounds like the wind over the roof tiles, but slowly she formed words that wrapped themselves around me like a familiar blanket. I could tell it off by heart even before I knew what the words meant. It's Freya's voice, not mine, but I can't help that: the Time of the Crisis was her story first.

The Time of the Crisis must always be remembered, so we are vigilant, and learn from our mistakes. This was the time before the rituals became solid and clear, and we were trying to decide how to live best.

It began with Green. Green came to Foxlowe very early one morning, while the stars were still out, and the dogs, the goats, even the chickens were still sleeping. It was the

Bad's favourite hour, black and cold as stone. So when Green came, it latched onto her easily, red and slimy, like organs ripped out. Freya knew it by the glisten of the blood and the way it screamed. It filled the house, and we all shrank from it, driving some to pack and become Leavers, the cries so full of spite that they ran away into the night.

Freya hoped that the Bad would leave once the sun became stronger, but instead it screamed and howled and scratched at her, it gnawed at her breast, it made her bleed. No one wanted to hold it, no one wanted to touch it. It was shut away in the attic until we could decide what to do. Freya knew it was the Bad, but the others were too afraid to say it. We survived it by wrapping it tight so it couldn't rage too hard, and not looking it in the eye, or touching it too much.

Freya felt the Bad all over the house. It made her weak. It made her cry and feel tired even when she hadn't done any work. The others tried to help, with food, and chores, and making things for baby Green, like shadows on the walls with their hands.

Things got worse. The rush of Leavers after Green's birth had weakened us. Freya was seeing things that could not be real: her mother standing at the foot of the bed, her father holding a small child's hand. There were whispers in corners. Secrecy. The Bad began to swell and grow in potency, inside the walls.

It was Richard who suggested we take baby Green out to the Standing Stones for Solstice. The group gathered up blankets and bottles of moonshine and set out with the baby wrapped in a quilt. Freya followed, hoping the air and light would deliver her strength. At this time, we would spend Summer Solstice at the Stones and meditate, feel the Stones at our backs, and watch the double sunset, a gift only we can see. So we sat around the Stones, and talked, and ate, and tried to ignore the Bad in Richard's arms. It was screaming, feeling the power of the Stones, but was holding on.

As we watched from the Stones, the sun dipped behind the hill called the Cloud, and shadows stretched across the moor. The Bad crowed in triumph, and we were afraid. Freya was cast down by the tiny hope that had flared in her, only to be extinguished again. Then the sun was reborn. It reappeared between the peaks of the Cloud, before sinking again. This is too much for the Bad, light renewed just as darkness sets in. It fled.

Freya held Green and kissed her, and loved her. This was the end of the Crisis, and Foxlowe became stronger and happier. We understood how the Solstice could help us.

* * *

But the Bad will always remember it lived in Green. It's still there, little traces inside the veins, little worms in the stomach. This is why the rituals are so important. Summer Solstice to drive the Bad away, and the Scattering to protect us when the sun is weak.

6

After we brought her back into the kitchen, muddy and cold, I never had a bad word or look for Blue again. In the years that followed we expanded, me and Toby, to let Blue in, and she became another Foxlowe ungrown. We taught her the best places in the house: the middle landing with its blue pool, the yellow room, the back stairs and corridors full of mice and cobwebs, and the empty rooms that sat decaying there, with their treasures of broken furniture and walls on which to draw in charcoal and chalk. By the time she could run, she made a good chaser with quick dodges and a hard grip, and wasn't afraid to slide down the banister or jump from the windows. When she was very little, she bit and kicked like we did, but me and Toby would attack each other if she was hurt by one of us, and because we rarely touched her, she stopped raging that way. When me and Toby fought, Blue took the side of whoever was left with the reddest skin, the deepest scratch.

We didn't need to teach her the way she had to live, like other new people who came. She was almost like me, almost a born Foxlowe girl. She learned our language and the rituals, Freya said, as new. It was how it should be for everyone, Freya said. We didn't have to explain that blood family didn't matter, because we were the only family she knew. We didn't have to warn her about the outside, because she couldn't remember it. I think she remembered her first Solstice somehow, because Blue always had ice fingers and toes. Freya would rub her feet under the sheets before she went to sleep. Gooseflesh, even in the summer. She could never get warm. Sometimes I watched her holding her hands in her armpits, or curling her fingers around a steaming mug, and wondered if her skin remembered lying on the icy ground, that night, with the scarf unravelled and the Bad all around her.

One day around five summers after Freya brought her to us, Blue disappeared. She'd slept in the attic with me like always; her drawer was too small for her now, and she lay with me on the mattress, and Freya sometimes slept on the rug, wrapped in her coat. I woke up alone, and when I found Freya in the kitchen, we both thought Blue had been with the other.

—Why don't you take better care of her? She's not a doll, Freya said.

She was sketching at the table, brushes and paints in a jar. Ellen and Libby were brewing tea and they looked around.

—What's that, said Ellen. —Little one lost?

—She'll be around, said Freya, but she swiped her brush in the jar, making black clouds there, and got up.

We searched the downstairs first, and the obvious places: the ballroom, where Egg and Pet were ripping up sheets for rags, the yellow room, where Libby said Blue liked to nap in the afternoons. —No she doesn't, said Freya, but Libby showed us the chair Blue curled up in, how it was out of the draughts. The back corridors with their empty rooms were quiet, and the staircases. In the big upstairs rooms, peeling wallpaper and rotting books, we found Valentina lying on her stomach and writing in a notebook, wrapped in a blanket.

—Not seen her, she said.

—October gone too? asked Libby. —Maybe they're together.

—No, we're playing hide-and-seek, said Valentina, turning over a page.

We tried the studios, and found Richard hauling sacks of clay, new delivered, ready for the pottery wheel, his tweeds covered in dust.

—Oh, he said, —I saw her in the gardens this morning.

—On her own? said Libby.

—Well, yes, he said.

Freya went to the window and cupped her hands around her face. —Green used to wander around all the time, she said.

—No, Libby said. —Toby was always with her, or you.

—She's fine, said Ellen, —I'm sure she's fine, but she went to the window too, and cupped her hands there, so she and Freya looked like they were speaking to someone, silently, on the other side of the glass.

It started to rain, and we went out onto the back lawns to search for her, calling her name, tripping over the leaping dogs. Raindrops turned into sheets. Toby showed up, in a thick red jumper that stretched in the drench, the sleeves flopping down to his knees. Valentina twisted one of them, splattering the grass, and said, —Inside, kiddo, don't want you catching cold. And Toby smiled his smile that was just for her when she noticed him, not half and crooked like the ones he gave to me, and obeyed.

—She must have gone back in, said Richard.

—We'll stay out and look here, Freya said, squeezing my hand. The others waded back to the house, some giggling and shrieking, others glancing back at the gardens and the moor beyond, brows creased.

Blue's name got lost in the rain when we called her.

—She'll be fine, said Freya. —Sure she's back in the house, drying that *hair* of hers.

Something about Blue's hair — the bright red had faded as she grew, but it lived in glints and streaks in the brown, and it was glossy, lovely like Libby's was — irritated Freya, and for her Blue's hair was always *that hair of hers*. All of her worry seemed to have drained away, and she stood smiling, cupping her hands to catch the rain.

—My Green, haven't you noticed?

—What?

—It's just you and me! First time in ages!

She gripped my wrists and we spun around, throwing our heads back so our mouths filled up with rain, and spouting the water out like fountains. Screaming happily in the wet gusts, we slid around on the muddy grass, throwing clods at each other and for the dogs to catch. Numb skinned, we gasped and pushed streaming water out of our eyes, ran and whooped across the back lawns, through walls of nettles, not feeling the stings in the wet. We darted straight into the copse and stood panting under the cover of a clutch of trees. I called for Blue again.

—Let's race, Freya said, and sprinted out towards the Standing Stones. The rain plunged in bursts when we rushed into spaces not covered by the trees, the soil churned under our feet, released its scent, making me hungry. Freya caught me and scooped me into a hug. I breathed in her skin, knowing I might not get her all to myself again, perhaps for years or ever.

—Well, she's not here, said Freya, panting.

—She might be at the Stones, I said. I didn't want to go back to the house yet, to the Family.

—Past the stone wall? Freya said.

—She might, I said.

Blue wasn't allowed past the stone wall alone. But she loved to clamber onto the Standing Stones, or try to loosen them with all her weight. Once, leaning down so his hair brushed her cheek, Toby had told her that he could move the Stones around like empty boxes, arrange them in patterns, that she could do the same when she was big and strong. Then we lay against the biggest stone, me and Toby, our feet resting atop one another, shuddering with laughter, watching Blue's toes slide on the grass, trying to shift the ancient markers, their stone roots running deep.

We were both quiet for a while, thinking about Blue getting bigger. Then we headed for the stone wall, made long before the Founders' time, spilling rocks onto the moor like broken teeth. From there we looked back at Foxlowe, lying under the rain like something glimpsed at the bottom of the fountain. Candles were lit in the storm-gloom, and the small shapes of dogs huddled against the back walls, shaking out their fur.

—Looks just like when I came, Freya said. —It was raining then, and I came this way, over the moor. She smiled at me, a full, open smile, and squeezed out my hair for me. —Come on, tramp, she said, and we set out towards the Stones.

—What's a tramp? I said. I had to shout over the rain and the rumble of the sky.

—An outside thing.

—Why am I one?

—You're not really, she said. —You have a lovely big home and everything you'll ever need. You're a scruff, that's all. Sometimes, Freya said, —sometimes I wonder how you'd look, if we, if you were outside, all scrubbed and dressed like them.

Then Freya was quiet, so I asked if we could play All The Ways Home Is Better, and I remembered them all, in the correct order:

1. We are FREE
2. We are a NEW BETTER KIND OF FAMILY
3. We have a NEW BETTER KIND OF EDUCATION
4. We are CONNECTED to the ANCIENT WAY OF LIVING and to the ANCIENT LANDSCAPE
5. We are SAFER because we know THE BAD and call it by name.

Beyond the stone wall, our copse merged with the moor and turned into a steep climb. You could hear the outside roar from here: a strip of road, the edge of the world. Today the rain cloaked the sound, and we climbed in silence, tugging at grasses.

The Standing Stones were eight stones, green with algae and moss, so they seemed to grow out of the grass. The Stones were as tall as Dylan, broad and solid, immovable. From here we could see the double peak of the Cloud, and the moor rolling down in valleys all the way to the road. We ducked under the barbed wire — *disgusting, illegal*, Freya called it. And there was Blue, sitting on the centre stone, with a man and a woman on either side of her.

I wrenched free of Freya's hand and ran, kicking up clods of earth, slipping into the Stones. I knew Freya would overtake me so I wouldn't have to speak to the outsiders.

The man smiled at me. He had a shaved face, his skin shiny where his beard should be, and wore a bright plastic jacket. I looked back for Freya, but she was walking slowly, her hands rammed into her skirt pockets, and then I lost her behind one of the Stones. The outside woman had lifted Blue into her arms. They'd wrapped something plastic around her, a brutal zip cutting under her chin.

—She was out alone, the woman said. Her hair was done in a way I'd seen before, an old Leaver had it like that, in sausages. *Dreads*. —In the rain, she said. —We were here taking photos and—

Blue stretched her arms out to me, and the woman put her down.

—She doesn't like to be carried, I mumbled. Blue was chattering. —It's raining, I got wet, my legs are all covered in mud, look—

The man was staring at my feet, so I looked there too, mud-caked in my socks. I wanted to tell him I hadn't known we were coming to the moor. A pair of boots from Jumble fitted me almost perfect.

—Is that your mum? the woman asked, and I looked to see Freya coming, shook my head.

Freya's cheeks were red, and her hands, released from the pockets, fluttered between her hair, her skirts, and wiping the rain from her forehead. Something was wrong, but I couldn't see what I'd done. It was right, wasn't it, to run to Blue, and I hadn't spoken to them, just answered questions. Freya ducked her head as she came close, and tugged at Blue.

—All right, the man said. —You from the big house, are you? That commune place?

—Are these your kids? the woman said.

When Freya spoke her voice was different, soft and sorry. —Thank you, she said.

—She was out all by herself, the woman said, angry.

I waited for Freya to tell them she was a Founder, you can't speak to her like that, but she was looking at the ground, so I said, —She ran away. We live just behind that rise. Foxlowe.

—Foxlowe, the man repeated.

And then the three of us were striding, breaking into a run, catching glimpses behind of the outside people, who were calling after us, hands held up to their eyes, still calling to us, until their voices faded. I grazed a Standing Stone as we rushed away, sharp pain in my elbow. When we reached our stone wall, Freya lifted Blue over roughly, knocking her bare legs against the rock. She tossed the plastic zipped thing into a bed of nettles in the copse.

We didn't speak the whole way up the back lawns to the house. The rain had drained away into drizzle. Blue's hand was sticky in mine, and I wondered if they'd given her outside food, like the chocolate we'd had once, brought by Ellen from a shop run. I lifted Blue's palm to my lips and licked, but I couldn't taste anything. I scrambled to make sense of all the details, assembled questions to ask her when we were alone. I'd seen outside people before, out on the moor, knew some of them by sight, the people who lived on the farms, and yelled at us if we jumped their fences. I'd never spoken to one though, or seen Freya with one so close, seen her turn into someone else, someone afraid. I tightened my grip on Blue's hand. On the other side of her, Freya strode, her face closed. Blue knew not to speak — we'd taught her, me and Toby, to be quiet when our nails dug into her skin, for times like this. I drew blood this time, spooked by Freya's lost voice and stooped back.

Meeting that night dragged on for hours. Cocooned together in the patchwork blanket, the warm weight of a dog across our laps, Toby, Blue and me nodded asleep, woke to more words and circling arguments, or were pulled awake by our own names spoken, calling us back to listen. The smell of coffee and smoke and, later, that day's leftovers, potatoes and leeks, reheated and passed around in mugs, floated over us.

Libby was speaking. —Never formalised things, about the children—

—But that's the *point*, Ellen's voice. —A new, better kind of education, a real childhood, no formalising—

—But when it comes to safety, to custody—

—But as far as the outsiders are concerned, it is all official. Richard's voice, faster than I was used to hearing it, less bored. —Everything is in order, but we want the children's *experience* to be that—

—They'll come here, Freya said. The glass in her throat was back, and anger thrilled through every word. —They were worried, they had that look. He knew us, knew the house. They're going to interfere.

—But they were right, Libby said.

Raised voices to this. Words that came up frequently at Meeting were thrown. *Freedom. Safe. Outside.*

—Should be more careful, Libby shouted over them. —The road is right there, the town is right there, there are walkers—

—Better to be more remote. Egg's voice, this.

—We can't help where Foxlowe is, Richard answered.

Freya's voice moved closer, as she joined Richard on the floor.

—We need to be near the Stones, she said. —This is where we should be, and need to be. It *can* be remote, if we block out as much as we can.

Later, Freya, Blue and me were in the attic, getting ready for bed. I plaited Blue's hair into thick braids, and asked her why she'd gone out on the moor alone, but she had shrunk into herself, smoothing her thumbnail over her top lip. Freya was sloughing dried mud from her boots with a knife.

—Blood will out, she said, a phrase of hers she often threw at Blue, never at me. We didn't know what it meant, but Toby thought it was a threat to cut her.

Then, Freya asked me, lightly, —Have you talked to Toby?

—Course, I said.

—About those outsiders?

I had told Toby all about Freya's sudden shrinking. He hadn't said anything, just raised his eyebrows in disbelief.

—No, I said.

—Good, Freya said. —It's not good to talk about outsiders. It pollutes the atmosphere.

Blue's hair was still damp and I sucked my fingers to take away the clammy chill.

—So, Freya said. —What shall we do with this girl?

I took my fingers out of my mouth and hid them in Blue's hair. She had started to twist into my lap.

—It's up to you, really, said Freya. —You were responsible for her this morning.

—I don't know, I said.

—Now, Freya said. —You *do* know, don't you?

—We can ask at Meeting, I said, thinking of Libby and how she would talk Richard around, away from Freya's suggested punishments.

—This is just about us, the three of us, our little family, said Freya.

Blue was burying her face in my neck now. Freya put down her boots.

—We could cut off her hair, I said.

Painless, and Freya would like it. That hair of hers.

Blue shook her head into my throat. Freya smiled, and shook hers too.

—I see, she said. —Clever girl. You're kind to her. But pain, you see, it's important, to drive the Bad out.

—Blue doesn't have the Bad, I said. —She was just exploring.

—Can't take any chances, can we? Freya said.

I was silent.

—I think it will have to be the Spike Walk, Freya said.

Of course I knew it would be the Spike Walk straight away, but Freya liked to tease it out. When it was me, she'd come and sit on the bed and ask me how I thought I should be punished, and I'd suggest ways, but it was always the Spike Walk in the end. Somehow it was worse to play the same game for Blue. It was her first time.

It was still a damp night, and the others would have taken their work into the kitchen, sewing and sketching by the aga, with the dogs lying over their feet. So we took her down there, crying now and clinging to my waist, and I stood at the yellow room end, whispering *Just think about tomorrow there'll be honey coming from the shop run we'll have honey cakes Blue just think about that,* and Freya stood at the ballroom side, pushing Blue back to the Spikes whenever she had done one Walk, telling her, —Now, run the nail along the same scratch, that's it, until it bleeds.

The next morning, Freya wrapped Blue's arm in a clean rag with wild garlic and lavender packed into the cuts. At breakfast I gave Blue my share of the new honey, and the Family stroked her arm or her back as they passed. Ellen clanged pots around, until Richard said, —Is there a problem? and Freya said, —No, no problem, and the others drifted out of the kitchen, touching Blue's shoulder or her other arm as they passed, while she nibbled on the honeyed bread, and snatched her head away when I reached to smooth her hair.

I didn't know then that I wouldn't have to do any more Spike Walks. They would all be for Blue.

7

Once I asked Freya about the Spike Walk, and she said there was a story for it, only we didn't tell it often, because it was clear as a summer sky what the Spike Walk was for. She told me the story anyway, and I told it to Toby, then to Blue when she asked, so it wouldn't be lost.

Foxlowe existed before the Family did. Many years ago, before long Solstice days, before the house brimmed with the smell of wine and candlewax, before home, Foxlowe stood alone. The Standing Stones slept on the moor with no one to imagine what they meant or to care for them. Every Summer Solstice the sun path lit up through the Stones, all the way up to Foxlowe's walls, and the sun set twice. No one saw it, or cared, or did things in the proper way. Freya was carrying her old name, and living in far away, concrete places, and only just beginning to understand how very wrong things were. It would be a long time before she and Foxlowe found one another.

Then Richard came, and Liberty, carrying their old names, and others with their old names too, people who lived at Foxlowe before the home we know. Foxlowe welcomed them with warm light and the blue stained glass made puddles on the wood for them to play in, and sunlit dust flurried in abandoned rooms. Richard knew the house from a long time before. He said the garden was full of things to eat but they had rotted away, swollen and burst, because no one had been there to enjoy them. They had to live for a little bit like the outside, paying money for all the food. But soon the paintings were taken down, and the furniture hauled away, and Foxlowe began to look like itself: the chickens, the vegetable patches, the fruit trees.

Most of the paintings were high up, and left squares of dark wood behind, in the way covered skin stays white in summer. In the Spike Walk, though, the nails stuck out low, and when you walked past them, they bit at you, snagging clothes and skin. In the first years, talk was of taking the nails down, and smoothing the wood with sandpaper and fresh varnish, but other jobs were more important, and everything had to be learned.

When Freya came, she said, —Leave them up. We'll call it the Spike Walk. No one knew why, but as in all things, they did as Freya said. Then many Solstices later, the children came. They were afraid of the Spike Walk and the ghosts at the end of the corridor. Freya understood that if the children got the Bad in them, you could get it out by making them walk up and down the Spike Walk until the skin bled a little. And then the others understood why Freya had told them to leave the nails where they were. Sometimes Freya's wisdom wasn't revealed for a long time.

8

As she got older, Blue would be punished again and again for disappearing alone, walking out onto the moor, talking to outsiders. Her arms would be streaked with scars, etchings of Spike Walk nights, and we got used to seeing her bandages. After that first time, she never cried in the Spike Walk. She held her arms out as though spinning on the moor for fun, holding Freya's eye. It was always me, in the end, who looked away. At Meeting, it was agreed that me and Toby were to keep watching her, and never let her out alone. But so often we lost her, slipping away over the stone wall and running so fast we could only wait for her to come back, a sickness rising, waiting for the night, for Freya to balance things again.

We knew, me and Toby, deep down, what it was that called her away again and again, and leached away when she bled in the Spike Walk, only to build again, because it was so old and rooted so deep; it had touched her when she was so very tiny, grown around her like a vine around a tree. We never betrayed her. Even she didn't know. When Freya would scream at her *Why do you do it?* Blue could only shake her head, and me and Toby held each other's eye.

Around a Solstice after her first Spike Walk, Blue had a bad run of them, her skin never seeming to heal by the time the next Walk came. So me and Toby taught her maze-making, one of our favourite games, to try to keep her attention with us, to hold her for a while. She'd kept watch while we stole the cogs of thread from the sewing box, fiddling with the fresh bandage on her arm. Toby showed her how to snap the line with her teeth, running the tongue over the tender parts of the mouth, avoiding the rot.

—Where do you chew? Show me, he said. Blue arched her head back and pointed.

—That one then, Toby said, and flicked at a tooth on the top of her jaw.

I remembered, briefly, those teeth coming through: the screaming, the sudden sharpness of her bite on my fingers. She'd lost many by then, sat twisting the loose ones in Meeting. Freya kept them in an old jar, with mine.

—Wrap the thread like this, Toby said, —and cut, and you have to be quick, because the chasers are coming for you through the grass!

Maze-making was best played on the sloping moorland near the Standing Stones. You had to catch the right time of the year: when the grasses were grown over our heads. A couple of dogs had followed us down, and flopped in the sun where the grass was lower.

Toby was the best maze-maker. He went in first, trailing a bright red thread, and disappeared into the green. The end was tied around the stile post, and the knot bounced and slipped as Toby made his path. The grasses crashed and snapped. Then a yell, —Now! and we plunged into the maze, following the thread line, the ground marshy beneath our feet, the crushed grasses like a carpet, and stones tipping us off course. Blue was faster than me, pivoting and making the quick turns with ease, leaving me squeezing through the grasses behind, trying to follow Toby's path. His counts carried over the air, and my very skin strained to get to him before the seconds disappeared, then suddenly Blue parted a wall of grass and fell upon him, as he yelled *Fifteen!*

—You did it! he yelled, rolling Blue onto his stomach, the thread still hanging from his thumb; she'd got to him before he could cut the thread on his teeth.

—Too slow, too slow! she cried. —My turn!

Toby solemnly gave the thread over to her with a little bow. He was tall now, so his jeans stopped at his shins, and it had made a kind of gap between us, as though it was him alone, then me and Blue lumped together, the smaller ones. Teaching Blue our game was another small ending of the world of us, of me and Toby.

Blue curled Toby's thread around her thumb as she collected it from the grass and we picked our way out of the maze, ready to start again. Through the green, I glimpsed a figure hovering near the stile.

The man was wearing a brown suit and his white hair was short, his face shaved. A smile played around his mouth as he took us in.

—Hello, he said.

Toby put his hand on my shoulder.

Blue tilted her head and waved. He copied her, making her laugh, then she danced, and so did he, waving his briefcase in the air.

—Playing a game? the man said.

Toby found his voice. —Are you lost? he said.

—Ah, no, just arrived, the man said, taking off his shoes. He perched on the old wooden gate, rolled off his socks, wiggled his toes in the sun.

—So nice here, the man said.

Toby looked at me, silently saying, *What now?*

The man had closed his eyes and was holding his face to the sun. I wondered if he'd forgotten we were there.

I shrugged back to Toby, and mouthed, *Just keep playing?*

There were no rules for outsiders who popped up on the moorland like spirits. We knew most of the locals by sight, and avoided them if we could. The thought that held me and Toby still and kept our hands on Blue's wrists to stop her shooting to this new plaything was that the man could even *be* a moor spirit, or the Bad, dressed up in a suit.

The man opened his eyes and his smile faded. —Oh, he said, —don't be frightened.

A dog bounded over and the man welcomed it with a kiss on its muzzle. She was Toby's favourite, a bitch with soft brown fur turning grey around the eyes. We both remembered her as a puppy, but Toby would play with her and try to teach her tricks, gave her a few different names that never stuck. When he saw the dog licking the man's face, Toby's grip on Blue relaxed and she rushed over to sit next to him.

—Why are you here? Do you have a name yet? We're playing a new game, she said. —It's with threads and you have to catch the maze-maker before he cuts the thread and I just won, how old are you?

—How old do you think I am? he said. He held up his chin and pushed back his hair, so she could look at his face. Toby and I went over to crouch in the grass.

—Old, she said. —*Eighty* Solstices.

—No, older, I said to her. —Look at his white hair.

The man laughed. Up close he was very real, with mud on his trousers, brown spots on the back of his hands.

—Do you live outside? Blue said. —We live at Foxlowe.

The man smiled. —I wondered if you might, he said.

I felt better. He wasn't a real outsider at all, but knew home.

—We should take you up to the house, said Toby, like it was a question.

The man gestured for him to lead the way.

We almost broke into a run, taking him back over the stone wall. We three had a huge secret, a gift, maybe even new family, and we'd met him first. The man kept stopping along the way to look behind us, to where the Cloud sat on the horizon.

When we reached the stone wall behind Foxlowe, the man's scalp under his white hair had burned red. He stood for a while gazing at the house, windows flashing in the sun. The garden was in full summer bloom; the sweet pea were bright, the fruit trees swollen. We three waited for the man to say something, about how he knew our home, but he only stared, then vaulted over the stone wall and dropped into the gardens, so we had to scramble to follow him.

Toby flung the kitchen door open and yelled into the house, —Everyone! Hey!

Egg and Pet were already in the kitchen, their arms around each other, Egg kissing Pet's forehead. They were always fighting and making up in Freya—Richard seasons, which this was. Mostly, it made life easy when Freya and Richard were together: Blue and I had the attic to ourselves, could whisper into the night. We'd find Freya every morning in the kitchen, where she'd kiss us both, though Blue would duck her head away, and give us pancakes soaked in apple syrup. She even laughed when Toby dropped a case of eggs when he tripped on the steps near the fountain. Toby had gone white, but Freya just made sketches of the mess, foamy yellow and the raw white like spit on the marble. But Libby spent her days with Egg in the ballroom, playing the tapes on the tinny stereo, and slept wrapped in his arms, making Pet's eyes raw.

They broke apart, stunned. I grinned; it was hard to surprise the grown. It took a second for Egg to recover. He strode forward, holding out a hand to the stranger.

—Hi, he said. —Are you lost?

—We found him out by the Stones, I said.

—He was just there, said Toby.

—We thought he was a moor spirit, I said to Pet, who'd told us stories about them, how they led you to bogs and marshes, told you riddles, made promises with hidden stings.

Noise drifted down from the house as the others caught the scent of gossip and clattered towards the kitchen.

—If only I were so magical, said the man. —I'm parked over at Ipstones.

Richard, Freya and Dylan burst in, followed by the others. Freya stood for a second, her eyes flicking from the outsider, to us, and then settling on Blue. She had her by the hair before me and Toby could move, and dragged her out of sight, towards the goat shed. The man's smile disappeared. Richard bounded over next to Egg.

—Hi, he said. —Welcome. Glass of water?

Pet filled a jar.

—We don't usually sell from the house, said Richard. —We have some goats' milk, jam and wine, if you're—

—Unless you're from a gallery, Dylan said. —We have some new craft pieces ready for market that you're welcome to look at, and our higher end stuff is in the back.

—Sculpture and pottery mostly, Richard said. —Some paintings.

—Are you lost? Egg asked again.

—Is the girl all right? said the man. —What's going on?

Folded arms and silence to this. Ellen and Libby were whispering to each other. Toby and I moved closer together. Valentina mouthed *Okay?* to Toby and he nodded.

—It's all right, I said.

The man studied Richard's face. —You're the owner, he said, not like a question.

—We live as a commune, said Egg, so who owns what doesn't really —

The man spoke to Richard again. —You're Ralph's boy, aren't you? Same nose, and the clothes—

—Oh, said Richard, and straightened up, grew taller. —You knew—

—I lived here for a while, when I was very young, the man replied.

A ripple went through us. Someone who knew old Foxlowe, before us — not an outsider, but something else, like an old friend we'd forgotten.

The man held up his briefcase.

—I'm supposed to mark them, he said. —Papers. I was on the train. I've kept on working, you know. Never wanted to retire.

He looked at the briefcase and down at himself. In the silence Freya's voice floated, *No more said about it.* It was her soft voice and so we parted a little as she came back with Blue at her side, hiding her hands in her sleeves, where the new scratches were. I pulled gently at her earlobe, and Toby squeezed her hand.

I found Blue's ear. —So, how old, do you think? Guess, I whispered.

She sniffed. —*A hundred* Solstices.

It was the oldest we could imagine. Freya was our eldest grown and she'd lived eighty-two Solstices, summer and winter.

The outside man spoke. —And then. I just, I don't want to, and I thought, it's so simple, and I realised I wasn't far from, well the train was coming through, and I just thought. I always wanted to come back and visit. Silly, really.

He trailed off and looked up at the archway and the old stone there, then looked back, smiling, like he was pleased to find something there. —I always meant to, he went on. — I was ill when it was Ralph's funeral, and then, well, I didn't know. You never know, do you, if you *should* go back, you know, to places you've ... He spoke to Richard again, —Oh, you're so like, he said.

Richard pulled at his shirt sleeves.

—Then it just kept playing on my mind, kept thinking about it, on the train, how much I loved it here. Your granddad and me ... He nodded at Richard. —Oh we had some laughs, when I was sent up here —

—*Maybe more*, I whispered to Blue.

—Um, said Richard, —well, I suppose, if you want to look around—

—I heard everything went to you, the man said. —I remember hearing about all that, and it's Ralph too, isn't it?

—Richard, Freya corrected him.

—How old are you? asked Blue.

—I am three hundred and fifty-seven today, said the man.

She laughed.

—Aren't you going to wish me happy birthday? he said.

—You say, *Happy birthday*, said Richard.

We did, copying the way his voice flew up and down on the words.

On his first day we didn't talk to Kai much. He told us his old name, and we tried to forget it, in case he stayed. He took a t-shirt from Jumble and wore overalls over it, leaving the brown suit folded in a carrier bag on the back of the kitchen door, ready to be cut up for patches. His first evening with us, he sang with Libby and Dylan; he was good at guitar. He found a mattress in one of the back corridors and Richard said he could have that room, if he wanted.

Days passed. Richard came into our attic and pulled out cobwebbed boxes from the eaves, things we didn't know were there. He and the man spread out photographs on the kitchen table, and the man found himself, so he said, a boy standing on the back lawns, wearing shorts, his hair cut short, squinting into the camera. He and Richard stayed up late together talking and sifting through pictures, writing things in pencil on the backs. Richard called us to look at them, Blue and me, pointed at dead faces, told us names, but they were like Leavers, just ghosts, and I said so, said, —But they aren't like us, they just used to live here, and Richard snapped the box of photographs shut. Freya packed them away again, put them back into the eaves. I didn't like them there, watching us sleep.

The man taught Toby how to play a game with an old ball he'd found in the sheds. He asked Valentina if she minded, and she shrugged and said she didn't care, then watched them from the kitchen windows. He told me and Blue stories about where he'd come from, Oxford, where there were books buried under the streets, and buildings made out of yellow stone, and Freya let him even though usually we weren't to talk about old lives, but she said his voice was nice, and she liked listening to it lilt and fall while she worked.

At the end of his first week the weather turned cool, and we made a hot dinner. I dipped bread in egg, pushing it under to make it soggy. Freya took the eggshells and smashed them in her fists.

—So witches can't use them, she said, and winked at me.

—Can't we have tomatoes? Ellen said.

—Yeah, no veg all week, said Dylan.

—We'll all get scurvy, said Pet.

There was a murmur of agreement from Libby and Egg, painting their toenails with tippex.

While we ate, Kai held the conversation. When others spoke, adding anecdotes, we all listened, but when Kai took up the thread again we leaned forward with our forks hanging. He didn't talk about the outside much but kept coming back to Foxlowe's old life, and how there had been fires lit in every room, and books covering the walls, and people who brought you things, who just lived there to bring you things, and how he and the man called Ralph had played games on the stairs that sounded like ours, using sacks to race to the bottom. Freya leaned on her hand and watched all this, chewing her eggs, smiling.

—Thing is, Freya said, as she took Kai's plate.

—Yes, yes, I know, Kai said, smiling. —I'm not an artist, I can't draw! Not at all! he added, cheerfully. —I heard in one of the villages that's what it is here now, an artists' place. Ralph used to paint, you know, he said.

—That's really not the point, said Freya. —We all contribute something. Richard and I, we can sell our paintings and sculptures, Dylan too, he just got a big commission from Liverpool — here everyone cheered —And I do most of the cooking and sell the wine and the jam and so on, and Valentina sews, Ellen brings in her contribution from the markets down in Leek, and Egg does lots of the goats work, and the garden …

—And I'm an artist too, snapped Libby.

Freya held Kai's plate out. —I mean, you just ate my eggs, and that's fine, but what do *you* put in?

—We're happy to take in anyone who can contribute, said Richard.

—I'm a teacher, a professor. I can teach the girls and October, Kai said.

Toby looked up from the eggs and caught my eye. —Like school?

—That's a great idea, Libby said.

—Who asked you? Freya said. —They're not *your* children.

—Nor yours, said Libby. —Right?

—Don't be a bitch, Liberty. Richard, tell your lady love it's unattractive to be such a bitch, it might make you lose interest, said Freya. She turned to Kai. —I hope you had a nice holiday.

Richard held up a hand and said mildly, —All right.

Freya went on, —You have to contribute, so we can buy the stuff we can't always grow ourselves.

—Well, Richard said, —it's not about *money*. It's about any kind of contribution. Want to learn some stuff? he asked Blue, who shrugged, slurping her milk.

—Freya's going to teach me how to make pots, I said.

—We should all talk about it, said Ellen. —I thought we were against institutionalising them, sending them to school.

—But this would be here, said Libby. —I never thought we were against *learning*, just—

—The point is they have the best education here, said Dylan. —They learn what's important, about how to live, how to be self-sufficient, so they don't have to worry about—

—Why don't we ask them? said Libby.

Everyone went quiet and Richard opened his hands, gesturing for us to speak. I tried to catch Freya's eye, to see what she wanted me to say, but she was licking egg yolk from her fingers.

—I don't know, I said.

—Blue's too young, anyway, said Richard.

—She must be seven or eight now, Richard, Libby said.

—We could learn to read, said Toby.

—Would you like that? Ellen said.

Toby looked at Valentina, who shrugged.

—I've got plenty of money. I'll contribute towards everything, Kai said.

There was a long silence. Richard rapped his hands on the table, playing it like drums, and Egg took up the beat.

Kai cleared his throat. —I'd really like to stay. I like it here. I feel better here. The money's just sitting there, he said.

—Well then, smiled Richard, and called Meeting, where Freya named the man after the crows that nested in the roof, and he was made our new brother.

* * *

That same night, after Meeting, we stayed out late on the moorland behind the house, watching the sunset. Me and Blue lay in our favourite way, spreadeagled on the grass, looking at the sky. We couldn't see the others and their voices gently buffeted us. Sweet smoke curled in the air. Cold seeped over my limbs but I stayed lying there, letting the shivers run up and down until I couldn't feel them any more.

Libby and Freya bickered lazily and their slurred words drifted over each other, like lyrics to Richard's guitar.

—I got it from the Oxfam in town, I remember, I got a sack of stuff, and you took a jumper, and I said I'd have this—

—You're too fat for it, look how it wrinkles on your arse!

Dylan's gentle voice rose. —Well, it's no one's, is it, it's not *your* stuff—

—Shut up, Dylan, you keep your stuff. Who else wears those jeans? And didn't you have a go at Richard for taking your boots? I heard you!

Snorts and laughter. Blue shifted next to me. Her raised arm came into view.

—What's that?

I didn't look. —The moon.

—Not the *moon*. You didn't even look!

I kicked her.

—Ow! She pointed again. —*That*.

—I dunno. A star, I suppose. Toby! I called out, and flung my arm up. —What's that?

Libby's voice floated across to us. —They've gone back to the house, him and Bitter Bambi.

—Why?

Silence.

—Hello? Libby, why's he gone?

—I dunno. Hungry?

Kai's face loomed in the sky.

—Hello, dear ladies.

—Hi, Blue said.

—Kai, what's that? She wants to know. It's a star, isn't it? I told her a star, I said.

Kai eased himself onto the grass with a sigh, and lay between us.

—Show me? Ah. That's … no idea. A star.

We laughed as though this was the funniest thing in the world.

—What a giggler you are, Blue, said Kai. —Where'd you get that from, I wonder. My mum, she was a terrible giggler. She used to cry with it, her mascara would run all the way down her cheeks.

—I don't know, said Blue.

—Maybe it's your mum too.

—Kai, will you tell us about the outside?

I knew I shouldn't ask, but with just the sky above me, it was like I was asking myself, or a blank space, and not really Kai at all.

—The outside?

—Outside Foxlowe, I said. —Where the Bad is.

Kai was quiet, and I thought about how it must be hard to describe, like trying to see your own face.

The voices and guitar notes drifted in the air near us, and the height of the sky made my stomach swoop, and I tried to feel the earth turn. Dylan had told me once how it spun, and I wasn't sure it could be true.

Eventually Kai asked, —Don't you know your stars, Blue? That's not a star at all. It's a planet. Venus. You can tell because she's close to the sun. Venus and the sun are in love, you know, but if they were ever to touch, the sun would burn up little Venus. So she stays just as close as she can.

—But it's *night time*, Blue said.

—You're making it up! I said.

I was delighted. He wasn't a teacher at all, just another storyteller.

—And what's that one? Kai pointed to another speck, glittering in the dusk.

—Ah, that's … no idea. A star! Blue cried, and we laughed again helplessly.

Libby's scent, apple and wine, drifted over our heads as she lay down next to us on the grass.

—Green, you remember me taking this skirt from Jumble, don't you?

—We're stargazing, said Kai. —Do they know their stars?

—Ah! Now that's one of *my* stars, said Libby, pointing. —I'm an Aries, and that there is the tip of my ram's nose.

—Aries, I repeated. I liked the sound. I thought of air and flying. —That can be one of my stars too.

— No, no. You're definitely a Leo, like Freya.

And Libby growled and jumped on my shoulder, making me squeal and laugh.

—Leos are fiery and have terrible tempers, she teased.

I laughed. —I don't!

—You *do*, said Blue. —Kai, look at my leg where she kicked me. And yesterday she made Toby's ear bleed.

—He hit me first. Look at the mark on my arm!

Libby's hand came into the sky, silencing us.

—And you are a little Cancerian, Blue.

—How do you know?

—Well, it depends on when you were born, said Kai.

—But we don't know our birthdays—

—But your traits are *so* pronounced it just *must* be so, said Libby.

Blue wriggled happily on the grass. —Cancer.

—It means you're connected to the sea, said Libby.

—Blue's never been to the sea, I said jealously.

That night Libby conjured up a world we'd never seen, of tides and the surface of the moon, all tinged with silver and green and the milky shine of moonstone and pearl. Blue became quiet, and I knew her eyes were closed and she was pinning the colours and the images to herself like new names. We'd heard about fire and earth and water and air signs before, but Libby said that was mostly rubbish and the stars were what mattered and they couldn't tell you the future but they could tell you more about yourself, and then we told Kai about Blue's name and how I'd given it to her, and Kai sang some of Blue's own song, of love and sadness.

When we stumbled back to the house, mud on our skin and clothes, grass in Blue's hair, it was late and quiet. We hadn't brought the torches, and no candles were lit, so we bashed into things in the kitchen, giggling, following the starlight across the flagstone floor. We jumped as one when we saw the figure, hunched in a sleeping bag at the foot of the staircase. Toby. Ellen shrieked and laughed, and we followed, started chattering to him. *What are you doing, you made us jump, why don't you have any candles lit? Where's Valentina?*

He opened his mouth, but no sound came out. His eyes were huge and startled. Blue went to him and put her arms around his neck, and the grown ups scattered through the house, calling Valentina's name. I kept asking, trying to make him speak. *Is she gone? Is she a Leaver? Toby? Is she a Leaver, then? Are you all right?* He just looked at me, and when the grown ups came back, shaking their heads, tears running down Libby's face, he curled up, as though to sleep, when they asked him about the Leaver, *Tell us how she went, tell us why*. In the end Richard said to just let him sleep, and Dylan carried him, like a smaller ungrown, into the ballroom, away from the hallway draughts.

Over the next days and weeks we talked over the signs. We knew there would be a story Toby would have for us, about how the Leaver went, what she said, but he was still telling it to himself in silence, getting all the details right. We told and retold the way the Leaver had called Toby in from the goats' shed weeks before, where we three ungrown were daring each other to uncover and spoil the curdling cheese. They'd spent the day together in one of the old bedrooms, and at dinner we'd heard their laughter as they came down, her arms around his neck, her thin hair the exact shade of his, breathing in the skin behind his ears. We talked of how the Leaver had missed Meeting, claiming a headache.

She'd left a pile of things for Jumble: clothes, books, her notebooks full of sketches and scrawl. Richard relaxed the rules, so things were held back for Toby — the notebooks, especially, no one was to take. But Toby didn't claim them, and they stayed in Jumble until Freya tore up the pages for kindling.

We waited and waited for Toby to tell. But Toby's words were gone. Valentina's Leaving story was never told.

9

This is the time the new stories came: the Time of the Healing. The most important is the Healing story itself, which was always in Freya's voice, and that's how I'll tell it.

The Healing was a gift brought from the Good to remind us how the Summer Solstice works to restore all things. Our new brother fell ill quickly after his arrival, not unexpected, when he came from the outside, where the Bad reigns; Freya understood at once what to do, and

Wait. I don't need Freya to tell it. Let me tell you. I remember it and it is my story now.

Kai taught us so many things, but it's the things we taught him in return that I remember him by: how to prick an egg so you could blow out the contents, leaving you the shell to keep; how to milk the goats, calming them first with an unbroken stroke from the head. We let him into our games, the only grown we did that for. His favourite was the first he'd seen, the grass maze game. When Valentina became a Leaver, Toby wouldn't play, so Kai made up the loss, playing with Blue and me. His first summer with us, whole hot hours were lost in the grass, us three nettle-stung and breathless and with bits of cotton hanging from our teeth.

A good maze-maker would make sharp turns, so the chasers had to turn and cross themselves and could never catch him before the line went slack. So, this is the way I think about Foxlowe sometimes: a lurching turn, grasses high over our heads. The last days of the easy time, I know, were when Kai came to us. So when I try to follow the turn of Foxlowe down the new path, like following a thread, there is Kai at the end of it, spooling out the line from his mouth. But that's not his fault. He was kind.

Kai's kindness to us was equally done: each of the three of us, Blue, me and Toby, got something. The first was for Blue. The day after we'd been on the moor, laughing at the stars, Kai had offered to do the shop run with Freya. I heard the old car spluttering down the drive and ran to watch from the ballroom window. At the end of the drive it stopped and Freya meandered towards it with the shopping baskets. Kai got out of the car and even from far away I could see his hands over his mouth and his bent back, and Freya's sudden quicker stride towards him. They leaned against the car for a while and Freya gave him a roll up and lit it for him, watching while he smoked. He held out his hands while he was speaking as though shaping his story out of the air and Freya was very still. Then she jimmied open the stiff passenger door for him — I had broken it the summer before when me and Toby were playing driving on the front lawns and I'd slammed it too hard — and she got into the driver's seat.

When they came back, Kai poked his head around the door and caught my eye, beckoned me.

In the hallway I said, —I saw you this morning. Don't you like driving? They won't let me, but I'd like to. Not away, but just around the fields and things.

He smiled. —Oh, yes, not a fan myself, he said. —Too many levers and buttons. Now … He bent closer, and I saw the pink tinge in the whites of his eyes, as though someone had mixed paints wrong. He brought a hand from behind his back.

—I have a gift for our young friend, I mean little sister, he said.

It was a jewellery box, silver and engraved with seashell shapes. He opened and closed it a few times so I could see the purple felt inside and hear the click of the latch.

—How did you? I said.

—I found it in town.

I was sympathetic. He was only new. —We're not supposed to get things like that. You have to take it back. See, it's just useful stuff, and you can't spend too much—

—No, no, he shushed me. —It's from a charity shop, and I swapped my briefcase for it. It's for the little one.

—*Just* for Blue?

—We're going to make her a present, you and me, Kai said. —Full of *Cancerian* things. A little identity box. She'll love it. We'll get things, some of the things we talked about with Libby. And put them inside for her.

—Does Freya know?

—No. She was buying matches at the market.

I wrung my hands in the cotton of my dress. I knew Freya wouldn't like it, it was wasteful, and not to sell, we couldn't take it to the craft fairs, and it was just for Blue, which wasn't allowed either. It should go into Jumble. I thought about Blue on the moor the night before and her quiet listening. I took the box and hid it in the attic.

Over the next few weeks we filled it with the plastic pearls, blue and white, that had snapped off Libby's bracelets. She kept them in a box in the yellow room. I stole pieces of blue and green fabric from the rag pile to sew into the lining, rippling them so Kai said it looked like the sea. Kai bought shells from the craft shop in town and we broke them and glued them back together into what Kai said looked like a crab. I found a cloudy piece of glass in the gravel at the front of the house, that could be moonstone.

When we gave her the box Blue didn't say anything, just sifted through the beads and shells, holding them on her hands, and then up to the candlelight. She opened and closed the box, clicking and unclicking the latch.

Kai whispered to me, —Ah well. Thought that counts.

—No, I whispered back. —She loves it.

* * *

My gift was a secret Kai taught me to make life at Foxlowe easier. We had lessons with him every afternoon. He taught us new stories, like Alice falling down the hole, wardrobes with witches in them; he acted out tales for us and made his voice shrink and swell for the parts. I asked him once how he knew so many stories, and he stretched out on the armchair, arched his back, and said, —My parents told me, I suppose. And I told them again, when it was my turn. Then he looked sad, so I said, —Do you miss it, outside? And he said, —Not the bad parts, and I knew not to ask any more.

He taught us old words and showed us how they made our own, then taught us new ones from the same root. I still see words like that, strung together by chalk, making loops across the board: *negare, negate, negative, lumos, luminous, numos, numinous*, while we listened to Kai's rasping voice making word trees in the air.

In one of those afternoon lessons, not long after Kai had arrived, he was making a word tree for the three of us from *mellus* (*melody, mellifluous* ...). My eyes were closed, better to see the sounds hanging together, and because, though Kai wrote them on the piece of slate, I needed to hear the sounds: the chalk didn't mean anything. Instead, I made pictures of honey dripping from musical instruments, and falling into soft pillows.

Now he stopped speaking, and when I opened my eyes he was looking at me.

—Green, he said. —Why is the name for a tree, tree?

I sat up. Blue was dozing in the armchair next to me, lulled by Kai's voice; Toby was looking out of the window, where our oaks were shivering. They carried old scars from us, scratching into their trunks, digging at their feet, stealing bark for the topping of mud pies and to see the smoother wood beneath.

—Because, I said. —That's … it's their name?

—Let's say it, Kai said. —All of us.

So we chanted *treetreetreetree* over and over again, even Toby mouthing the word, waking Blue, who laughed and joined in, tripping over the sounds, until it didn't mean anything and then we looked at the oaks outside the window and they had shaken off the sound, standing serene.

—What does *tree* have to do with what a tree looks like or what it is? said Kai. —Nothing at all. So, he said, placing a hand on my shoulder, —when someone says something, something upsetting, it's just a sound, and the truth of things is very different, something far beyond the noise we make for it.

I understood he meant for me to let Freya's words drop off me, like the trees shaking off their names. So that when she told me about the Crisis, reminded me how I had the Bad threaded through me like stitching in a dress, I could imagine her words floating above how things were, just sounds. Kai couldn't know how Freya's words were written on the inside of my skin, how they weren't like other words, how they could never be only sounds, with a different truth. But I loved Kai for his trying to rip Freya's words from me, even as I held on to them ever tighter.

For Toby, Kai had a gift of a different sort, also given that first summer he came to us. He had left a note in the attic room for us one morning, on our pillow: *Back Lawns*, then a drawing of a clock showing 2 o'clock. Blue and I got the time first, then sounded out the words. *Back* I knew, from cutting out the coupons on the back of cereal boxes, *on the back of this pack*. *Lawns* was harder, but I knew *L* from Libby's name, and then we worked it out because with *Back* it was the only place that came next.

So on that sticky afternoon we sat out on the back lawns, picking at grass, Kai, Blue, Toby and me. Blue's hair was loose, stuck to the back of her neck in sweaty clumps. She had new bandages from disappearing again and talking to a group of walkers. Kai was barefoot, showing his painted toenails, flaking tippex and black resin. —Like a piano, he said, and wiggled his toes, then pretended to play a tune by pressing his fingers on each nail. His hair had grown a little since he'd become one of us, and it puffed around his ears like white cloud.

Toby's jeans were rolled up to show his brown shins and the scars I'd given him around his ankles. We sat cross-legged so our knees touched, like a meditation.

Kai clapped his hands together. —Well! Toby's thirst for knowledge has called this little gathering! You were trying to read one of my books, weren't you? he asked Toby. He had this way of talking to Toby I liked, as though the silence wasn't there, as though at any moment, Toby would simply speak again.

Toby poked at a soggy peach I'd brought out with us. His cheeks were red.

—Nothing wrong with wanting to read, Kai said. —Words echoing around your head. Other worlds, other lives. A thousand, thousand stories. Would you like to learn?

—But we can read already, I said, nervous. I closed my eyes and reeled off, —Keep away from Children. Ingredients. Ballroom.

—How did you get on with my note? Kai asked, grinning.

—Fine, I lied.

—Well then, let's try something more difficult! he said.

The grown read books and traded them with each other for ounces of grass to smoke or for soap. Kai brought one out from behind his back and waved it, grinning.

I split a long piece of grass into two long strips, wound them around each other to make a bracelet I knotted around Blue's wrist. Kai watched, and said, —It's okay if you don't want to—

—Yes, Blue said.

I glared at her. —Blue, it's not—

—I talked to Richard, Kai said. —You're not doing anything wrong.

He opened the book and its spine gave a satisfying crack.

—All right, said Kai. —I'll read it out, and you follow the words on the page as I go. That way your brain will start to make the link between the sounds I make and the black ink shapes.

We crowded around the pages, Kai crouched behind us so he could read over our shoulders. The story began in a room with a chair and flowers and a lamp. The room was described so you could see it in your head, and after a few pages I stopped following the ink and it was like listening to any other story. I kicked the back of Toby's legs in a bored rhythm.

Kai stopped reading and sat back on his haunches. —Maybe this is a bit hard to start with, he said.

—I don't want to, I said.

Blue tugged at my hair. —I want to, she said.

—What if you go on a shop run? Kai said. —You have to read then.

—One of the grown will be there, I said.

—Or be a Leaver, you need it for being a Leaver, Blue said.

Toby started.

—Don't be *stupid*! I said.

Blue looked blank. Kai rolled onto his back and sighed. —Look at those clouds, he said. —That one's a chimney, look.

I tried to catch other shapes and shout them out, but after a while Toby's quiet spread over to all of us.

—What you have here, children, it's magic, Kai said. —Hardly anyone in the world has the chance you have, to grow up this way.

Then Kai asked us to meet him every day for new lessons. Not stories, proper reading lessons. Toby was beaming that day. After that he disappeared every morning to make the markings on the pages speak to him, and Blue went too. I hated that they had this together, without me. In the attic Blue would never show me how to do it, she said I had to go myself. Libby had spoken for us at Meeting, Richard had said it was all right. But I was Freya's, and what Libby said didn't matter much for me. I knew it would be a bad thing.

That was the first time Blue mentioned becoming a Leaver. She'd only seen seven Summer Solstices then.

10

Damp air seeped into the kitchen, the windows streamed. The year had rolled around again and it was close to Summer Solstice, but the house was full of shadow, and cold fog skulked across the gardens. I picked a flake of skin off Toby's scalp, making him flinch. Richard was making a house of cards at the table, Libby in his lap, while Dylan boiled the kettle, his huge frame blocking the weak window-light. Freya's scissors made a sound like teeth into an apple, as she cut string into worms she then laid on the table.

—New piece? Richard asked.

Freya snorted. —You're confusing my art with Liberty's bits of string glued on a toilet roll. It's to tie herbs together, for tea. For Kai.

From the chair by the aga, from which we carefully held our eyes away, a painful breath scraped in and out. I didn't turn at first, but then I saw that the grown were looking.

Kai was curled up, his feet tucked under him. A blanket folded under his chin was moist at the edge. Stained rags were scattered around him. Someone would have to collect them for boiling at the end of the day.

It had started with the wheezing that crept up through the air at night, and Kai's plate, that we stopped setting, because he ate nothing, and then he was sick anyway, though the water wasn't bad. Every day the kitchen smelled of ginger and mint, but it didn't help. For weeks he slept by the aga, in the warm, where the dogs napped in the afternoons, but every morning he was worse. The boxes of pills Freya delivered for him, ever since that first shop run they'd taken together, he now kept with him, clutching them like Blue with a blanket she had loved when she was very small. At first me and Blue sat on the edge of the thick-armed chair and he read to us or just smiled. Then we stopped going to that side of the kitchen.

—Kai, Freya said. —You're all right.

Her voice was soft. We all spoke quietly those days, as though loud words could hurt him.

—Are the taps on? Libby asked Richard.

—No. Well, do *you* want to pay it? he said, as Libby tutted her way out of his lap.

Dylan held out the kettle. —I just boiled the last. There's more in the rain bucket.

—No, it should be cooled, Libby snapped.

Dylan looked stricken. —He can have mine, he said.

Dylan crouched before Kai, peering into his face. He and Libby looked at one another.

—Should we … I don't know. Call someone? Dylan said.

Freya put her mug down firmly. —Right. Kai. Let's try getting you out to the Stones tomorrow.

Kai's eyes opened. —Oh?

—It'll help. Let's go tomorrow.

—Yeah! Libby can lead a meditation, said Dylan. —Do we have any weed left?

Libby and Dylan left on a shop run to get Solstice treats, and Richard disappeared to the studios, where he was working on new sculptures made of bracken and plaited grass. The others were in the gardens. Kai's breaths deepened and we let him sleep.

—Should start making yourself useful, Freya said to Toby, —now you're alone here. You've had plenty of time to wallow. She's been gone two Solstices now.

Toby stared in silence.

—Start by cleaning those eggs I brought in this morning, she said, gesturing to them with the scissors. —They're covered in shit.

—I'll help, I said, and Blue got up too, but Freya stopped us with a sharp turn of her head. She got up and chose a bowl from the side, shook dust from it. She put water on to boil, adding steam to the wet air, and we three watched in silence. I thought about the steam soothing Kai's chest. Toby was limp in his chair, seeming to see nothing, he and Kai like dolls in the room.

Freya poured water from the singing kettle, and placed the bowl in front of Toby. The eggs she wrapped in a dirty cloth and placed next to the bowl. She settled opposite him, smiling. We waited.

—Go on, she said.

Blue bit the skin around her nails, but I was still. I knew I shouldn't watch, but I didn't move or pull my eyes away as Toby sank his hands into the water, snatched them out, sank them again, a cry.

—There's your voice, Freya said.

One of the eggs cracked in the water but the others he cleaned all right, laid them back on the cloth. Freya threw them away, ruined she said, by the water too hot. Then she left to work on a painting. Blue threw her arms around Toby, snuggled into his chest.

—Freya doesn't feel how hot the water is, I said. —She's used to it, so.

—No, said Blue. —She knows it's too hot. She knows it hurts.

Toby just held up his scalded hands, the red skin like gloves.

The next morning was still wet, but we all trudged over the gardens to the Standing Stones. Kai wheezed and retched and we stopped to rub his back and give him boiled water we'd brought in a pail. Libby was wearing a long purple skirt with beads stitched around the hem and a purple scarf knotted over her breasts. Seeing her pimpled flesh, I said, —Libby, aren't you cold? and Freya replied for her, —Our Liberty likes to dress well for meditations, all eyes on her.

We cleared beer cans from around the Stones, and leaned against them, hugged them, tried to feel the hum of the ley line that ran through them. Libby clapped her hands and we settled into a rough circle around the Stones, in the cold mud, making sure we all touched one. Freya and Richard shared a large mossed stone at their backs, and left Kai propped against its twin. Blue and I shared another, our hips squeezed together to fit. Toby was next to us, his legs stretched into the centre. Richard handed around sweet scented roll ups, and we took deep breaths of smoke each time one came into our fingers. We'd taught Blue how to hold the smoke in your mouth so it didn't make you feel sick, but she breathed as deep as anyone.

Libby held up her hand to her face, and showed us how to breathe: first a finger, then a thumb over each nostril in turn. She used to lead us through a guided meditation with forests and gardens, tell us to imagine ocean waves, but it came up at Meeting, and they asked us ungrown what we saw when Libby spoke. We couldn't say, and there was talk of confusing us. So we just breathed.

I fell into the familiar pattern, trying to ignore the needling cold in my bare arms and legs. As Libby counted, *One two three four five iiiiin* … we held one nostril, then the other, forcing air through each time, rocking with collective breath. I felt the ground under my thighs, and the stone on my skin, imagined the roots of the Stones far underground, the ancient things buried underneath. Blue leaned into me. She got dizzy easily. A warmth flooded into my arms and legs, and I twitched my fingers and toes to feel the needlepoint tingle there. *One ... two ... three ... four ... five ... ooooout.*

Then Blue was shaking me, and I opened my eyes. Everyone was standing over Kai.

Pet knelt by Kai's side. —How do you feel?

Libby knelt down next to Kai. —Are you okay there? she asked, so softly.

—Kai? Richard said, quiet too.

—Better, I feel better, Kai said. —Did I cough? You didn't hear me cough, did you?

—It's just because you were sitting still like that, said Egg.

Freya pushed a pin back into place in her hair. She turned to face Richard and said, —Well, we're not finished yet, are we? She turned to include the rest of us. —This isn't *it*. It's the Summer Solstice that will really do it, just like the Crisis. *This* is just to help, to begin. Meditation can't hurt, but it's the Solstice, the double sunset, that really—

—Oh shut up, Freya, said Libby. —It was stupid to bring him out here. I mean, look at him.

Freya uncurled herself, and I knew a screaming row was coming, but then Kai tried to get up, saying, —I'm fine, see. He coughed so long, so deep, his back bent over, and no one went to rub his back or offer water this time, we all just watched, stuck, and I wanted to go to him but Dylan's hands over his own mouth, and Libby's face crumpling, stopped me.

Kai sank back onto the stone.

—Kai, Libby said. —Kai, you're ill. I mean you're really ill, sweetheart.

—Yes, Kai said.

—We should take you to a doctor, sweetheart, don't you think?

Kai looked around at the circle of us. —Can I stay, please can I stay? he wheezed.

—Yes, you can and should stay, Freya said.

She glanced around at everyone, and I followed where she looked, a trick I'd learned. It avoided her gaze, but also made her happy with me, as though I was with her. Dylan was pale and miserable. He looked between Kai, still slumped against the stone, and Freya. Richard stared at the ground. Libby glared back at Freya. Ellen and Pet were biting their nails, their eyes damp. Egg was staring at his feet, his hands in his pockets. Toby knew my trick and stared right back at me, blinking slowly. Blue rocked from foot to foot and ran her thumbnail over her top lip, calming herself.

—Everyone knows you should stay, Freya said, putting a hand on Kai's shoulder. —It's all right.

—I'm staying, said Kai. Freya took his hand. —I won't be any trouble, he said.

—You need a hospital, Libby said. —It must be your lungs, or, I don't know … Maybe a disease. You might have cancer.

—She's right, said Dylan, and I hated him suddenly, his spit bubbling at the corners of his thick lips.

Kai's face seemed to shrink. —I don't want to go there.

—Liberty, Freya said. —It's not for you to say.

—Oh, you'll be washing him then? Changing him? Libby said.

Kai reddened. —I won't be any trouble.

—Oh Kai, Libby said. —It's not right for you to stay. It might get very bad. You can't ask us to —

—It's my home here now, said Kai.

—You can't leave, I whispered.

—Libby doesn't understand, said Freya. She was speaking to Richard now. —It won't come to that.

—There's no doctor here, Ellen said. —We'd have to drive him down to the villages.

—We can help him, Freya said. —The Solstice is coming.

—This is surely the best place to be, said Pet.

—Exactly. Fresh air, fresh food. It can't hurt, can it? said Egg, his thumbs tucked into the waistband of Pet's jeans.

—Look, Kai, said Libby, and she sounded different, more grown up. —Are you saying you don't want any treatment? Because that's your choice—

—Thank you, Libby, said Freya slowly.

—But if that's your choice, we'll have to contact your family, to take you home, or to a hospice—

—Hospice? No, no hospice. Not like her, not like that, said Kai.

—You *do* want treatment then, Libby said.

—Yes. I can be treated here, said Kai.

—We could find somewhere locally, so we can visit, said Ellen.

—Foxlowe can heal him, Freya said. —It's the Bad, making him ill. The Solstice will drive it out. She looked around. —Isn't that what we all know? Don't you remember the Crisis?

Libby stood up. —Freya, this is different. It's not … that might have been a coincidence, this is serious.

—What do you bother living here for, if you don't think Foxlowe is special? Freya spat. —Why do you bother, if you don't think there's anything to it?

—Mia, said Richard.

Mia was a name Richard gave Freya sometimes. No one else was allowed to use it. Once, a rare blush flooding her neck, Freya had told me it meant *mine*.

—It's time we all started taking this seriously, Freya said. —Kai is. I always have. It's not a game.

Spots of red had risen in Libby's cheeks. —But exactly, it isn't!

—I'm sorry that you can't understand, said Freya.

—You've lost your mind, said Libby.

Richard kicked at the ground, avoiding Freya and Libby's eyes. —I mean, he said, —we do believe, don't we, that the Solstice can help? The Crisis showed that.

Freya and Libby were very still.

—But, Richard said, —but it's a case of … here is someone really sick. The Crisis, that was … I mean … I don't want anyone to be harmed here, he said.

—It's two weeks until Solstice, Freya said. —Two weeks and I'll show you. Everything will be different.

—No, Libby said. —I'm going into town tomorrow to phone his family.

—It's just two weeks, Freya said.

—He might not have two weeks! What's the matter with you? Libby said.

—If I'm wrong, I'll become a Leaver, said Freya.

Libby stared. No one moved for while, then Libby raised her arm, a vote to agree, and the others all followed, hands rising as one. I watched Freya, and when she put up her hand, I did too.

11

That night under the blankets we made a tent, lit orange from the candle glow outside, and traced the inside of the wool with our fingers. The air pressed down, but Blue's arm was cool next to mine. The dogs barked and raced around the walls outside.

—Cancer, we whispered. —Cancer.

It had a pretty rustle to it.

—Like drowning, Blue said, and silently I followed the thread of her thoughts back to the jewellery box that sat on the shelf, hanging in a web of thoughts that connected Kai and us. *Cancer*, flowing soft through our teeth, would always be greens and blues and water, and Kai's voice rising and falling as we lay on the grass with our arms spread out, and how we knew he was kind, because he tried to give Blue an answer to the question *Where do you get that from, I wonder.*

— No, I said. —It's not like that. Not drowning.

—I *know.*

—I know.

—Dying, they said.

Blue pushed the blanket high, let it fall. I ballooned it out again, making the candle flame shudder.

—He might become a Leaver, I said.

—Or *die*, he might *die*, Green. Where would he go? she asked. —Where do they take the dogs?

— I don't know. We buried the last one by the rockery, but sometimes they take them away somewhere.

Blue pulled at my earlobe.

—But Freya says he won't die, I said.

Blue blew gently at the sheet so a tiny shaft of candlelight peeked through and shone onto our faces.

—Things die, like the dogs, she said simply.

—Freya says she'll be a Leaver if she's wrong, I said.

—Yes, Blue said.

—Don't you care?

—Of course, Blue said. But I heard the empty in her voice, like dead seed husks in winter.

Later that night I tried to ignore the thirst that scraped around the inside of my mouth. We hadn't had the taps on for a few days, so we had to be careful with the water, but I'd used my share to rub into my itching scalp. The attic was warm, and I licked the sweat from my arm; that made it worse. I listened for two clock strikes before I got up.

A torch had been set on the kitchen table, making a ring of electric light. Kai was in his chair by the aga, the glow of the torch making harsh shadows on his face. Freya, Richard and Libby were around the table, the tail of an argument, *Why don't you, How can you?*

—Sorry, I said.

—No, no, Libby said.

Freya was mashing something in a bowl.

—What's that? I said.

—A balm, she said. —For Toby's hands, you know.

I went to the sink and tried the taps. Nothing.

—Milk in the pail, said Freya. I found it and gulped it down.

I picked at the wooden table. Some ants were racing across it: *scuttle-freeze, scuttle-freeze*. I set my finger against the wood, let one scramble onto the smooth plateau of my fingernail. Libby placed a finger next to mine and my ant stopped at the tip of my nail, seeming to assess the new ground. We watched. The ant crawled onto Libby's finger, and we smiled at each other.

—What's going to happen? I said, before I could stop myself.

—Nothing bad, said Libby.

—We're still deciding, said Richard.

Freya's bowl clattered.

—Liberty wants to change everything, she said to me.

Richard put his hand over Libby's. She had been about to speak, but then seemed to change her mind about the words.

—We were thinking, Green, she said. —Since Kai can't teach you any more.

—He'll be better after Solstice, said Freya.

—Since he's unwell, how would you feel about going to school?

—We'll talk about it at Meeting, said Richard.

Freya spooned the balm onto a cloth to cool. In the morning she'd smooth it onto Toby's scalded skin.

—No. I don't want to go to school, I said, and went back to bed.

Toby, Blue and me sat in the yellow room at the end of the Spike Walk. It had become Libby's space, where she often slept in Freya—Richard seasons. Her clothes and jewellery hung from the backs of chairs and over the wardrobe doors. It felt like a safe place, quiet except for the scuttling of the mice and the gentle settling of the house around us. When Toby went that way I followed, ducking under the nails, and Blue followed me. I took her hand in mine and followed all her ghosts from Spike Walk nights, their bleeding arms and steady stares.

Toby took the mouldy armchair and folded his legs under him, and sucked at the skin on his arm, making a red mark he then inspected. His hands were bound in cloth, the balm underneath. Blue drew in the dust, and I knew I should stop her because the creatures that lived in it made her broken skin flare up and we'd be putting compresses on her hands for days, but instead I sat next to her and watched.

—Will she be a Leaver? said Toby.

Libby had told us, Blue and me, that we should act normally if Toby spoke, just keep him talking, but I saw Blue reach out to touch Toby's bare toes, a brief stroke, and I had a sudden urge to make her get out, so I could hug him.

—So, he said, smiling, and I realised I was staring. —Will she? I think she will.

I thought he was talking about Valentina, that he still thought she would come back, and I meant to say, *Yes*, but some glint in his eyes made the word stick.

—Freya, he said.

I laughed. —Of *course* not.

—Why d'you say that? Blue asked, not looking up from her dust picture: a flower growing out of a pot.

Toby cleared his throat, spoke slowly at first, then the words tumbled out. —She's lost, hasn't she? No one's doing what she wants. They're sending Kai away, I'm sure they will. Libby and Richard are back on again. Libby's strong now. Did you see how she led, at Meeting? She talked right over Freya, and no one even said anything. And Freya just sat down, and she hasn't got back at Libby. I think Libby's going to lead more now, her and Richard will. It's going to be better, even if Freya stays. She won't hurt us any more. I think Libby will stop her.

Blue and I were silent for a while.

Then, —Yes, Blue said.

—You're being stupid, I said. —*No one* should leave. Kai should stay and, Freya *is* the leader, you can't say that she isn't, and Libby just *isn't*, that's not how things are, and she hurts us sometimes because of *the Bad*, Toby, and *you* should know why she has to worry about that—

Toby was stretching out on the chair, trying to look like he wasn't bothered, but his voice shook a little when he said, —I don't care, I just think she'll go, that's all.

Blue looked up from her drawing again and frowned. I made a leaf in the dust, and curled it around the flower she'd made. I was hungry; no one had made bread the night before, so there had just been the peaches, soft like Kai's old skin, tasting of perfume. I dusted off my fingers, slowly, my head to one side, watching the particles fall.

I separated. It was like that. I can't think of another way to say how I felt then, and at the other times when Freya spoke through me. One part of me looked on and felt sick and sorry, but the other half, the speaking half, the half that everyone could see, did this: she fixed Toby with a stare he would recognise so he would go cold and she saw him begin to turn away because he knew what was coming and then, —Shut up, she said. —Valentina didn't want you, and now we know it's because you're a hateful little shit.

As though the air was all sucked out of the room.

I knew it was Freya, somehow, and so did Toby, but he got up anyway, and as he left he pushed me into Blue and she fell into the dust. Her face fell into the picture and I lashed out but missed him as he slammed the door behind him.

I pulled Blue up, brushed the dust from her cheeks. —Don't mind him, I said, shaking. —He's a bastard.

—Don't call him names, said Blue. —You made him do that. You're the bad one.

She turned away and smoothed over the floor, making a new canvas.

12

Summer Solstice is a day of great celebration. The sun is strong and light will flood over the moor stretching into the hours of night; this is a day the Bad must shrink and flee. Hang garlands from the doors, and wrap them around the throats of animals and small children. Bring the gardens inside the house, and eat the ripest fruit. It is a day of fresh things.

This day is the safest time, so be outside: on the moor, enjoy a day entirely free of the Bad.

This is the day of the greatest gift. When the sun is sinking, go to the Standing Stones. Take gifts of fruit and flowers. Watch the sun drop behind the hill called the Cloud. The Bad will rejoice. But then the sun will appear again, before a second sinking. Even the sun is reborn on this day. All broken things are made new. All sickness is healed.

13

Summer Solstice came. In the attic, the beam above us glowed in strong, Solstice sun. You could tell what time of year it was by the light. Solstice was near when the sun reached across the centre of the room and lit up a knot in the wood above our heads. All the rain had drained away. It was a good sign. I pinched the blanket over our heads so the air was warm underneath.

—It feels all wrong, I said.

—Not like Solstice, Blue agreed, with sour morning breath. Everyone was tense, and arguing. Freya wouldn't let Richard touch her, slapped him once in the kitchen. He slammed doors for a few days, then ignored her. Blue had found Freya crying up here, lying on our bed, and crept away before she was seen. Only Libby was happy, dancing to silent music through the house, her hips swaying.

I sniffed at my damp armpits, and wriggled my toes to feel the dirt there.

—Is there time to wash? I said. —It's Solstice, we should.

Blue scratched her scalp. She slid out of her wrinkled dress, revealing a yellowing vest and knickers underneath. We rooted around under the bed for new underwear. Blue got back into her dress, and added a cardigan that she waved out of the open window and sniffed afterwards. In a pile of clothes on a chair I found a skirt, too big, but I safety-pinned it and tucked the t-shirt in, added a cardigan with paint stains on the cuffs. We looked at one another.

—Fine, I said, and Blue smiled. We'd missed the warm water anyway. It was on for an hour on Solstice days; she hated to bathe in the cold.

Toby waited for us at the bottom of the staircase. We three had made up quickly, needing the solidity of us when the grown were making everything feel unsafe. A cluster of dogs dozed in a sunbeam at his feet.

—It's bad in there, he said, nodding towards the ballroom.

—But it's *Solstice*, said Blue.

—Freya didn't come to do our hair, I said.

Toby nodded. —It looks shit.

I slapped him lightly. —Not as bad as *yours*.

He was wearing a bandanna made from an old patch of fabric, blue with a pattern of apples. It made his eyes seem bigger, without his hair to distract you.

Dylan smiled at us when we came into the ballroom, where everyone was gathered on rugs with the incense and candles for later, but it was a second-smile, and then he started to chew on the skin around his thumb. Freya stood at the ballroom windows, her back rigid. Her hair was done up with fresh flowers in it, as it should be, but none of the other women had done it this year, so hers looked lonely and strange. Libby watched the ballroom door, as though she could see through it across the hall and into the kitchen, where Kai would be dozing by the aga.

—If Freya becomes a Leaver, Toby whispered, —will you go too?

My throat closed.

The whole day the Family were distracted, half-finishing the Solstice tasks, falling off the edge of conversations, wandering around rooms. We gathered around Kai in clumps, wiped his face with the dirty cloths, rubbed the back of his hands, sang in low voices. Ellen abandoned the flower-gathering to whisper with Libby in the ballroom, and Freya pulled the flowers up herself, brought an armful to Toby, Blue and me. We strangled the bright sweet pea and feathery grasses with both hands, plaited them into circle-wreaths, and hung them on the doors, around the necks of the dogs, the goats, to protect them in case the Bad tried to fight. I laid one around Blue's neck. —Don't need one now, she said. —I'm nearly a grown. I ignored her, tied the stems fast behind her throat. In the kitchen, Richard laid out the Solstice stores, saved for months: butter, cream, the herbs dried over the hot weeks; and then others fresh picked that morning: mint, thyme, parsley. A hen Freya killed the night before drained blood into a bowl. Honeycomb dripped into jars, ready for the sweet cakes. Egg and Dylan cracked kindling over their knees in the garden, the sound like broken bones startling Kai awake, wrenching coughs from him, until they left that too, wandered inside, just to watch Kai shake and retch.

We held Meeting that day in the kitchen, so we wouldn't have to move Kai. We carried the lit candles, moulded into leaves and roses and stars, and trailed the incense from the ballroom, dotted the lights around in alcoves and on shelves, along the edge of the aga, where the chicken roasted in cream, the dogs drooling on the flagstones. As the light faded we'd thrown all the windows open to the summer air, and from the kitchen we could hear doors slam, ghosts wandering between rooms.

Freya didn't talk about her promise to be a Leaver if Kai wasn't healed, or try to convince us any more. It was just like a normal Solstice Meeting. Richard spoke about the year, wished the Leavers well, and we thought on them for a full minute, the only permitted time, holding hands, our eyes closed, Toby's grip tight on my fingers. Freya spoke about the Bad, and the Time of the Crisis. Between them, Freya and Libby told the story of the double sunset, wrenching the lines from each other like a fought-over new dress.

Ellen and Egg gave out bowls of chicken casserole and bread with blackened crusts that burned our fingers. A vat of moonshine was dragged in and we sweetened it with honey, drank deeply, wetted Kai's lips with it. The sky began to glow.

—Okay, said Freya. —Can you bring Kai, Liberty?

At the Stones, Solstice light beamed strong through the circle, hitting the centre stone like a jewel. We laid Kai on it, bathed in light, and piled up the gifts: fruit, flowers, wine and honey. We sat with our backs to the Stones, feeling the ley line's hum and watching the sun path flow strong. We didn't sing or meditate or smoke or drink or dance between the Stones, no one had brought the guitar or the drums, there was only our breathing, and our willing Kai better.

The sky started to blaze, and pink lines trailed across the huge sky, stretching from the horizon and behind us to where Foxlowe lay quiet. There should be singing, and wine, and all of us holding hands, but we were too afraid, that Kai would be healed or not healed, and we stood alone and separate from one another, and watched the sun sink in a sky on fire. Kai leaned on Freya's arm, speechless. The sun disappeared behind the Cloud. I took Blue's hand and shivered in the sudden shadows, and all around me I felt a shift as we moved close to each other. For a few seconds we held collective breath, and the Bad danced. But then the sun was reborn above the second peak of the Cloud. It was a beautiful one, clear and a true double. We watched as it sank again. Freya scooped Blue and me into a fierce hug that hurt my ribs and whispered hot in my ear, —Now we'll see.

Afterwards, no one wanted a party or to dance out on the moor; we finished the stew, and spent the rest of the evening prying the spilled wax from the ballroom floor to remould later. Freya took Kai back to his room, carried him warmed stew and tea, and banned everyone from smoking in the back corridors.

—Is she packing? Toby whispered, as we watched Freya pace from ballroom to kitchen to back rooms, from where we sat on the middle step. I dug my nails into my palms, and Blue traced her thumbnail across her top lip. We waited until the candles burned down, and the dogs began circling to make invisible beds for sleep, their wreaths shaken off or hanging torn around their ears. The house quietened.

It was the next day that it happened. We all woke late and stumbled around brewing tea and chewing on the remains of the Solstice bread. Sun streamed in and the house was warm and sleepy, a day for dozing, lazy sewing, easy cooking. Freya and Libby circled each other, their eyes never meeting.

Libby moved first. Most of us were in the ballroom, busying our fingers with nothing useful — I plaited and unplaited Blue's hair, finding the red in it like glints in the moorland stone. Libby shook out her own hair, twisted it on top of her head, let it go. Waited until the room was gazing.

—Think we should see the results of Freya's experiment now, she said.

Freya's smile was slow and wide. She'd been knitting, and set the needles aside with a clatter. Her long skirts cracked as she strode out.

—Wait here, she called over her shoulder.

Libby did a quick dance, her bare feet pointed. Her bracelets jangling as she turned was the only sound in the room.

Kai came into the ballroom on Freya's arm, but then he let go and walked in alone. His breaths came deep and almost silent. I realised I hadn't heard the coughing the night before.

Freya held out her hands as though asking for quiet, though we were already dumb, and the room shifted towards her.

—Kai is healed, she said.

Libby laughed. —I said you should just take him, she said to Richard. —While she was asleep.

—The Solstice did it, the double sunset, said Freya. —It drove the Bad out of him. Come and show them, she said to Kai.

Dylan caught at him. —Are you all right? he asked. Kai turned deftly and put his finger to his mouth. I thought of his playful face and the dancing from foot to foot when he had shown me the Cancer box. I clutched at Blue. —It's all been a game, I whispered.

—Kai, how do you feel? asked Freya.

—Much, much better, he said. He spoke in a strange rhythm, nodding with each word, and then sighing after he'd said it, seeming pleased.

—There, Freya said. She beamed at us all, clasping her hands together.

—Amazing, called Libby. —Freya's Jesus. Praise the Lord!

Freya cocked her head at Libby and mouthed *Fuck you.*

Kai came around us all, and I studied his skin and the clear whites of his eyes. I saw how he walked easier, and heard his soft breaths. Ellen had started to cry and was hugging Freya, her huge arms across Freya's throat. Pet pulled Egg into a circling dance, but Egg wasn't smiling. Dylan and Richard were both looking at the floor.

—I'll sleep now, said Kai.

We watched him go, all listening, straining our ears for any coughs; there were none. The ballroom door shut.

Freya picked up a glass from the floor, lifted it. —Wine?

—Seriously, Libby said. —This is …

—He's fine, isn't he? Freya said. —Can't you see that he's fine?

—So he wasn't that ill in the first place, Libby said.

—You all saw him, Freya said.

—You did something, with the pills, said Libby. —That must be it. What did you do?

There was silence. Freya looked around us all, and then threw her glass against the wall behind her, where it smashed and left a trail of red along the wood.

—What more do you want? I told you I'd show you what Foxlowe can do. What more do you want?

—I believe you, said Ellen.

—Richard? said Libby.

—Hmm? He spoke as though he'd thought he was alone in the room.

—I just … Maybe we should still, said Dylan.

—Richard? Libby said again.

We all looked to him. It was easiest. He didn't answer for a long time.

—Kai *is* better, he said.

Raised voices, slammed doors. Libby barricaded herself in the yellow room, wouldn't let Richard in. We danced and drank long into the night.

Later, once the attic door closed on the weak summer light from the windows, the darkness on the landing was absolute. None of the candles were lit, and our own had drowned in itself. I held my hand in front of my face, straining my eyes. I tugged at Blue's arm.

—It's too dark. Let's go back, I said.

—No, Blue said.

We counted steps forward, along the landing. Toes pointed and stretched, feeling ahead. The banister was smooth, with three small dips, before the lurch downwards. I counted them out for Blue, my other hand in hers. We stopped again at the top of the stairs. The space gaped before me and my stomach seemed to stretch towards it, wanting to fall.

—Freya?

Blue shushed me.

I crouched down and felt on the floor until it fell away. The edge of the top step against my wrist. I shuffled onto the floor and swung my legs down, pulling Blue with me. Slowly we edged forwards until we sat on the step below. I knew that a few steps down, the stained glass window would make a blue nightlight. Then shapes formed in the dark, moving.

—Can you see? Blue whispered.

In answer I grabbed her fingers, flapping in front of my face, and she smothered a squeal. She brought her face up to mine. —I see you, she giggled.

It was a candle, swaying with the familiar carried motion. We turned gratefully to see its golden pool reach the top of the stairs above us.

—Girls? What you up to? Don't you have a candle?

Libby's voice was low. She crouched on the step above us and I took in her jeans and trainers, old winter clothes, and the hooded jumper that I'd never seen before.

—You look funny, Blue said.

Libby set the candle down before us on a lower step, so that our shadows loomed on the wood around us. On the high ceiling our dark forms ballooned, and I had an urge to yell, to make the echo come, but Libby was quiet, and everything was softened to a whisper that night.

—You want to see Kai, Libby said. I didn't know if it was a question or not, but I nodded.

Libby touched the tip of my nose with her finger.

—You worry too much. He'll be fine now, you saw at Meeting.

—Is Freya up?

Libby shrugged. —I don't think so, I think everyone is asleep now but us. She reached back to something, outside of the light, and fumbled there. She brought out a small torch.

—New things! Blue said.

I said, —When did you? What else is there?

—No, Libby said. —This is mine. It's really old. I brought it with me when I was new here.

We just looked at one another then.

—Here, Libby said. —I have this. She swivelled the top of the torch, and it shone into our faces. I winced. —You take the candle back to bed, she said.

She smiled at us. A sudden image rose of Libby's hair how she used to wear it, under a scarf, and a jasmine perfume she didn't wear any more came drifting in my head.

—Let's make the echo, I said.

Blue looked at me. —We used to do it before you came, I told her.

Libby laughed. Her snaggle tooth caught on her bottom lip. —Then we stopped, because you were such a noisy thing.

—Always crying.

—Sorry, Blue said, and Libby kissed her head.

—We can't, Green love. Sorry, we'll wake everyone up. But let's play it tomorrow.

She stood, lighting up the steps below us. I concentrated on breathing, counted, as she'd taught me, Libby. Even now, if I have to, I can find her voice, counting breaths, dragging out the expelled breath so it made you dizzy.

—Is it because of the Healing? I said.

Libby sat down again. —Oh, Green. You don't believe it?

Her eyes travelled over our hair and the edge of our faces, and we did the same back, memorising, because that's what we did, for Leavers, if we had the chance.

—Richard will take care of you, she said. —And you take care of each other and Toby. Take care of Toby, won't you?

—Can I come? said Blue.

My stomach dropped. —Shut up, I hissed. —Don't say things you don't mean.

—You could come too, Blue said. —We can wake Toby up, we can all go.

—We live *here.* This is home, I said, and I sounded calm, sure, like Freya, but panic fluttered under my ribs.

Libby kissed Blue on the head. —You should stay here with Richard, she said. —Sorry, sweetheart. Her eyes were spilling over.

The front door sounded lighter than normal as it closed. Perhaps she had a trick for it. We didn't ask her where she was going or if she would be all right or if we would ever see her again. But the next day when she was missed I realised that no one had seen her Leaving but us, there had been no farewells. We searched for notes, and the small tokens Leavers sometimes hid away, and then as time went on we waited for postcards or parcels or letters. Nothing ever came.

14

Things didn't change at first. Every Meeting, one of us would ask if anyone had heard anything from Libby (*the last Leaver*, we would say, but we all said her name in our heads at once) or if Richard had written a letter to say he'd found her. (In the kitchen, one of the windows still taped up with cardboard, Richard's knuckles bloodied up, and Freya's snarl, *Go after her then*, and her tears afterwards, in the attic, curled up under the blankets for days.) Freya would shake her head no. She held Meeting every two days now, but no one drank wine or smoked while they happened, or started singing. Now Richard was away, only Kai was good enough at guitar to start up music, but he never did, and no one was sure what Freya would say if that happened.

That's how things were in the first months. Freya never made new rules, or said things had changed. She smiled extra-sweet and hugged us all the time, but when she spoke she used her hard glass voice and it was safer not to do things, just in case. So it stuck, and it was too frightening to strike up in the middle of that silence and say, *But this isn't how it was before*, because then we would have to admit the *before and after* that had appeared in our thinking.

Then we fell through another Winter Solstice with no word from Libby or Richard. Freya made the Scattering alone with her steel capped boots stamping through the door, so the year started, she said, with a bang. Then a summer, another winter, another summer, until Richard and Libby began to fade, their things around the house gathering dust and falling into piles that toppled and were kicked into Jumble, until we shared them out. At Meeting, instead of talking for the three of them, saying *We the Founders*, Freya began to say *I*.

Every Meeting she made long speeches about the Standing Stones and the Solstice and how we could use them to make Foxlowe a better place to live and work. Then at the end she brought Kai forward, under the cracked mirror, and reminded us what Foxlowe had done for him, and everyone clapped. When I looked around some people's smiles were strange, like they'd been pulled back by little hooks in their cheeks. Sometimes Kai's cough came back, on damp, misty days; and then he wasn't at Meeting, and Freya didn't mention him at all. He haunted the back corridors, a Leaver who had stayed, who sometimes didn't remember us, or either of his names.

In this new way of things, I felt safer. I missed Libby, but I didn't miss the way the room felt stifling, even the huge ballroom where there was so much air, when Freya and Libby and Richard were in one place, or the way Freya would lie awake some nights, twisting her ring, or the way only one of them, Libby or Freya, could be happy at once, laughing and playing with us or with the dogs, while the other shrank. Now Freya was the only Founder, she made all the decisions, and life was simple.

But Blue suffered more. She couldn't learn to give all the control to Freya, couldn't see how much better things would be if only she could. The more she had to take the Spike Walk, or be Edged, or stand outside on winter mornings in only her underwear, the more she fought Freya; she held her eye when she should look down, stole food when it had been denied her, and more and more, ran out onto the moor alone, sometimes staying out so late we thought she'd become a Leaver.

One day when the year was new, Winter Solstice only weeks gone, Blue and I stood at the attic window, watching Toby as he was driven away. It had been raining for hours, battering the slate roofs, soaking the dogs, who whimpered, shaking out their fur. Foxlowe sang a chorus of drips into pots and chipped mugs all around the house, the low notes under the leaks in the ballroom calling to higher ones in the upper floors.

—Can you see him? Blue said. She lifted her heels, showing the blisters there. —I think I can see his hair in the back, she said.

I rubbed at the condensation, strained my eyes through the drops, but the back window of the car was dark and shrinking.

—Maybe he didn't go. He was a bit scared, Blue said.

—No, he's gone, I said.

We laced and unlaced our fingers, counting. Blue's were slick with tears and snot; I wiped them on my skirt. It took twelve counts for the car to disappear. The dull ache pulsed in my stomach. Overnight it had taken root there and boiled up my insides.

Blue curled underneath the bookcase and took down the Cancer box. She picked up some of the plastic beads and dropped them one by one back into the pile.

—That's three things now, she said. *—Libby*, she mouthed, because it was taboo to say a Leaver's name out loud, and especially that one. —Richard, she whispered. —And now Toby gone without us and now he won't be our friend, he's already not with us most of the time.

I sat next to her, poked around in the box, and took out the crab, which had a leg hanging off, the glue stretching like chewing gum. —He'll be back this afternoon, I said.

I didn't mean it though. I thought, like she did, that Toby might slip away, find a bus station like the one Pet had described with its roar of engines and plastic chairs, or simply get lost somehow, and never find the road home.

—I thought we'd all do our first shop run at the same time, Blue said. —It's wrong that he'll see it, outside, and we won't.

—He's older, I said.

—Are you going to go without me too?

—Probably, I said. —But I'll tell you everything, I swear, and I'll bring new things that we'll hide up here, I won't put them in Jumble. They'll be ours.

Blue rolled onto her back and stretched her whole body, her toes pointed, her face screwed up, arms lifted over her head. She did this when she felt trapped and angry and bored, when the outside pulled at her, and it worked to stop her breaking things, or yelling at Freya, which could only make things bad for her. I waited until the tension drained from her limbs, and she lay limp on the floor.

—Come on, I said.

We went to the empty kitchen and drank foamy goats' milk from jugs left out on the sill. I sniffed it first and poked at the gluey skin; it had started to turn, and we drank with the sour edge of it flooding our mouths. Every few seconds Blue craned her neck to see into the gardens and I kicked her bloodied heel under the table to stop her looking for him. Then I'd do the same thing, listening to the clatterings around the house. I thought about the glittering road across the moor and wondered if Foxlowe was visible from that far away.

Egg was gone too. Toby had been begging him for weeks to take him. It had all come out the night before, at Meeting. Toby had put up his hand when Freya said, *Is there any other business?*

—I want to go on the shop run, he said.

I'd started to make a pile of dust. I liked the grainy feel of it against my hands. When I looked up Freya had her eyes on me, and everyone had followed her to stare. I thrust my fingers back into my lap.

—No, Freya said, after a long time. —Too young, you're all too young.

—Not the girls, I'm not asking for them, Toby said. He wore jeans I'd patched myself, using bits of the quilt Libby had made for Blue when she was little. Pieces of it were already sewn into draughty curtains or used as cleaning cloths. I didn't like it, felt it was bits of the baby Blue being passed around and dirtied, although she was long gone and the Blue I knew was next to me on the ballroom floor. He wore a faded silk handkerchief of Richard's as a bandanna, whether to soften or irritate Freya, I didn't know. In the light that day, the fuzz over his lip and the down on his cheeks showed; he could have been one of the grown, holding his hands out, addressing the room. —It's just a request, he shrugged. —Just want to say I'd like to, and if everyone is happy then I would like to go next time.

Rehearsed. I knew he'd practised, maybe in the goat shed, where he liked to go and breathe in the sweet smell and listen to the animals' gentle shifts.

—Yeah, said Egg, but it came out croaky. He smoothed the greasy moustache. —Yeah, I'd be happy to take him next time.

Freya was still looking at me, and my face burned. The tiny dust-mountain in front of me had a hair on it; I made my eyes focus and refocus on it, blurred and sharp, blurred and sharp.

I'd hoped the milk would drench the heat pain in me and make it cool, but it curdled into a hot sludge. I wanted to be moving, walking; but rain gusted against the windows. Dylan came in, peeling off his overalls and throwing them over our heads, revealing badly fitting cords and a t-shirt underneath. Blue grasped at the overalls like we were playing piggy in the middle. He swooped to wetly kiss my cheek.

—Want to help me clear out one of the back rooms? he asked.

After the Healing, Kai had stayed in the back of the house, where the rooms were small and warm. Last Meeting Kai told us there were rats back there, where the dogs couldn't catch them. —I can hear them he said. —At night, scratching around the walls. I can't stand it, I can't get any peace. Then he'd had one of his turns, where he cried but couldn't tell us the reason, and stared at us like he didn't know us at all. Freya said we had to start clearing out the old servants' rooms, all boarded up from before our time, to flush the rats out.

Through the studios, we waved at everyone and mostly they ignored us, busy in the strange places they went to, with their paints or pencils or thumb-printed clay. Freya flicked under people's chins if they ignored her. I wondered how long I would have to wait before I could start to do that.

We came to Freya's studio last. She had a huge canvas on the far wall, a sky and landscape, sketched in pencil and charcoal. She was smoothing the top of her head when we came in, looking out of the window over the back lawns. She heard us and spun around.

—Visitors! Are you bringing me tea?

—Sorry Freya, Dylan said. —Didn't think.

—What do you reckon? she said, nodding to the black gashes in the paper.

—The moor! I shouted first, so neither of the others could.

—Yep. She flicked her pencil towards the canvas. —Look closer.

It was the double sunset on Solstice day. Two discs sat above the double peak of the Cloud.

—Not my best, Freya shrugged. —I can never get it right, the angles. Anyway, I'm waiting for the paint to come back with Egg. Golds, for the suns.

Freya's pencil twirled in her hands.

—Spit it out, she said.

—It doesn't look gold at Solstice, I said. I glanced at Blue and she nodded, her hair in her mouth. —It goes like grey, I went on. —Like, things are dying in it, and then it's pink and red and even purple sometimes, like — I twisted to show a bruise on the back of my leg

—and even the grass goes that colour, like night-time colours.

Freya looked at the painting again.

—Don't hog my girls too long, she said to Dylan as we left.

The back rooms were through another door and then down a narrow wooden staircase, nothing like the one at the front of the house. The worn carpet was slippery under my bare feet. Dylan flicked a lighter on. The stairs came out at a lower corridor. We used to play down here, with the bells that had the names of the rooms on, only they had different names to ours: *Parlour, Master Bedroom, Nursery*. It was fun to ring them and listen to the echo down the corridor. But we hadn't been in this part of the house since the Healing.

Kai peered around a door in his grey vest and underwear, holding a razor, his face covered in cream.

—What is it? he said, as though there were some emergency.

—Kai, you shouldn't have that. Where did you get that, hey? said Dylan, gently taking the razor from his hand and, with a flannel from the sink behind Kai, sponging away the cream. Underneath, his beard stood intact, grey and white, snow on slush.

Dylan settled Kai back into the best chair from the ballroom, leather with thick arms and a deep creaking seat.

—Oh, said Kai. —Oh.

—We're going rat catching, Blue said.

—Come watch, I said.

—Kai's tired, said Dylan, and kissed his forehead.

Two doors along was the new room. Dylan kicked at the handle and then shouldered the door open, revealing a small wallpapered space, with furniture piled along the walls, and a fireplace full of newspaper. Every surface was littered with things: glass and ornaments, and papers, and even candles that had only been half used.

—But, Blue whispered.

—All this *stuff*! I said.

—Yeah, load of rubbish. We have to clear it out and take it to the ballroom, in case anything can be used, said Dylan.

—*Rubbish?* Look at the candles! And I bet there's clothes in that wardrobe and oh I asked Toby to get me a candle to keep biters away look I bet one of those would do! Are there more rooms like this? We might never have to go on a shop run again! Does Freya know this is here?

—Green, we still have to eat. And this is just … it's all mouldy and dusty, it's things Richard didn't think we'd use when he came, I think. Come on … He picked up some papers. —Let's get the place cleared out, for starters. Dylan shook out a bundle of sheets, showering us with dust, then chased Blue with one over his head, enveloping her in it and spinning her around in his arms until I thought she would choke with laughing.

Dylan kicked boxes out into the corridor, and threw the candle stubs into a pile. —I'll take these upstairs, he said. —Keep going, and if you see rat droppings don't touch.

Blue and I striped the fireplace ash on our cheeks, rubbing it into our hair to tell each other how we'd look when we were old. Then I found it. My nail scratched against it while I was scrabbling at the back of the grate. A mirror. It was small, with a pretty handle made of something like bone.

Blue was frantic. —What is it what is it?

I held it out to her, and she smiled wide.

Mirror hunting was something we'd started the summer before, when a heat wave burned the gardens yellow and it was too hot to sleep under the wool blankets in the attic, where the heat rose and pressed against the roof. We all slept in the ballroom, the windows open, fighting for places close to the air. It was so sticky some mornings that we stripped off and bent our bodies under the garden tap, crouching against the wall, Blue and me. The water gushed onto the gravel and made it swell, and you could dip your feet in the puddle.

One morning I was standing dripping off with my arms held out to the sun, letting the water run off my hair in streams, when I caught Blue looking at me with her eyes screwed against the strong light.

—Your hips are all funny, she said.

I thrust one out, putting my hand on it and pursing my lips.

—And there— she pointed to my breasts.

—Yeah.

I cupped them, but I could never see them properly, not from above.

Blue looked down at her own girl's body.

—I'm older, I said proudly.

—How much?

—I remember when you were a baby, so I think I'm around four or five summers more than you, I said. —You have four or five more summers until you change.

—I don't want to, she said. —It looks ugly.

I made a face and put my cotton dress on. It stuck at my back where I was still damp.

I turned back to Blue. —Fine, I said. Let's look for a mirror and see who's ugly.

—Don't need to, she said. —We can see each other.

—Don't you want to know how you look?

She was still crouched under the running tap, holding her knees. The sun caught on the water fanning behind her head. She nodded.

We'd agreed to find mirrors around the house and arrange them so we could see ourselves head to toe without needing each other as talking mirrors, not distorted like the warped image in the ballroom windows, and not in pieces like in the bath, *knee foot elbow stomach*. We'd already found two small ones in the rooms at the top of the house, near the attic, where Pet and Egg liked to sleep, frameless with sharp edges, sweat spots left by blu-tack around the edges. We needed one more piece, and this was it.

Blue snatched for the mirror and I kicked her away. It was covered in a mouldy speckled skin that I tried to scrape off with the sharp edge of the mantelpiece. Dylan's footsteps rang down the corridor, and his low voice, speaking to Kai, his *Hush* and *Shush*.

—We have to wait, I hissed.

—Let me look.

So I held it up above us both. The cracks ran in two seams down the centre. We could see in pieces: eyes, freckles, lips. We pressed together so our faces split amongst the mirror and I had to blink or stretch my skin to find the pieces that were me. My eyes were dark like Freya's and I had shadows under them; Blue's were lighter. We closed and opened our eyes to watch the irises bloom.

—Let's put them all together, Blue whispered. —We can put them in the attic where no one goes, we can see all of us.

I held the mirror further away and dipped it so I could see a dim and fragmented view of my body. My stomach pulsed, a cramp. I was used to hunger cramps and held my breath until it passed, but this one stayed. I stuffed the mirror in the back of my jeans. The glass was cool against my skin. Blue fumbled at my back, —Come on, let's … and I whipped around and caught her by the arm.

She struggled but I pinched her until the skin broke under my fingers. She kicked me but I held on until she looked at me.

—Stop. Being. A *baby*. We have to wait.

She wrenched away from me, and slammed into Dylan as he came through the doorway.

—Blue? he said, but let her go.

I knew she would stamp up the stairs, breathing in gulps. By the time I guessed she'd reached the top of the first staircase, twenty-nine steps, I was sorry, seeing the red on my fingers. I'd do something nice for her. I'd collect up the mirrors on my own, somewhere quiet, secret, and show them to her. It would kill time until Toby came back, if he came back, when he'd tell us about outside, the things the others didn't bother with, like what colour the ground was, and how the air tasted, and how the money felt in his hands.

—Is it lunch? I said. I wasn't hungry but I wanted to get away, to put the mirror together. And perhaps the shop run was back already.

—No, not yet. But let's get a drink, Dylan said.

We wove our way to the kitchen, back through the dank narrow passage and up to the art rooms. Freya was gone and the canvas stood lonely without her. I saw that she had struck deep charcoal cuts through the sun. I took

Dylan's arm, like I was much smaller, and he patted my hand and said, —Good girl.

The kitchen was still Freya's place; her thumbprints on every surface, her herbs and drying grasses hung from the rafters; I was tall enough now to hit the lower hanging ones if I stood on my toes. She worked in here sometimes, her paints and brushes scattered across the workbenches. Everyone knew not to use them. The space Libby used to cook in, when it was her turn, or when she and Richard were hidden away for a while and came in here at strange hours to burn toast and giggle together, was now draped in Freya's aprons and paint sheets. The mirror still lay flat against my spine, snug under the waistband of my jeans.

Freya was scattering flour over the kitchen table.

—Taking a break? Dylan asked.

—I'm done for the day, Freya replied. Then, —Dear, would you let me have Green for a couple of hours, leave the clearing out for now? We need bread for lunch.

Dylan gave me a half hug as he left. —Later, alligator! he said.

I couldn't remember the other bit he'd taught us, so I just hugged back and smiled after him so he wouldn't be hurt.

Then we were alone in the kitchen, me and Freya. She pulled me close, and I smelled white spirit and soil. The mirror seemed to burn at my back, her hands pressing me just above it. —I miss you, little one, she said, releasing me. —I never get to see you these days, do I?

I shook my head. —Yes? Freya said to me. —Play in the kitchen with me a while. You used to love that. When's the last time I had you all to myself, hmm?

I tried to remember. Some old, old time. Before Kai came, before Valentina became a Leaver; even further back. Before Blue came? Blue's skin under my nails.

—I'm … I want to find something. Can I look first? I said.

Freya's head moved sharp from side to side, a joke, but her grip on my shoulders dug in until I said, —Yes, okay, yes, yes.

I kneaded the dough hard, pushed it into the wooden bench, and it stuck; I'd forgotten to sprinkle the flour first, but I kept pushing, because I placed my own stomach there, in place of the dough, and it soothed me to imagine the roll and press of my hands on it.

Freya loved rolling dough. She thwacked it onto the bench, pummelling it with her fists. I gave up mine, stuck to the bench in stringy clumps, and watched her. A thick line of white ran through her black hair, which she wore twisted up in a high bun. Her long skirt was pulled down over her hips, and above it she had tied her t-shirt in a knot. Silvery lines zigzagged over her skin, around her back.

She caught me in her eyes. In the gloom of the kitchen there wasn't a fleck of colour in them, so dark they made the whites seem to glow.

—Why the staring, Green dear?

Sweet voice. She was in a sarcastic mood. She uncoiled her arm, so long, and prodded my dough.

—Can we still use it? I said.

—We'll have to, you've used the last of the flour, she said.

—I can go on the shop run, next time—

—Oh, can you?

She surveyed me then, coming close. Her eyes lingered on my body and she pulled me away from the bench, held me at arm's length. Then she darted a hand behind my back, under my clothes, and whipped out the mirror.

She laughed, rocking her body in her way.

—What have we here? Is this what sent Blue sniffle-running back through the studios without you? Did she get a shock when she looked? She wiped her eyes. —What about you, my Green? You looked?

Freya brought her arm around me, and held up the mirror, just as I had done with Blue. Split by the cracks, our eyes and brows and lips came back to us disassembled, and I saw how much my eyes were Freya's eyes, how they narrowed at the ends, how the lashes didn't curl like Blue's but stuck out long and startling.

—What a beauty you're growing up to be, Freya said.

I smiled and one of the broken lips curled up, showing straight stained teeth.

Freya laughed again, holding her nose, like she was underwater.

—Oh! Poor Green. I don't mean it. You can't see, you're a skinny *rag*, no flesh on you, your arse is flat and you've no boobs at all, and your hips jut out like *knives*. But don't worry— she pulled my hair. —You're a good girl. Want to keep it? Finders keepers?

I knew the answer to this one.

—No, it's everyone's. I'll put it in Jumble to share, I said.

Freya waved the mirror by its handle. —You should have one, I suppose, never thought of it. But don't think you really see yourself. Only I can do that. Keep it, she said.

Then Freya hugged me from behind, putting her hands on my stomach, and I winced.

—What's that? she said. —Don't want your Freya pawing at you?

—It hurts, I said. —My stomach.

—Don't guzzle all the fruit then. I told you.

—No, it's not like sick, I said. And when she released me and tilted her head in that way, so I knew I couldn't stop there, I said, —It feels all tight, like wound up, like …

She frowned. —It's the bleed coming.

—Oh.

I knew about the bleed, of course: the women kept tampons from town under the sink in the bathroom, but sometimes, if no one had been on a shop run, or we didn't have enough money, they used rags instead, then washed them out in sudsy water and laid them to dry on the rockery; in winter they'd sit over the aga, dripping, holding their marks. The men flinched if they touched them while they were cooking.

—Oh, I said again.

—Be careful. The Bad is attracted to it.

I went back to the dough. I didn't want to talk about the Bad. As I rolled and slapped I felt a need to look in a mirror, stronger than before. I stared at the door without knowing I did it. Freya hummed and lit the aga. Then she hitched herself up onto the table and nibbled on the skin around her thumb, eyeing me.

—What is it? she said. —Is it Toby gone today, is that it? You're not missing anything.

I dug my nails into the palm of my hands.

—Not missing *her*, is it?

I kept still.

—Or *him*?

She looked out over the garden. —They're probably together somewhere, she said. —He'll be back. He'll be back, she said again, and tore off a strip of skin with her teeth, sucked the blood that came up there. I wondered if the bleed felt like that. —Well?

—Nothing. Nothing's wrong, I said.

—Come here.

The weight in my stomach dragged on me, but I went. She was still sitting with legs swinging, high on the oak table, next to our mirror.

—What's wrong with you? Here.

She pulled me forward, held me in a double knot, arms and legs. Her t-shirt smelled of wood smoke.

I swivelled my head towards the door and it was stupid because of course she'd feel that, she'd notice that. She moved so quick that when the hit came I lagged behind it. My head whipped back, pain in my neck. I had my eyes closed, so there was just the colour behind my eyelids and the familiar salt taste.

—Sorry, I said. I swallowed hard, opened my eyes.

Freya's lips were sucked in. It had been a while since she'd hit me full force.

—Well, she said. —Well. Your precious October is away for one day and you can't wait to get away from me and you think I don't know the Solstice, what it looks like? Perhaps you think you're all grown up now your bony little body is spitting out blood. But— she jabbed my shoulder so I rocked back, —don't get too full of yourself. I think I'll take that mirror after all.

Pet came through the bead curtain, Kai on his arm. His face was painted with inks from the studios: a line of red kohl around his lips. He took Kai over to his chair by the aga and slid a blanket out from under a dog, tucking it over Kai's knees. —He's cold today, Pet said. Then he looked into Freya's face and turned to me.

—All right? he said.

I clicked my jaw, swallowed. Freya wiped her eyes.

—Oh, just a tiff, she said.

—Blue's all in tears too, upstairs, said Pet. —I found her in the attic, she told me to go get Kai, that he looked cold.

—They're jealous of Toby going, Freya said. —I thought it wasn't the greatest idea, but … She shrugged. —He's older, and they're both spoiled, thinking he can't have something they don't.

She used her apron to wipe my face, though I wasn't crying. She held my face in her hands. —Let's say no more about it, she said.

Pet nodded, smiling at me, and poured coffee granules into a mug of hot water.

—Don't look so tragic, Greenie, he said.

When the door beads stopped their tick tock against themselves, and the footsteps were gone, Freya gave me a smile.

—You hurt Blue, didn't you?

I looked at the floor. From his chair, Kai gave a low chuckle as the dog pushed its head under his hands to stroke.

—What did she do? Did she try to get out alone again? Did she tell you about an outsider she spoke to?

—She didn't do anything bad, I said. —It was me, I lost my temper.

—Because she was being naughty again?

—She was trying to see in the mirror, that's all.

Freya nodded. —Vain. Blood will out.

—Why can't she go out on the moor alone? I said. —We go, me and Toby, we go all the time.

—She's not like you, Freya said softly. —She doesn't love her home.

Ellen rattled the curtain, grinning.

—I smell bread. Is it done? We're starving!

She didn't wait for an answer, but hollered back into the house and the others began to pile in, squeezing around the table. Toby and Egg still weren't back, and Blue didn't appear. Freya sat with her legs dangling, laughing with Ellen. Dylan was on lunch. Tomato soup. I went over to sniff. It smelled sour, and my stomach twisted.

—Can't we wait for the shop run to come back?

—This will be gorge, Dylan said. —You'll see.

I waited for him to yell out, —Okay everyone, and the surge for bowls and spoons and the push towards the smoking pan, and I snatched up the mirror, returned it to my back.

I sat between Pet and Ellen, who wove me a bracelet out of some loose wicker on the fruit basket. When the bowls were in the sink and the roll ups came out and there were murmurs of warmer air and a night in the gardens, Freya gave me a nod, so I could go.

In the attic, Blue lay on the bed, facing away from me. She was curled around her arm, and as I came close she curled tighter. I sat on the edge of the bed.

—Hungry? Soup and bread downstairs, I said.

I took out the mirror and balanced it on the blanket next to Blue, waving it like a toy.

—I was going to set them all up together for you, I said, —but Freya …

My cheek ached. I wanted to lie down, to sleep. I edged onto the bed next to Blue.

—I'm sorry, I whispered. —Is it bad? Can I look?

She thrust her arm up, and I saw the red welts on the skin.

—Look, take the mirror, I said.

—Don't need to. I can see.

—Ah, got you talking …

I peered around into her face. She didn't smile. I leaned closer, making stupid faces, and began to poke her in the ribs, until she kicked me and rolled over to the far end of the bed.

—No! No! You hurt me! You bitch, she said.

—I'm sorry, I said, to her back.

—I hate you.

—You don't.

—I hate it here.

—You don't! This is Foxlowe, this is home. Listen, All The Ways Home Is Better, I said. —One …

—Shut up.

—Toby will be back soon. He can tell us all about it, outside, the shop run.

Blue kicked the wall and the bed shuddered, its old slats creaked.

—Get out, she said, and she sounded like she was the older one, and I the younger ungrown, and her fists were clenched as though ready to punch, and I did as she said.

I went to the goat shed, a tiny room tacked on to the side of the house, with cobbles beneath the straw. We had three goats, who tottered around the garden, bleating when the dogs came near, chewing up sheets left to dry on the rockery. They came inside in the winter, and I watched them now, weaving in the straw, nudging each other, imagined their secret conversations. I would stay there until my tears stopped.

When Toby appeared, I wasn't shocked, as though my thoughts had simply taken shape in the air.

—Is it Freya? What's she said to you now?

He crouched in the straw next to me. The smell of apples and milk. He must have come from the kitchen, where the others were probably mashing them together and adding new-bought sugar.

The end of my nose was dripping and I wiped it with my sleeve.

—So what did Freya do?

—Just, I said.

—Let's talk to Dylan. I'm sure he'll say something at least—

—No, I said.

His hair was tied back in a rough ponytail so his face was uncovered; his skin flushed pink from the cold. I hadn't been this close to him for a long time.

—There's a load of new stuff. Come on, he said.

He was grinning, excited. The outside clung to him. It seemed like a long time ago that he'd been driven away from us.

—Toby, remember at Winter Solstice, that time?

He blinked. —What? He sat down next to me. —Green, you have to get on the next one. It was great. I'll take you, I bet I can drive soon. Okay, so there's these rows of stalls like tables all put together, and they have *everything*, and it's crowded, like imagine a thousand more than us—

—Don't pretend you don't remember. I put Blue out for the Bad, remember?

He sat back, crossed his legs.

—Of course I remember, he said. —It's all right. We've taken care of her since then, haven't we? She's all right, isn't she?

I nodded.

—Stop now, he said. He rubbed my cheek roughly with the collar of his shirt. —Stop crying.

—Is the sky the same there?

—Of course! It's only the other side of the Cloud.

—Did you talk to outsiders?

—Yeah, in a shop. I changed a mirror for a pile of blankets at this shop where you give things instead of money, I mean you just give like one coin and it's all Jumble like here—

—A mirror? You gave one of the mirrors away? Toby, we need them! We've spent ages collecting them all up! I only just got the last piece!

—All right, all right! What d'you need a mirror for? There's one right in the ballroom.

—It's too broken. And it's too heavy for me to get it down on my own. How could you just take one without asking? Did you take it from the attic? That's *our* room!

I gave in to the rush of sobs, burying my face in my knees.

Toby's hand stroked my head. —All right, it's all right. Green, I can show you where … Come on, come in and I'll show you, and we'll fetch Blue too, and you can make up.

—There's nothing to make up. What d'you mean?

—Come on, you only cry when she's not speaking to you, or Freya's been a cow. So if it's not Freya—

He gave me a rag to blow my nose on.

—Leave Blue. She'll calm down, I said.

—Okay, just us then. He pulled me up and held on to my hand as we left the shed.

In the hallway, the Family was spilling onto the stairs and chucking material and boxes to each other. Toby tugged me past and silently headed through the Spike Walk, to the yellow room.

No one came in here any more. Libby's jewellery still hung over the corners of things, and I picked up some beads, wound them around my wrist, and missed her.

Toby had let go of my hand and was biting the skin around his fingers, looking away from me.

—What? I said. I'd meant it to sound sharp but it came out whispery, like I was excited too.

—Okay, he said. —It's not a new thing, but I don't think you know it's here.

—What? You don't know Foxlowe better than me!

But I was already casting around the room. There was the chest of drawers that Freya had taken Blue's first bed from. Toby went over and bent down to peer into the gap.

—Still there! Look, he said.

The dust balls skittered at my breath. A cloud appeared. I stretched a hand through and tapped with a fingernail. I turned to Toby and his face was closer than I thought; I could see the new hairs on his lip.

The chest of drawers was heavy but we shoved it in tiny diagonals until a shore of dust had formed at its edge. Then we wrenched the mirror out from its hiding place. It was another beautiful broken thing: gold leaf split around the edges, and it was speckled with brown spots. It had been here all the time. Of course Libby would have a full one. She used to dress so the ribbon hem, hand-stitched on the bottom of her skirt, matched the bands on her wrists and the flowers in her hair. It was big enough so we didn't need the others, the small scattered pieces. We propped it against the wardrobe, standing side by side.

No cracks, so it was how we really were. We looked at each other first, what we already knew, then at ourselves. My face I knew in broad strokes, from the attic window. Little sharp nose, eyes dark, lips too big. The lower lip fuller than the upper one. Up close I saw how the skin under my eyes was dry and red, studied the roots of my hair, the chip in my front tooth that I'd felt with my tongue for years.

—We should get Blue, I said. —She'll want to see too.

But we didn't move. We listened; it was easy to hear someone coming along the Spike Walk.

I peeled off my jeans first, Toby his t-shirt. We'd seen each other like that a thousand times; further back, we'd been naked together all the time. I took off my vest, showing the new breasts, and slid down my knickers: the elastic had gone, so I just had to wriggle my hips a little.

I was aware of Toby doing the same. We stayed side by side, shivering, untouching, and I looked at him in the mirror, him me. He was still thin and dirty, streaks along his belly, probably from the car. A new pelt had grown along his chest and down to his navel. After a long while I got bored of Toby's body and turned back to myself.

It was like Freya's, my figure, skinny and tall, with sharp bones seeming to stick out everywhere, and long arms and legs. I swung my arms and then posed with them on my hips, leaning forward to get a better look at my breasts. I'd been cupping them on bath days, trying to see the nipple. I knew you got two types, either the brown ones like Libby's, or red like Freya's. Mine were pink. I lifted my arms to see the dark hair there, saw that between my legs it was less than it seemed underwater. I stared at myself for a long time. I posed with my back to the mirror and twisted to look at myself, and tried different ways of standing to make my hips rounder; with legs apart, or one before the other, but either way, they stuck stubbornly out. I remembered Blue under the taps. Ugly, she'd said.

—Okay, I said. —Thanks, Toby.

We dressed again in our own cold air, watching each other in the mirror. Then because things felt strange between us, I gave him a hug, putting my head under his chin, snuggling into his chest. My arms at the small of his back, feeling the hard spine under the cotton. When I leaned back he pinched my nose so I gave him a shove, laughing. I didn't hit him. I sensed that we wouldn't touch each other like that any more.

15

Spring came, and we pulled the blankets from under windows and doors, shaking out the dust; our fingers unfurled from hot mugs. We wrapped our jumpers around our waists and went barefoot. Ellen and Pet made scrubs of salt and porridge oats, and sat in the gardens, massaging it into their dry legs.

The bleed came just as the cold thawed, and I wrapped a rag around my knickers and went to the kitchen like it was a normal day. I told Freya, and she made me tea full of honey, used the very tips of the mint leaves, the freshest, sweetest parts.

Toby and I never talked about the yellow room, but I still used it alone — sometimes standing in early morning light, before Blue and the others were awake. All the rest of that winter, when I couldn't sleep, and restlessness ran over my skin like an itch, I'd taken a candle to look at night. I touched myself afterwards, lying on Libby's abandoned mattress, before I went back to our attic bed. I always felt wrong then, lying in the thick dark, feeling the Bad twitch and circle inside me. Blue slept heavily and I watched her, feeling guilty for abandoning her for this new strange game. I knew we would never tell her about the yellow room mirror. The hand-held glass from the cluttered room lay next to her Cancer box, and I left it to her.

Toby's downy top lip and tall frame couldn't be ignored any more, and at Meeting he'd been declared one of the grown. There was no more playing with us in the gardens or out on the moor; he had to make a contribution. He helped with the practical side of things, like mixing paints and resins, or measuring and cutting canvas. He'd taken to looking after the goats more and more, and so, in the way of Foxlowe, it became his role.

He worried about it while he brushed the goats down and checked their underbellies for ticks. I perched on the edge of the goat stall, a kid nosing my lap, steaming mugs at my feet. Some of the dogs were scratching around the straw, sniffing after a rat. I liked the sound of Toby brushing the animals, a satisfying scratch, and felt the rush of blood as though it were my own skin.

—You could do sculpture, I said. —That's just making stuff.

—But it's all supposed to *mean something*, he said, waving his arms and making his voice high and floaty in such a good imitation of Ellen that I burst out laughing.

—If I can't make anything I'll have to leave, he shrugged.

I drew my sleeves down over my arms, chilled. —But *I* don't do anything. I don't even help them, really. Neither does Blue.

—You're younger, he said. —It will start to matter.

—You're only one or two Solstices more than me.

I could see his back stretched under the goat, and his hand put down to steady him as he smoothed the other over her stomach.

—Maybe, I said, stroking the kid's nose, —you could do the pottery. Richard's, I mean the Leaver Founder's, stuff is all still there, and it doesn't look like he'll come back now. You're good at that, you can use the wheel, and … or something else. We'll think of something.

Toby came to perch next to me. He smelled of the warm straw and, under that, a mix of sweet goat's milk and acrid manure.

—Kai already tried to help us, he said. —We should start again, see if we can find a way to learn, to get ready.

—Kai's gone, I said. —He's here but he's gone.

—I know, not Kai. Someone else.

—I can't, I said.

—She can't stop you, Toby said, but his voice was empty, and we knew Freya could do anything, now Richard and Libby were gone. I didn't need to tell him that, so I just said again, —I can't.

Toby went quiet and turned his back to me, and I knew he was angry but I'd only told him the truth. I left the shed, went back into the house, and followed Freya's voice cackling from the ballroom. There were other sounds: Egg, Pet and Dylan, swearing, laughing too. I put my eye to the slats of the ballroom door. They were dragging furniture, Freya with a notepad and pencil, wiping laughter tears away with her free hand. Egg held his foot, hopping. We were going to sell some of the old things, it had been decided at Meeting. A flash as something caught the sun: the yellow room mirror.

I went back for him, still with the goats' brush in his hand, and he began to speak, to say sorry perhaps, or explain, but I got in first. —Let's climb the Cloud, I said.

—Can't, he said, but smiling. —I've got to—

—Come on, I said. —Please.

We left Foxlowe, flicking at the algae on the fountain as we passed. A storm cloud on the horizon was sucking all the air up to itself. We glanced back to watch Foxlowe glint in the light, until it sank behind the ridge and we passed the Standing Stones, and carried on along the moor path.

The moor path wasn't really a path, more like a track we'd made over seasons of tramping on it. In the summer it grew over with nettles, but you could always spot our way; the grass was lighter, newer, the ground itself had been sunk into the earth. There were times when we had to go by the thin roads or on the walking routes, to keep the peace, but after a while we'd always go back to our way. The path took us past horses grazing next to stone walls and through fields of grasses that came to our waist, down steep drops of sharp rock.

On the horizon, tiny cars flashed like jewel beetles.

—Is that where you go, on the shop run? I said.

Toby shielded his eyes and looked at the road. —Yeah, he said. —It's not far.

I looked away from the moving ribbon on the horizon so all I could see was green.

The Cloud hides itself as you get closer, the rocky outcrops hidden by trees growing on the lower slopes. Huge slabs of moorland stone mark the path upwards, some smooth and pooling rainwater in the grooves, others broken, split into sharpness, making natural steps. Beside the path, tiny white blossoms of self-heal, flashes of purple foxglove, carpets of green fern amongst the trees. I picked self-heal, knotted it into a crown as we walked, ringed it around my hair, hoping it looked like Libby's used to. Ahead of me, Toby stopped to rub dock leaves on his nettle stings. As we climbed higher the sky widened again, the trees falling away to show the moor rolling away on every side, and the rocks grew into huge crags, dangling over the drop. Pink heather lay in clumps; higher still, it reddened, a sunset in bloom.

We went to the very peak, a flat moorland giant that lay looking over to the horizon, and sat with our legs swinging into the emptiness. Below us, patchwork fields and the villages, and far in the distance, the blue hills of the impossibly far outside, another country. We sat in full sun, watching rain ghost to the ground far in the distance, and fields split into light and dark by moving clouds.

—We should do rituals up here, I said.

—Freya decides those.

—I know, I said. —I didn't mean it. You'll have to do it in secret, the reading, if you start it again. Freya won't like it.

Toby fell back onto the rock, letting his body bend in two, and I fought the urge to hold on to his legs, in case he fell.

—I hate Freya, Toby said.

—I love her, I said, over his words.

—She doesn't love you, Toby said, not nastily.

Toby couldn't know about my and Freya's secret things: her plaiting my hair, and cutting out the knots, the safety of sleeping against her back, and her stories, just for me. I watched the steel men straddling the moor, sharing wires like skipping ropes. Far away, they seemed in motion, thin giants loping across the world. Toby raised a hand, as though he would say sorry by touch, hovered around my cheek, then dropped it.

—Why d'you keep going in the yellow room? Toby asked.

He pulled at a sprig of heather as he said it, and sprinkled it over the grey rock. I guessed he'd been wanting to ask for a long time.

—You do too, I said. —I can tell, you always move the mirror so it's slanted differently.

In the purpling light his blush looked almost black.

—They're taking the mirror away, I said. —I just saw them.

—Oh.

Behind us, shouts from outside people, the walkers. They didn't like us sitting on the edge.

—It's okay, Toby said. —When I'm a Leaver—

—Stop it!

Toby rolled onto his side and watched me with his face cupped on his hand. A blade of damp heather stuck to his skin and I wanted to peel it off. Somehow it made me thirsty.

—It's okay to just think it, he said. —Like a story.

—What's it like? I said.

—Just so many people, he said. —But it's the places. Think of all the places we don't know. Look, that place, he said, and pointed to one of the grey patches moulding on the moor.

—It's just a town, I said.

—But you've never seen one.

I shrugged. —Just like the villages but bigger.

—Bet there you don't have to run around to feel the strain in your legs just so you don't hit a wall you're so bored, Toby said.

—Bet you can't, I said. —No space, is there. Freya says it's all boxes, people live in little boxes.

—What would you do? Toby said.

—What?

But I knew what he meant.

—Come on, he said. —How would you do it?

The heather between my fingers soft, like hair. I should say, *We shouldn't talk about this*. I should say, *Freya wouldn't like it.*

—I'd go at night, I said. —I wouldn't tell anyone, so Freya couldn't try to stop me, and after a party so everyone was really deeply asleep. And I'd take the blue jumper from Jumble, the warm one with the high neck.

—Where would you go? he asked.

—I'd walk to the big town, to Leek, then … I'd work it out.

—You can't walk from Foxlowe, he said.

I laughed. —So? It's just a story. Anyway, I bet I could walk it.

Toby tucked his hands behind his head and we watched the dark clouds sink.

—I always thought I'd go on a Meeting day, he said. —Announce it at Meeting, have a meal with everyone. But I like your idea. It would be good to go at night. That's what Valentina did.

—And Libby, I said.

It felt safe to say her name, all the way up here.

—We could find them, he said. —And find a new house, a smaller one, that isn't so cold.

—And with no fleas, I said, picking at a bite on his wrist, and he laughed.

—But we don't know how it is outside, I said. —When's anyone said it's good? It's always, *Here* is better. *This* is better. I rolled back so I lay next to Toby, and the sky was endless above me. —It's perfect here, I said.

—Let's say it anyway, he said. —Let's tell it like a story.

After that me and Toby spoke about Leaving whenever we were alone. We'd go to the goats' shed after breakfast or in the long empty hours of the afternoon, tell the story to each other, adding detail each time: the smell of the inside of the car (I'd go on a shop run, just with Pet, and tell him while we were in town), the layered clothes (Toby would go in winter, in the busy week leading up to Solstice, so he'd need warm jumpers). My stories always ended at the end of the road leading out of home, because I didn't really know how things would be after that, and I focused on the goodbyes, and which things I would take, how I would tell or not tell Freya. Toby's were different. He liked to talk about the moment of walking away, but then he'd talk about what he'd do afterwards: into town, and he'd describe the things there, shops and places to eat, and how there was a station with metal tracks going all over the country. He'd go, he said, to London, the biggest city, where he'd come from. Valentina had told him that's where he used to live, and that's where she must be now, along with the rest of his outside family.

After a while, our stories got tangled together. Then it was, *We'd do this*. And later still, *We'll do this*. Sometimes Toby brought Blue into the tale, but I never did. If I thought of her, I had to stop. I told Toby it was hard to imagine Blue in the outside, exposed like the soft belly of a puppy. To myself I told the truthful version: I liked the story of just me and Toby. I liked to pretend, just for stolen guilty minutes, that Blue did not exist.

16

As the year ran on, Blue shrank into herself and lived in the corners and edges of rooms, near to doors, so when I turned to check on her, she'd have slipped away. It was as though she'd been Edged. One day when she'd dissolved into shadows out of the kitchen, I found her in the gardens, sitting against the red brick wall at the back of the goat shed. I peeled her arms away from her forehead where her face was hiding, ready to see tears, but her cheeks were dry, and she touched her face, around her lips, like a sign language I didn't know.

—What? I said, lightly, but my body was already tense with jealousy. *What do you have? What did you find out? Why is it you?*

She turned her face away. Freya called me.

—Stay here, I said. —I want to talk to you.

When I came back Blue was gone, melted back into the house. It was like this for weeks. I only found her again at night; she still slept with me in the attic, coming to bed long after me, and feigning sleep when I whispered to her.

One night Blue stirred next to me, kicked the blankets off. Freya's mattress lay empty; she slept in Richard's old room now.

—Too *hot*, she murmured.

When she opened her eyes, she held mine and I knew then, this was the time to get it out of her.

—What is it? I whispered.

She whipped her head into the pillow, giggling.

—Nothing.

I tickled her sides, and she screeched and gasped for air.

Something Freya had said once came to me. —You can't keep secrets from me, I can open up your heart with a knife and read your secrets there, scribbled inside the flesh, I said.

—I'm asleep.

—Then if you tell me, it will just be like you spoke in a dream, and it won't be real, so it's okay.

She smiled into the shadows. Shook her head, and it wasn't a game now. She had a real secret and she wouldn't tell me.

—Okay, I said, the threat of tears in my voice.

She stroked my lip with her thumbnail.

—I'll swap a secret for one of yours, said Blue.

—I don't have any, I said.

Blue stroked my lip for a few seconds longer, then turned her back on me.

—Then neither do I, she said.

Her breaths got low and heavy, and I started to fall asleep myself, but then Blue spoke again.

—Do you ever think about the Leavers?

—No.

—If you left, would you take me?

I rolled over so I could see the dim outline of her face.

—I mean, just say. *If*, she said.

She knows, I thought. She's heard us.

—I wouldn't be a Leaver, I said. —We'll stay here forever, you and me. We'll be like Freya.

—Yes, she said simply, and turned away. Before we fell into sleep, she said, so quietly I might have dreamed it, —Tomorrow, I'll show you a secret.

Blue was quiet on the way down the back lawns, glancing behind her to check I was following. She wore Valentina's old yellow boots and in the morning mist I followed the spots of them when she darted ahead too quickly.

I'd guessed since we'd woken up: new things, squirrelled away from a shop run, hidden in the gardens where only we could use them. We'd talked about doing it, but never dared. Or an animal wandered off the moor, a fox. Blue only shook her head, smiling.

In the lower gardens, I wished I had boots too; the nettles grew high. I tucked my hands into the sleeve of my jumper, but I couldn't save my bare feet, ankles and shins. Blue pressed on.

—So where is it? I said.

—Come on, Blue said.

We came through to the stone wall and dropped onto the moor side. I thought she was taking me to the Stones then so I said, —Too far, you're not allowed, but she said, —It's all right, this is it.

One of our trees, a young spindly thing, stretched branches over the stone, leaning away from Foxlowe, trying to jump the wall. Blue led me to it.

—Can you see it? she said, pointing.

Thin light branches, buds of blossom, young leaves. My toes had gone numb, and I worked them into the mud. A low bird call sounded from our side of the wall. On a low branch, a cluster of twigs.

—Oh, I said, and moved closer, standing on tiptoe. —Is that it?

Blue had a thing for birds' nests. Toby had stolen one for her when she was little, and it decayed slowly on her shelf next to the Cancer box. She loved to hold the perfect curve of it in her palm.

—Look, she said. She pulled the branch down gently, so we could see inside. There were four eggs. I thought she wanted to eat them, but when we'd done that before, it had caused lots of arguments, and it wasn't worth it. I started to tell her this, but she whispered, —One of them is wrong, look.

They were all the colour of oatmeal, freckled with green. One was huge.

Blue pointed to it. —It's an *imposter*. Hear that call?

I knew it. It was one of the moor sounds. A low hooting bird call.

—That's its real parents, Blue said. —But they leave it here so another bird looks after it.

—What? How d'you know?

—I've been learning, Blue said.

—Kai taught you that, before?

She shrugged.

—I can't believe you got me up early for that, I said.

But we stayed and looked at the nest a while longer. Blue wouldn't let me touch it, even though the eggs looked warm and smooth and like they would feel good in my chilled hands.

Later, after breakfast, Toby and I were on our way to the goat shed, we said to clean it out and brush the goats down, but I knew we would lie on the straw or sit with our legs swinging, or balanced lightly on the goats' backs, and tell our Leaving story to each other. I had a piece of toast hanging from my mouth, and Blue pulled it out, bit into it.

—Let's show Toby, she said.

—No, I said. —We're busy. I made my voice low in a growl like Freya's, but Blue didn't shrink from it, and next to me, Toby was already taking Blue's hand. She leaned against his arm as we walked down the gardens.

At the nest, the eggs were gone, and we found them smashed on the ground. There was one chick, worm-pink, its mouth an orange gash.

—Blue! I said.

—It wasn't me. Look, said Blue. —It killed them. It pushed them out. We missed it, I wanted to see. It puts them on its back, and throws them out.

The baby bird made a shrill cry, and we huddled down next to the wall, settling on our haunches.

—It killed its brothers and sisters, Blue said. —It's not supposed to be in the nest. It's a different kind of bird. It comes in when they're laid, the eggs, and it pretends, and then it kills the others, and the parents feed it. And then it flies off to be with its real family. She looked at us. —Do you see? I'm going to kill it, she said.

I watched the chick. —Where's the parent birds? I mean, the ones who built the nest?

—They won't come while we're here, said Blue.

—It's just, I said, —it's just, they think it's their baby still. They'll come back and they'll *all* be dead. We should've done it before it killed the others.

—And, said Toby, —I mean, how does it know it's not really supposed to be there? It was just laid there, and it was born, and it woke up and its parents were there. So it doesn't *know*.

—It didn't have to kill the others, said Blue.

—It might be like the dogs running after rabbits, I said. —Can't help it. It's like Toby said, it doesn't know it shouldn't be there, it doesn't know what it is.

Blue pushed past me and flung the nest to the ground, stamped on it once, twice, the sound of crushed twigs and the slosh of mud under her boot. Toby sucked air through his teeth, like he'd been cut.

—Fuck, Blue, he said.

—I'm being kind, Blue said. —It did know. It knew it didn't belong. Do you see? she said to me, and I shrugged, not wanting to fight with her.

We talked about it later, me and Toby, in the goat shed, kicking up dust from the straw after Blue disappeared into the house, shaking us off, our hands falling from her back and shoulders.

—So it goes back to its real family, I said. —But how does it know it has another real family in the first place? It doesn't remember them, how can it?

Toby sat up to whistle a low sound to his favourite goat, Astra, who was head-butting a post.

—I mean, how does it *know* it's not supposed to be there? Doesn't it just think the birds feeding it are its family, like us? I said.

—You can feel it when it's not really your family, said Toby.

—No you can't, I said. —How can you tell the difference?

—I know Valentina was mine, he said.

—Only because you remembered that from before, I said. —If we'd told you it's Ellen, or it's Freya, you'd feel the same way.

Toby rolled back onto the straw, and tucked his arms

behind his head. The shed ceiling was cobwebbed from beam to beam.

When we told each other the Leaving story that day, we made it with more detail than ever before. We told how I'd leave Blue the almond scented soap that I'd saved since Winter Solstice, that she inhaled with the bar to her nose, deep sniffs, saying it made her hungry. How in the dawn light, before even the animals began to cry out, we'd walk as far as the town road, along past the big green signs, until an outsider car picked us up.

Then, —But we'll take her with us, Toby said. —Blue.

I imagined her between us, each with a cold hand in ours, but I forgot, I was always forgetting, she was bigger now, and would walk ahead of us, glancing back at Toby, her bright hair falling over her face, and before long, a new body budding under her clothes.

—I thought it was just us, I said.

He turned to face me. —Okay, he said.

I laughed. I needed to break the game, because I was afraid we'd gone too far, and the outside was pressing in, waiting, and if we fell into it we'd keep falling, like in a dream, and we'd never find our way back home. Toby stood up; he didn't like it when I broke the story. Brushing straw from the back of his legs, he nudged Astra aside, and rapped on something with his knuckles. I sat up.

—See it? he said.

Dust settled in a film on the mirror.

—I moved it in here, Toby said. —Took it from the van they hired to take it all away to sell. Kept it here for you. For us.

It was still a new thing, Toby's kindness to me. I didn't know how to say thank you or do something nice in return. The strange ground we walked on now, where Richard and Libby were gone and Freya was distant and towered above us all and Blue kept secrets from me and stroked my lip like she was the older one, and she had to take care of me, this was part of it, and so I froze, not wanting to change anything else.

Toby's eyes on my face, skidding around the curve of my ear. I knew it well from the mirror and my own fingers, it had a ripple in the middle, his fingers would catch there if he stroked my hair, then down, to the new swelling breasts, the stupid nipples, should I cross my arms, no, best not move, eyes further down, and the urge to fold my arms, turn away was there, but I stayed still, and I could see myself in the mirror behind him, arms curled around my legs, my dark hair loose.

Libby or Freya in Richard's arms, Pet and Egg folded into each other, their arms seeming to disappear. I wanted it to be like that, but when he pulled me up my arms stayed stuck, so the hard edge of my wrist dug into his collarbone, and my shoulders hurt, but I didn't move away, his mouth on mine. And so we stayed like that, and he only held me there, and his hands stayed at the small of my back, and we didn't use the mirror, not at all.

That first time it was easy, laughing so hard I thought we'd never stop. *Did you know that would happen? Dylan said but not that much oh my god look it's all over your —* heaving laughter into the straw — and yet, *Let's do it again? Yes, yes, yes, let's do it again.*

I went back to the shed every day, and wanted to stay there longer and longer. In Meeting, or crowded around the kitchen table, snatching at the jam and milk, me and Toby stayed our old selves, never touched each other this new way, and no one saw how the air around us was different. We made a secret lie between us that we could keep the goat shed just for us, and even though no rooms at Foxlowe were locked, and everyone wandered everywhere, we pretended we could hide away there, and we were lucky enough for the lie to hold.

Somehow Toby became unknowable and exciting even though I knew his face better than mine, knew how far he could spit, and there were old scars on his legs and back that my nails had made; even so, it was a different boy I was with in the goat shed, and he said the same to me, *like you turned into someone else.*

—I know this thigh. That scar is mine, he said.

A kiss for the thigh he knows.

—Freya will kill us, he said.

A little thrill of fear in my spine. I shrugged. —Bet she was younger than us, so.

—Still. She will. She'll kill us, he said.

* * *

Later, I felt the springs of the attic mattress make tired jumps as Blue rolled from one side to the other, sweeping her hair over her face to hide whatever was there. She had new bandages on her arms, spreading down to her hands, and I felt guilty that we'd abandoned her for our new secret world in the goat shed, not been there to comfort her afterwards, or even to know what she'd done.

—Blue, I said.

—Um-hm?

—How did you know all that stuff about the birds?

—I told you, I learned it.

—Kai didn't teach you that, I said.

Silence.

—Why are you always in the goats' shed? Blue asked. She leaned on her elbow, and somewhere deep below us a spring broke.

—Tell me first, I said.

—It's a friend I made, Blue said.

—An … outside person?

—He's really nice, Blue said. —He watches birds. He knows all about them.

—You talk to him?

—He found me with that nest. He said I shouldn't touch it. We argued about it but then he wasn't angry any more and we talked about other things.

An outside man, with one of those pink, shaved faces. Talking to Blue, teaching her, peeling back the film we made between ourselves and the other place, the other side of the moor. I fought down a thousand questions, and only said, —You'll be in so much trouble.

—Now tell me, she said.

I could just make out the swell of her shoulder. Her face was blank, full of shadow.

—It's nothing, I said.

Blue rolled back so I could see the outline of her face, the soft round of her nose, so unlike my sharp one.

—I was thinking, she said. —I was thinking, the three of us, we could … My friend. He would drive us.

—Don't, I said. —Don't.

17

Here is a way time and stories work strange: I told the story of Blue's first Scattering, and naming her, and the world before she came, because in one way that is the story of the end of the things I knew and the world and Freya and me and all the Family, and happened over the years, slowly. But in another way, it happened in one small turn, not even the time between Solstices, only seven sleeps, maybe less. It started with the front doorbell ringing.

The Family was in the ballroom, sewing, writing in notebooks, mixing paints. I sat under Freya as she combed through my hair, looking for lice. We were quiet except for the tearful whispers between Pet and Egg, in the last hours of a row.

The sound soared up into the staircase. I'd never heard it before. We went to look. The bell above the front door was rusty and full of cobwebs. It moved again, cascading dust.

—Go on then, open it, Freya said behind me, chewing her nails.

—Richard wouldn't ring, I told her.

—I know that, she said. —So open it then!

In the glass around the door, a dark shadow twitched. I felt sudden fear, like the Bad had made itself into a person, that could come and ring the bell like that, and when I opened the door it would eat us all. I felt Toby on the stairs behind me. I opened the door.

Two of them. Both women, with ironed hair cut in jagged shapes. One was in a suit and her nice shoes were caked in mud and grass. The other wore sandals and a dress with a jacket over it. Her toenails were painted red.

—Hel-lo, red toenails said.

She held up a card on a string around her neck.

—I'm Mary. This is my colleague Pam.

Muddy shoes Pam nodded.

—We're from Social Services, Pam said. —May we come in?

Long seconds in which they looked me up and down, and glanced at each other. I heard the group move forward and Freya pulled at my skirt, awkwardly dragging me out of the way. Instead of going to Toby's side I curled into Dylan's waist. He frowned down at me. Everyone was quiet, listening. The sing-song *hellos* again. Freya's voice very low. An outsider name, *is he …? Procedures are such that … So just a visit, to see how you're all getting on …* Then Freya's back straightened, she seemed to have made a decision, and when she stepped back she had put on a mask I hadn't seen for a long time, eyebrows arched up, girlish laugh hovering at the corners of her mouth.

—Of course. We're just getting ready for a summer party, so it's all a bit of a mess—

—Not at all, said the suit and the dress. —Lovely, lovely. And the children, are …?

—Come through to the kitchen. Have some tea.

—Actually, we should have a look around first, if we may, and then—

—It's this way.

The group herded them into the kitchen, and they took out folders and notebooks.

—So. Who is in charge here?

—That's me, Freya said.

—And the owner. He's no longer residing here?

—He's … away.

—Do you know when he'll be back?

A smile from Freya. The women blinked around the kitchen, at the pans flashing in the light and the beautiful oak beams, and all of us gathered around the doorway.

I thought of the fish we used to watch in the fountain. That somehow they knew how to swim together, talked to each other, *This way, now this way*. The shoal. That's how we were, when real outsiders came, not like Kai, but to pry us open like nuts. In the kitchen doorway we were hanging off each other, smiling carefully, our hearts beating fast together and wondering what was going on and what was Freya going to do and they are in suits and suits are dangerous, and we moved together, a lean forward, sideways, to catch the conversation.

—So, could we talk alone for a moment?

Freya turned to us and the shoal spilled out back into the hallway. Dylan pulled at my hair.

—Where's Blue? he mouthed.

I shrugged. We crept around the door. I knew it was serious, but still I loved the game of it, everyone straining to keep quiet, moving slow and awkward now, trying to stop the floor from creaking.

From the kitchen, new names, and Freya's voice soft and low. Then the shadows lengthened towards the beads in the doorway and we made a giggling scramble back.

—Hello there, nice shoes says to me. —You must be Green.

I looked to Freya to tell me what to do, but she whispered to Dylan, her hair hiding their faces, so I smiled and looked at the floor.

They haunted the whole house, checking cupboards, asking questions. *Home schooled? Oh, yes. May we see …* Old books provided, Pet talking in a new voice, vowels stretched out like a dog in the sun. Kai dozed in the kitchen, and the women smiled, glanced at notebooks, moved on. Everyone smiling and nodding at each other, the words just sounds and the smiling-nodding the real language. I knew how to speak it: keep your mouth shut, smile and nod. We clustered behind them as they went all over the house *—Where do the children sleep?* — up to the attic *—Ah yes. Is there heating? —Ah-yes-nod-and-smile.* Through the studios and into the gardens.

Then we were on the back lawns, and the women were putting files back into their briefcases. Suit swung lightly on her heels.

—So. There's just the question of …

She riffled through her notes. Blushed.

—Um, sorry … we don't have a name. The child in question is understood to be living here … it must be the younger home-schooled girl?

Her plastic pen was chewed at the edges. I liked her for that. I chewed things too, and got into trouble with Freya for it, ruining the brushes.

—Blue, I supplied, and Freya massaged my shoulders with a strong grip.

—*Blue*, she repeated, and made a note. —Green and Blue. I see. That's, nice.

—I named her, I said. —It's after—

—And where is she?

Just like that her dot appeared near the copse, shaking her jumper over her shoulders, now the sun had gone in, so I pointed. We twisted to watch her come. People cleared their throats, shifted on their feet. I saw Blue was in trouble, which wasn't fair, so I said, —It's okay, we always go out on the moor. Red toenails nodded, unsmiling. Behind me, Toby took my hand, and whispered in my ear, *Listen*, but everyone turned to us then, the air too quiet, the whisper too loud, and he stopped.

Blue was slow and she kept stopping to twirl; she still did that, I'd stopped it ages ago, but she loved to make herself dizzy. She saw us and waved, then as she came closer she felt the stillness and the quiet, and she must have seen the strangers, and Freya's hands on my shoulders. She drew her hands into herself, avoided us, looked over our heads at the house. I felt for her. By the time she drew up to us she was scarlet, and stood with her arms in a knot over her stomach. The sleeves of the jumper twisted in her fingers.

—Hello, red toenails said. —You must be Blue.

I tried to catch her eye, but she was looking behind me, to Toby. She gave a tiny nod.

—Nothing to worry about. Your mum— she turned to Freya, and in the second before she turned back Blue's face fluttered confusion —says it's okay if we have a chat. Your guardian, I mean, she said, as sandals pointed at the notes. —Okay? she chirped.

The floor sunbeams had travelled far before we got her back. They'd taken her to the kitchen, and we went into the ballroom, sat together on cushions. I ached for arms but I didn't know if they were Freya's or Toby's I needed, so I sat with my own around my knees, cold in the late afternoon weak sun, murmuring with the others.

—Must be something. Her mother? Ellen said.

Freya shook her head.

—Maybe *she* contacted them, Pet said.

—Who? Egg said.

—Blue. Maybe, maybe she wants to leave, and she didn't—

—No way, I said. —No.

Then I thought about her secret in the attic and my own secret seemed thin and pale next to hers, a burning thing that had brought outsiders here. The outside man, Blue's friend, pushing out the edges of the world, so the hugeness of it threatened to suck us out and throw us to far away places. Beside me, Toby was sitting back on his hands, like he was ready to run, and I felt sick, that we'd invited the outside in with our stupid game.

Ellen was the least worried. —Happens all the time, she said. —They just want to check there's food in the cupboards and stuff, beds, you know. Mine used to get checked out every so often, she said. —Do they know you, from before?

—A bit, Freya said. —Then when … she nodded at me.

—Just to update their records, then. Don't worry about it, Ellen said.

But Freya was staring through me as though she was thinking about something else.

—All they need to do is see her arms bare, she said, and the grown all dropped — eyes, hands, heads, as though strings holding them had been cut.

When they brought her back in, Blue was pale as I'd ever seen her. She held the woman's hand, and for a second I thought, *Oh my god, they're right, she is going to become a Leaver, this is it, I'm never going to see her again, just like that*, but then she let go, and came to crouch at the edge of the group.

Freya and Dylan led the women to the front door; more low voices, and the *slam-shudder* of the door sealing us in. I whispered to Blue, —What is it? But she shook her head, staring at the floor. For a long time we stayed listening as the sounds of a car faded. I saw from the ballroom window the huge front gates opening and closing. They would have rust on their hands.

Freya stood in the doorway. —Meeting, she said. —Now.

Blue's secret was pulled out and flapped around all of us. Freya's voice got high and soft, a long-ago voice, from the time we would snuggle under her arms, wrapped in a blanket.

—I have a new story, Freya said. —Once, a girl who had everything she could ever possibly want, who was loved and cared for by good people, and didn't have to live in the city or go to school, decided she would make a new friend, a secret friend, on the moor. An outside person. An adult man.

Freya left this hanging, looking over Blue's head while Blue tried to catch her eye, tears pooling on her cheeks.

—After a while this new friend starts to ask lots of questions, and the little girl tells him all about her happy life. But she doesn't know how to tell things as they really are. Instead of explaining how happy and free she is, and how much she is loved, she says that sometimes she is cold, and sometimes she is hungry, and sometimes she wants to wash but there is no water. And when her new friend asks her about school, she doesn't tell him that she is learning about the world in a way he can never understand; she knows what the ley line he is standing on means, which is more than he does, and that her friends at home are trying to teach her the best lesson, which is how to be content. Instead she says, I don't go to school, and I can't read, and I can't write, and because she is a stupid, thoughtless little girl, she doesn't say anything else.

Blue quieter and quieter, even her breathing a silent shallow thing. A space forming around her like she had a disease.

—So, because the outside man doesn't understand, he decides to make some phone calls. So he calls up these people in suits, and they are so happy, because they have wanted to come and trample all over Foxlowe forever, and ask questions.

Freya looked at Blue then, smiling. —The end, she said.

A long quiet came, and I thought I might inch closer to Blue, or catch her little finger, so she wasn't so alone, but everyone was so still that I didn't dare.

—But what did they say? said Pet, picking paint from his nails.

—We'll never get rid of them now, said Dylan. —She'll be, what's it called, she'll be on file, or whatever, they'll keep checking.

—I said I was happy, said Blue, her voice steady. —I lied to them, I said I was happy. She looked right into Freya's face. —So stop making things up, she said.

I kept quiet when the yelling began. Blue put her head down so when the tears came they dripped onto her knees. I thought about the secret Kai had given me, and wished I had passed it on to her like a story, wanted to ask her if she remembered the nameless trees. She was running her fingers over her scarred arms as Freya circled around us, her voice rising over the group at times, other times sinking beneath other attacks, throwing in agreements. Freya came to stand behind me and I felt the sharp edge of her boot in my thigh.

—It was stupid, Blue, I mumbled. Then I said it louder and louder until Freya moved on.

When the shouting died down, Freya hugged a few of us who were trembling or crying, shushed us and smoothed damp cheeks, whispered things like, *There now, it's horrible, isn't it? It's all right now.* Blue was hunched now, her nose almost touching her crossed legs. Freya went to her and lifted her chin.

—So, she said.

Blue held her eye.

—We were always headed here, Freya said. —You've always been like an outsider, Blue.

Blue stayed silent. From where I sat I could see her fingers splayed out on the floor, red and veined like autumn leaves.

—Do you wish to become a Leaver? Freya asked.

Someone breathed in sharply, Toby or Pet, but no one moved.

Blue was quiet for a long time, Freya's finger under her chin. I could hear my heart in my ears, and felt somewhere behind me Toby radiating panic too.

—No, she said.

Freya waited a beat before she replied, so I knew she was surprised.

—Right then, she said. —Right. But what shall we do with you now, since you broke our rules so entirely? What should we make of this? Freya turned to us. —Is it the Bad, putting words in her mouth she speaks to outsiders, pulling her out onto the moor alone? What should we do?

—She's always been like this, Ellen said, fondly. —Remember when she was little, she just loved running around, exploring. She's just taken it too far. We need to explain to her again.

The Family took up this thread guiltily, steering us away to a kinder place, away from the sharp drop of the question of our baby, our youngest little sister, becoming a Leaver. We were more indulgent of Blue than was normal, and spoke about how different it was for her, because she didn't know about the world, and we should only try to make her understand, so that she didn't misstep again, and when Freya pointed out that I, Green, was even more of a born Foxlowe girl, but I was good, and I knew how to behave, I could only say, —Blue *doesn't* have the Bad, she just *doesn't*. And then the group began to grumble about hunger, and talk turned to food. Freya stepped over Blue and gave her a look that said she hadn't done with her yet, and there would be a Spike Walk for her later, and then gave her a nod to dismiss her.

Blue left, slowly, and I thought, she'll look back, and then she'll go to Freya and cry and Freya will say *All right, you've learned your lesson*, but she didn't look back, she walked slow and straight-backed and closed the ballroom door behind her with a thud.

I counted for her. Twenty-nine steps to the first landing. She'd go to the attic and lie on the bed. She didn't have anywhere else to go. I could go up after her, lie with her, stroke her hair and tell her it would be all right, but I was afraid of her hurt, the row we would have, *Why did you say, why didn't you say*? So I stayed on the floor playing with the frayed ends of my jeans.

The old chipped bath full of moonshine was hauled in; we dipped broken crockery into it and drank in gulps, burning our throats. Ellen went to the kitchen and brought back thick slabs of bread filled with fried eggs that burst yolk onto our fingers. We plunged into one of those long nights that happened around the Solstices, the type we lost ourselves in, when we loved each other and our home hard. We tried to make Blue, sad and alone upstairs, fade a little in our minds. The light seemed to weaken fast, and I stopped counting the clock strikes. I lay for a while with my head in Freya's lap, sipping the moonshine from her mug. —Good, isn't it? she said, then shifted so my head hit the floor with a crack, and the drink caught in my throat. —You can help me with Blue later, she added softly as she drifted away.

I propped myself up against the wall, watched my family. Dylan was at the head of a small circle, his arm around Ellen, lighting up and laughing. His beard glowed briefly blue with his lighter flame. Egg lay on one of the battered old sofas in the centre of the room, his legs crossed up in the air. He laughed at something Pet said, holding his stomach. Freya stalked through everyone, touching shoulders and bestowing smiles and nods. Kai had wandered in, and sat cross-legged with his back against the wall, just staring into his hands. I waved, but he didn't catch it. Toby was gone, probably to soothe Blue and wipe her wet cheeks with his sleeve. I drank more. Someone brought a guitar and the room hummed, dancing began. Foxlowe held us warm and slipping with drink and sweat. Dylan lifted Freya up and started to spin her around; I slipped away as her laugh rang around the walls.

Music, shrieking, laughing, all sealed away behind the closed ballroom door. The setting sun, an almost-Solstice sun, made the wooden walls and the banisters warm to the touch and glow golden. I resisted the urge to stop on the middle landing, only wiggled my toes in the blue light as though I'd dipped them in the water of the fountain. I'd go to Blue, and we'd talk it through and then she could start healing things with Freya. She'd have to do a Spike Walk, when it was late and the others were drunk and could pretend they didn't see or hear, or remember the next morning; we still had her, though, she was still here, and the Solstice was coming, to heal all things.

At Foxlowe voices were absorbed into the walls, swallowed by the scale of the rooms. We all learned how to recognise a voice pitched for secrets. We knew to hide outside the door, tilt an ear, like the dogs, how to breathe silently; in winter, to cover the clouds of our breath with our collars. So I stopped on the upper landing, crouched by the wooden finial, when I heard Blue and Toby's voices, heard the tears in them, knew this was something secret and real.

—No, no, shhh. It's okay, I know, Toby was saying.

—What if we never get her to come? Blue said.

A silence in which Toby might have shrugged, or looked at the floor. —Or she started crying, because—

—Hey, hey. So soft, he spoke to her. A voice I knew from the goats' shed. —She'll come to it, I know she will. We can't tell her right out, we have to be so careful with her. She'll tell Freya, that's just how it is, we can't trust her. It's working, the story, I know it is, she keeps adding details. I know she'll come to it by herself. It won't be long, I promise.

I edged into the shadowy space behind the door, looked through the gap where the cobwebbed hinges rusted. She was in his arms. He kissed her forehead, said, —If it comes to it, we'll go without her.

Freya's hand in mine was damp with sweat, the familiar calluses where she painted and gardened ran under my thumb. She smiled down at me while I interlaced our fingers. Behind us the Family danced, slipping in the spilled wine and crashing into each other, laughing with tears leaking down their cheeks.

—What is it? Freya said.

I gripped her hand tighter, pulled her away to the stairs. She caught my silence and followed me quietly. Somewhere underneath the rage that surged in me like boiling water I felt the strangeness of leading Freya, making her wait.

We sat on the middle step. I heard Blue and Toby moving above us. Freya pulled me to her, and poured her dark hair around us like a curtain. She kissed my nose, sharp wine breath, and pressed my forehead to hers.

—I have to tell you something, I said. —A story. A secret.

I remembered Freya telling me I could have no secrets from her, that she could read the inside of my heart. I watched her, seeing if it was true. An outsider would never have seen how shock played on her face. Her eyes were a steady glare. She held a breath. Her hands worked over mine, grasped, clutched, bent back my fingers.

I took a breath. All the little things I had ever done to hurt Blue — they all led here. I told Freya everything.

PART TWO

Jess

18

When I try to think of a good name for this time, I can only think of *Afterwards*, but glass tube boy gave me a better name: The Mulch Time. He'd smoked too many of the pearly rocks in the glass tube he carried in his jeans pocket, the jeans that stank and hung from his hips, and sometimes words like that came, little truths, but he couldn't remember saying them afterwards. I liked the smell of the stained jeans. Everything else smelled too clean in that place. They sprayed the corridors with bleach every night, and it crawled into my nostrils, made my eyes itch.

The hostel was an overnight kind of place. People came with big backpacks and played table tennis in the games room, or football along the corridors. In the mornings, doors creaking open on their hinges, the zoom of vacuuming, the bleach. But we stayed a long time, glass tube boy and me.

My first night, I felt something smooth and cool under my pillow. A bag of weed. Things felt better. Glass tube boy let himself in just then, talking about money in the outside way.

—A tenner you said, a tenner, oh, it's not you, he said.

We looked at one another.

—Let's be friends, he said, and offered me a rizla from his shirt pocket.

Sometimes he'd come into the shared kitchen and talk, while I boiled the kettle and tried to work out the packets of dried food. One of those kitchen times he was telling me a story about a girl he used to know. He called her *this girl from my Mulch Time*. I split the packet of noodles open and poured over the boiled water, dribbling it everywhere, waited for the gelatinous worms to swell.

—Mulch Time? I said.

But he was already on a new track, talking about the water in the taps.

—Poisoned, he said. —Boil it. Always boil it, and we'll get iodine too.

The next kitchen time, I asked him again. He was breaking eggs into a bowl.

—I like the ritual of cooking, you know. I like the old routines, he said.

I scooped up the egg shells and crushed them.

—So witches can't use them, I said.

He nodded, smiling. —Exactly.

—You know before, I said. —*The Mulch Time*.

—Huh?

—You said, *this girl from my Mulch Time*. The other day.

—Don't remember, he said.

—Okay.

As he left he offered me the plate of scrambled eggs he'd made. When I shook my head he tipped them into the bin. At the door he stood for a second, pulling his crusted jeans up. A small shake had begun in his hips there. He shook a lot.

—It's the lost time, he said. —You're still in it.

Then, Mel found me.

A squatting witch, something pressing — the sheets, kick them off. Little stinging crescents on my palms where my nails have bitten in. The ceiling is a white paint ocean, brushed-on waves lap at the walls and the light fitting. Seasick, I stare and sway in bed. The wall blurs where the radiator heat shimmers.

I have strategies for mornings like these, when dreams of old faces, old fear, spill in. The best one I know is Mel's. She says, *Count all the things you are happy about in the now*. Mel says lots of things like that. It's just *count your blessings*, a tired idea, a needlepoint design for paper-skinned old women. But it works. So. I lift my index finger.

It's Sunday, which means no appointments today, no meetings in circles with biscuits and enthusiastic applause for stories. Which means lying here all morning if I want. Second finger. It wasn't a nightmare. Not until.

Swallow. Keep going.

Ring finger. I slept, didn't need any chalky pills coating the back of my throat. Pinkie. I'm twenty-five years old, they tell me, they think, and I've only got one wrinkle, across my forehead, I can hide it with a fringe. Thumb. Okay, my brain doesn't always work properly, but I have really long legs.

I must add to the list: I have a home here, I'm not lost any more; but still there's a feeling like hunger, a heart-ache that lives in the throat. I'm too old to feel homesick. But being too old for things doesn't matter much, the way I live now. I never made it to grown.

The smell of toast rises up through the carpet. I could sprawl here all day, looking at the walls where I can make scenes play out, an imaginary movie projected onto the floral wallpaper. An oval mirror with a mother of pearl frame sits on a lace doily on the bedside table. There are so many pretty things in this house. I wonder what sound it would make, if I smashed it against the wall. Things are muffled here.

At the foot of the bed Mel's laid out my clothes for the day: a pink jumper with lace on the shoulders, a skirt that puffs at the hips. I pull a dressing gown from the back of the door.

It took me months to shrink into this neat, symmetrical box, like the houses children draw. The bedrooms sit over the lower rooms in perfect alignment. The stairs are straight, the landings neat little squares. Thick carpets and heavy curtains wrap us all up and keep the house in a permanent hush. Everywhere is lace and pink and cushions. Throw myself down the stairs and I'd bounce. Outside, the streets of Highgate lie leafy and serene.

I pad down the stairs. Breakfast, sit. Maybe look at the book, it might help. Richard and Mel will be in the kitchen, in joggers, loose t-shirts and flip-flops. They like to stay in on Sunday mornings, supine over armchairs. Then we'll walk Jimmy on the heath, Richard will work in the afternoon and Mel and I will talk in the conservatory or she'll read me stories from the Sundays, about affairs, lost children, cellulite.

The glass door into the kitchen catches the winter sun as it opens and my twisted sheets, my slow finger counting, they spill in here. Something's wrong. Richard leans on his hands at the table, his fingers curved around his skull, like a passenger in a crashing plane, something from the television. Mel is stroking his back. The radio burbles as Jimmy ambles over to lean against my legs, unbalancing me with his warm weight. He blinks at me from his wizened face. He's a lazy retired greyhound, and like me he ambles from room to room, goes for walks, eats, dreams. Our world is small and comfortable.

We all watch Jimmy push his thin head into my shins. What do people do, when there are no pets to deflect attention, to buy a few seconds? Mel smiles at the dog, still smoothing Richard's back up and down.

The first time I met Mel, I had her down as a bitch. Her sharp cheekbones and thin nose make her face pointed and hard. Her thin lips turn down a little, making her look permanently irritated. I was wrong, though. It's only when she speaks, or when her eyes do, that you can see how soft she is. Her eyes are grey. Her kindness sits in them, and also in her small hands. She should have children to rock and coo over.

We stay like that, pretending nothing's wrong, for long seconds. Mel clears her throat.

—Sleep well?

Richard pours coffee.

I shrug. —Yeah, it was a good night.

—Dreams?

I nod. I wish I'd stayed in bed with my wallpaper movie. I take a triangle from a rack of toast, spread a thick layer of honey, and a dollop of chocolate spread. In the bin under the sink are the empty wrappers of my late-night binge: cardboard sticky with ice cream, orange and purple foil I have licked clean.

—Just one as I woke up. Is something wrong?

Mel chews the inside of her cheek. I swallow more toast, the flood of sugar making my teeth pulse. Richard plays himself like bubble wrap, cracking his finger bones one by one. Jimmy's drool swings and drops onto my toes.

Mel starts the conversation over, a rewind-erase she uses when I say the wrong thing.

—Not getting dressed today?

I shrug.

—Go on, she says. —You know I like you to look nice.

—After a bath, I say.

—Okay.

—Okay, I echo. —I'll just … I click my tongue for Jimmy to follow me into the study.

This room is the only part of the house that's cool, the window blocked by heavy ivy. I bury my face in the downy fur along Jimmy's back and make babyish noises until he flops onto the rug, grizzling happily. A green coat, Richard's, lies over the back of the chair. I wrap up in it and rub my feet into Jimmy's belly.

The laptop buzzes and grumbles to itself. The sound is wrong, not a Sunday sound, a break from routine. The website flashes up, *Listen-and-read*. I don't want to work but I hate feeling in the way, the intruder on secret marriage politics. It's usually small stuff, Richard picking at her sometimes. *Bins, dishes, where's my keys?* But his head in his hands, I've never seen that, not here. It's something bad. I don't want to take a pill. I'll take five minutes with the book.

The book sits on the shelf next to Richard's art books and boxes of photographs. Across the cracked laminate jacket *The Secrets of Pompeii* is emblazoned in orange font. A museum ticket stub is tucked into the first page, and a photo of Mel and Richard in wide brimmed hats. This is how the book works. There's a picture on each page of the modern ruins, cracked and yellowing stone under holiday blue skies. Then you turn a plastic page over it, a *palimpsest*, Mel told me, and the ruins are covered with the ancient city, as it was. You see dead people in strange clothes buying fruit and carrying children in their arms along the stone foundations. The stone is whole and clean and its paint restored. I love to sit with it, peeling the pages over, laying the past over the present. Now I only get to the second page before Mel's shape approaches the glass study door.

There's nowhere for me to go, I have to stay and listen. Something bad. They want me out. I'll have to leave Jimmy behind. I graze his nose with a knuckle.

Richard comes up behind Mel. She folds her arms and looks at the floor. He speaks flat words, so I have to work to make the sounds mean anything.

—Freya Marsh died last week, he says.

I close the book and place it on the desk, smooth over the cover.

—I had a call from the lawyer about the house this morning. We weren't sure if …

He opens his hands, raises his eyebrows to say, *I'm reasonable*.

Jimmy's fur is matted, I should brush him.

Freya is gone.

Richard leaves. He said her full name like he didn't even know her.

Mel settles down next to me, links her fingers through mine. She's brought a glass of water and a diazepam. The pill makes a queasy ball with the tea and toast.

—You've had a shock, Mel says.

She counts and I breathe. Then she makes me stretch out my hands.

—Do you want to talk? Mel says.

Freya reaches from my throat and sews my lips shut. Mel picks at the seams.

—Richard won't talk about it, she says, tugging at my fingers.

Freya's face, her veined cheeks, dark eyes, crooked teeth. Her rough hands cupping my head. Her low purring voice weaving between Blue and me, binding us close. Her black hair, smelling of soil. I bury my face in Jimmy's fur. The study door clicks shut.

The rest of the morning is sluggish, the three of us stuck to furniture and floors. Richard on the phone, floating old names around the house. *Foxlowe, Freya.* Mel sits with tea in the kitchen where she can watch both Richard and me. I catch her gazing through the glass doors. The diazepam suspends me in the air.

Jimmy starts to wriggle and pace. His teeth chatter and he loops around me, nudging hands and knees. Mel goes upstairs and returns with wool jumpers in her arms. She lays one in my lap.

—Come on. Fresh air.

The jumper is one of her hand-knitted ones, a horse's head surrounded by roses. I take off the bathrobe and pull the jumper on over my t-shirt, then drift into the hallway where Mel is already clipping a coat over Jimmy's back. She sits me down against the dresser and lifts one foot, then the other, rolling socks onto them, then stuffs my feet into trainers. In the mirror behind her, I'm glazed under a serene expression. Richard goes up the stairs behind us, the phone hooked under his ear.

Mel leads Jimmy and me along the High Street. We make wild sounds when the wind cuts under our coats, passing closed charity shops and patisseries with empty stands. Jimmy slopes along, tripping over his own feet. Mel stops and huddles into me, and I follow where she's looking: The Flask.

—Mulled wine and fires, she says. She bends over to rub Jimmy's muzzle. —Shame we've got *you* or we could sit in the pub all afternoon! she says.

I should laugh, I should help her. But it's too late and we are walking again, towards the mud and the grass.

They brought me to The Flask the first night I moved in, a long-ago summer. We sat outside on the picnic benches, Jimmy's lead hooked around a table leg. My arms were still sore from the hospital and I wasn't supposed to drink; I nursed a coke. The needle bruises in the crook of my elbow and the back of my hands twinged when I picked up the glass. Mel's face was set in a smile and I felt the ache of her face, wanted to say, *It's all right, you don't have to*.

—I was thinking, Mel said. —What we should call each other. You should call me Mum.

—Um, I said.

She smiled. —Well. See how you feel. And, perhaps, do you know what—? She turned to Richard, lowered her voice. —What's her real name? she said.

—It's Green, I said.

—But that's not really ... Well. A fresh start? How about Jane? That's my favourite book, Mel said. —*Jane Eyre*. I could read it to you—

—I don't care, I said. —Call me Jane. Or Jess. Call me Jess, if you want.

Mel pulled me into a hug, her tiny arms digging into the back of my neck. —Jess, she said. My Jess.

Richard stroked Jimmy.

—Strange, isn't it? he said.

Mel went inside to the bar. It was the first time he'd spoken to me.

—It was all her idea, he said.

—Yes.

—Not that I don't want you. If you want to stay, that is. If you think, you know, you'll be all right.

He was dressed differently then, in a tailored suit jacket and dark jeans, expensive shoes that squeaked. His face was clean shaven, lined now around the lips, the result of years of puckering around roll ups, and his eyes had lost their colour somehow, washed out. His hair was grey now around the temples. His voice, too, was different; gone was the bored drawl, the long pauses. He spoke in the outside way now, quick, floating ideas, constantly checking: *You know, if, that is, you know what I mean?*

Jimmy pushed his head onto my lap, offering his ears to stroke.

—He's lovely, I said, without feeling. I didn't know how much I would love Jimmy then.

—Mel got him from a rescue centre, Richard said. —They were going to put him down, he's got something wrong with his legs, can't race.

An old memory surfaced, Freya with a dog in her lap, cradling it as it died. Had she given it rat poison? *Never be sentimental about animals*, she was saying. *It means they suffer longer.*

—Didn't Freya use to …? I began.

—Now, look.

Richard leaned forward, as though to take my hands, thought better of it, and let his own fall between the glasses.

—Mel and I have a lovely life here, and she'll look after you. This is all, it's for her, you know, this is *her* thing. She feels … Well. She's angry with me.

He leaned back, opened his hands, as though I would reply, *But how unfair!*

—You know, she thinks this is the right thing to do. But I don't want to hear about any, any of that time, you know, the house, the … Everyone there with us, it's all done. I'll pay for you, like before, if you like, and you can do what you want. But I don't want this … He circled his hands. —Oh, remember when, and Oh, we used to … okay?

I nodded. —Fine.

—I mean, just look what happened to you, with the … and Mel having to, and all that.

—Fine, I said.

I watched him dig under his nails. He was still looking for Foxlowe dirt, crusted there, to scrape out and wipe on the grass.

—Do I call you Dad now?

It was an easy shot. Blood flashed up Richard's neck. I buried a rush of triumph in a gulp of coke.

—Richard is fine, he said.

I raised my eyebrows. —Your Foxlowe name. Don't see why I can't be Green then—

—I changed it a long time ago, he said. —I'm too old now to … And it's a *normal* name.

He flicked a bit of dirt away. Jimmy snapped his jaws as it sailed past.

—Mel said I could call her Mum, if I wanted.

—For god's sake, Green. She's only a few years older than you. Let's just keep things simple, all right?

It was Freya he meant. There's to be no talk of Freya. Blue too, because they trail each other, one hanging off the other's name.

Mel pulls us along, and we leave The Flask behind, down the wide streets with iron gates and sleek grey cars in the driveways. When we reach the muddy path with its map of the heath, I breathe more easily. I love it here. The trees mute the traffic and the sky is wide. We trudge along past woods and the hidden bowers used for picnics and sex. It's the hill we're heading for, the view. Mel grips my arm painfully and rubs it, rustling her glove over the nylon coat.

—All right? she says.

Jimmy shies and yelps at a leaf. I pull him into my legs, whisper, *Stupid dog*.

—Richard wants to go up there. To Foxlowe, Mel says. The name sounds strange in her voice. —Well, I mean, he has to, you know, to sort through the house.

—What's going to happen?

She takes my hand and hugs it into her shoulder. —You'll stay with us, of course. We'll put some of the money from the house into an account for you, and everything will stay just the same.

—I … that's not … I fumble in my pocket for dog biscuits, find ancient ones in the lining, throw them in the air for Jimmy to catch.

The crest of the hill is before us now. On the horizon, some kids whoop as their kite catches a gust and swings upward. Mel cranes to watch it.

Quick, before she changes the subject.

—So, he's selling it, I say.

—It's in quite bad shape, apparently. I don't know why he kept it on.

The funeral. Freya's funeral. Surely it will be at the house. The ballroom, the garden, the wide staircases. The attic room. Surely the others will be there.

We walk on, up the gently sloping path, until we reach the wide hilltop. All the benches are taken and we stand a while, Jimmy plodding in contented circles around us. Then Mel yanks us, and marches, shouldering a woman out of the way. She apologises with a smile, and we sit. London shines below us. I'm always surprised by how small it looks. I can span from the Eye to Liverpool Street with my fingers.

The kite we saw from the path crumples in front of us, making us jump and sending Jimmy tearing away in fright. The children, two boys and a girl, rush to pick it up. The tallest boy fiddles with the string while the younger two idly push each other towards a puddle.

As they run away again, the little girl turns and waves. Mel's lips sag and she pulls me to her.

—I like that children fly kites still, she says.

I stroke her fingers where they grip my waist.

Jimmy careens back into Mel's legs and pants clouds of stinking breath over us. She nuzzles his head and kisses his ears. I look at the trees along the edge of the hill and the muddy grass. Then the city glinting and smoking below us.

—I'll go with Richard, I say. —To Foxlowe, I mean. I'll go with Richard, I say again, because Mel is staring at me as though she doesn't understand what I've said.

* * *

After the heath we plunge back into heat. Mel wrenches the door handle up, sealing us in with a *thunk*. Jimmy collapses at the foot of the stairs and I step over his skinny legs, stuck in the air as he pants on his back. Through the glass I glimpse Richard smoking, using a teacup as an ashtray, and it makes me laugh, with surprise, or fear, as though the old Richard is coming back, the past has punctured the smooth membrane of the house. Mel's pulling at my coat so I shrug it off into her arms. I want a bath. I head to the bathroom, shedding clothes as I go.

Naked, I sit on the toilet lid. Mel runs the bath. The *whoosh* of the water makes me realise how quiet we are.

Mel wrings her hands. —Oh! Towels, fresh warm ones. She answers herself as she goes out. —Yes, *towels*.

I lock the door on her. She knocks and then I hear her settle on the stairs to listen out for me.

The water is like little knives on my ankles, then thighs and back. I force my body down, water spilling over the sides, and regard the rolls of fat, my roasting feet. When the water covers my shoulders my heart flails around. In the jagged beats I find my morning's dream, and Freya lays the past over me, like turning a page of the Pompeii book; here are things I do not think about in waking life, things I had forgotten, coating Mel's house so we are buried under the film. Silently I scream Freya's name; the drugs keep my tongue still. The only sound in the bathroom is the slosh of water as I run the water over and over my knees.

19

Now that Freya's death is in the house, Mel's turned to food to weigh me down. When I first moved in, she searched my room for hidden sweets, even put a lock on the fridge, but after a while she brought things for me, treats, and left them on my bed, and in the evenings she poured hot chocolate into mugs, crowded with marshmallow and dusted with cinnamon sugar. —My poor baby, she'd say. —You'll never go hungry here, not with me. Clicking her tongue, while Richard's face flooded red.

Now the kitchen steams up in the afternoons, when she boils and roasts, and I draw patterns in the windows: downstairs, flowers and stars; in my room, a stick-figure porn show, an orgy across the pane.

We eat late, around the doily-covered table, mash smothered in butter, pies, sticky carrots glazed in honey, sponge cakes. Food smells hang in the air, making it hotter. My armpits itch with sweat. Still I eat, clearing my plates, sit dazed and slack in front of the TV afterwards, letting the things I don't understand wash over me, Jimmy asleep over my knees. I go to bed making fierce resolutions, but every day I sleep late, doze in the afternoons, until the house is dark and heavy and I can only return to bed, stepping over the piles of folded clothes ready to pack. I count the pills in the bathroom every night. But there aren't any drugs in my food. When she came back, Freya brought Blue. Together they hang on my shoulders, pull me down to rest. I'm too exhausted to go.

Being tired, that's the thing, since my life changed. It's just so fucking tiring all the time. Even now, when I understand so much more, and I am curled up in this little house, smothered and buried in sugar and soft things, outside it is all waiting to assault me: the shouting, heaving, screaming, noisy mess of it.

The first thing was the light, as though on a bright day someone had thrown open the doors, and the sun bleached out the edges of the world. But this isn't the sun; it is a constant buzzing, glaring thing, assaulting through drawn curtains, bouncing off cold, painted walls, absorbing into eyelids, so it's never a true dark. Then the noise: a thousand voices, some of them real, spoken soft at first, others swimming across the crackle of radio static or stretched in the waves of the TV, all of them screaming secrets. They washed through me like rags rinsed clean. After a while the voices left traces, teaching a million tiny lessons: pull the eyelid and look up so the kohl doesn't smudge, men walked in the dust of the moon, new songs of buy-this and money, the tune of the train, *You have arrived at your destination, ping pong ping pong*. Here is a map of the world, here is you, where is home? Here is England, here is London. Scrutinise the dot, imagine Toby living amongst the pixels. But here is more, the ocean — a vast moving moorland made of sky colours — there's a building called the Taj Mahal that looks like heaven, and enormous towers made of the silver from knives and forks. These places live in posters on people's walls. There are places where the moor stretches on so far you can't walk across it, made of sand or ice. Wash between your legs and under your arms every morning, and at night before you go to sleep, and you brush your teeth like this, with the gritty paste, like frozen mud.

I tried to share the things that I knew: All The Ways Home Is Better — but the whole of the world and all the things that have happened before, layers of time and people that must be learned, and where the lines of named places are drawn and killed for, and all the names for things, all of this was stacked against me. If you placed the things I knew on a kitchen scale, dusty with flour, and placed all their lessons on the other side, then the things I knew would float up and bounce against the ceiling.

Now, though, there's a weight to the things I knew, because Richard has spoken names and Freya has clawed her way into Mel's life, and now, perhaps, the time of Mel's house is ending, and there's a new time coming. So

I try again. Beef pie congealing in my stomach. Globules of gravy are spattered on the tablecloth; grease pools around them. Mel counts out the three pills and arranges them in a triangle, next to my orange juice.

—I wanted it to look like a heart, she says. —But it doesn't.

—It does. A heart, I see it, says Richard, and I snatch the pills into my mouth, to shut them both up.

—When are you going, Richard? I say, through the orange syrup.

—I don't see why you have to go up there yourself, Richard. You're not family, Mel says.

—But we *are* Freya's family, I say.

Mel gulps water. The skin on her throat is so thin that as she tips her head to swallow, the veins stand out clear under the white flesh.

—I'm responsible for the house, Richard says. — But there's no need for you to come, Jess. Might be, you know. Upsetting.

—It could set you back *months*, Mel says. Her eyes are threatening tears. Her knife screeches on the plate. With each crunch a distant panic scrabbles towards the surface: *I can't stay I have to leave I have to leave now.* I could go tonight, pack a few things — the photograph, the pills are in the cabinet above the bathroom sink. Get the train from Euston, like before. I could take Jimmy with me, they let dogs on trains, and he's well behaved, just goes to sleep. I could get up from the table and say, *I'm not wait-*

ing for Richard, I'll go myself. I'll meet you there, people say that, casual —*I'll meet you there*. I could sleep at Foxlowe tonight, in the attic room, in my old bed.

—I think it would be good for me, I say. —To go back.

—You are not leaving here without our permission, Mel says. —You're not well enough.

I don't answer, and Mel slumps back in her chair. Her mouth droops. She isn't wearing any make-up, and the hard edges of her face, unsoftened by powders and blush, look so sharp I imagine pricking a finger on them like a needle. If I can make her see she loves me, she's my ally, surely I can make her see. I fumble for something she'll understand.

—Freya was like my mum, I say.

Mel leaves the room, and Richard pulls at his earlobes. It's an old Foxlowe habit. Freya, or Libby, I can't remember who started it. Grip the skin between your thumb and forefinger for headaches; pull your earlobes for calm.

—Look, he says. —It's not a good idea, you know? You can't come.

—You can't tell me what to do, I say, unsure if it's true.

—Well, he says. —It's not a good idea.

—I should've gone ages ago. Don't you feel like we just fucked off and forgot all about her and left her there? Richard?

His head hanging back, he blows air at the ceiling. There's a strange smile on his face, it twitches at the corners, perhaps he is going to cry.

—I don't know why that should be, why you think that.

He looks at me. Curious, gentle, like a hospital visitor.

—I just don't know why that should be. How can you? I mean, how can you miss the place where Blue … I mean, what's the *matter* with you?

I don't close my eyes when he speaks Blue's name.

—The Family, I say. —Please tell me where they are. I know we agreed, but …

He leans back now, his hands behind his head, the deep lines etched around his eyes and lips mimicking a smile.

—What's the point? he says.

I stayed in my room for the first weeks of the Mulch Time, hearing the whine and slam of the fire doors. There were signs everywhere. Fire. Warning. Do. Don't. Numbers. Not a safe place. I'd ventured as far as the corner shop where the man behind the counter had a kind face and let me hold out my hand so he could count the coins he needed for things. He showed me how to use the card machine and held his fingers in his ears when I tried to tell him the number I needed, because I'd forgotten it was a secret. But even the shop wasn't always safe. There was a long road to get there, and people tried to speak to me and held out bits of paper with urgency, *Take it, take it,* or pushed me out of the way. Glass tube boy didn't like the outside either. When he went too far from the hostel, he heard people talking about him into their phones. So we began to set each other little challenges, to stop us being frightened.

Glass tube boy set the first challenge: get a bus. I liked that, the roar and beep and the soothing voice announcing each stop, and the seat I liked best under the stickers that peeled off neatly, kissing the glass as they went. His turn: to the shop on the far side of the street. Not the kind man one, the other, with fruit outside and long queues on weekdays. He made it. My turn.

—Take the tube to the river and back, he said. —But don't. Don't. *Don't* lose the blue card, or you'll be fucked. Arrested. By the police.

I was sitting on my bed, getting noodle sauce on the sheets. I knew police. I remembered the flashing lights and the questions and how I saw in their faces that they didn't understand at all.

—Not afraid of *them*, I shrugged. —They aren't clever.

He stared for a moment, stroking his hollow cheeks.

—London police are different.

—Yeah?

—They kill you, he said.

In the escalator tunnel, gripping the sticky moving banister, I felt for the card, and it was there, smooth in my pocket. Follow the signs with the black colour, he said, not the green, and he wrote the name for me. I held it up to the map on the wall, to see that the shapes matched. I looked at the map a while. I liked it. It was like our winter snow footprints at Foxlowe, seen from the attic windows. All interconnected, weaving different ways, and then finding each other again. I stood at the map too long. Someone shouldered me out of the way, pushing me into another body, and I stumbled. You can't stand still for long in the tunnels. I felt again for the card. It was gone.

Tunnels led to walkways and onto underground bridges, up and down flights of stairs, down escalators to deeper places. All the time, checking and rechecking pockets, turning my bag upside down on the platforms. Then I worked out that I could stay on this one, yellow, line, and it kept going round in a loop. I just needed to stay here until I caught my breath and found the blue card.

So I was scrabbling deep into the bag, feeling the slimy remains of a banana in there, when she pushed past me to an empty seat and I saw her face.

I tried to remember the last time I saw her, and couldn't. But I'd seen a polaroid of her, stuck to the pinboard in the ballroom, every day for years. Toby used to move the postcards and letters around so you couldn't see her photograph, but someone always moved it back. It was her.

I could see her reflection in the window. In the hard light of the carriage, she sucked in her lips and bit them, scraping away some of the red paste. I remembered her doing that. Her eyebrows had been stripped away and painted on in high arches. Her hair was pinned messily to her head. A streak of grey in it, around the hairline. The rest was dyed orange. She wore a t-shirt with a dolphin on it and some writing underneath.

We pulled into Bayswater. I followed her out. I hadn't yet learned how to speak to people this new way. Make an excuse: the time, directions. I didn't know that then, so I just reached for the hood on the back of her top, tugged it, and said, —Valentina.

She swatted around her back. —Get off, she said, sounding bored. Kept walking.

—Valentina, I said again. I sped up to keep pace with her. —It's Green. From Foxlowe. It's you, I know it's you, stop!

She made little darting movements of her neck, to catch me in glimpses. Then she slowed, and faced me. The crowd in the ticket hall jostled us. Someone's bag caught my shoulder and dragged me a few inches. Valentina pulled me back.

—Fuck, she said. —Look at you.

She tried to pull her hands away, but I gripped them, in case she left.

—It's you, I said, stupidly.

She looked around, and twisted her hands away from mine.

—What's your t-shirt say? I asked.

—What? Oh. Um, it says, Everyone smiles in the same language.

—Oh, I said.

—Look, I'm late for work—

—I lost the blue card. I've been hiding until the police go. In case they wait.

She frowned. —It's okay, Green. Don't … Just relax, okay? Let go of my hands. Come on. Like this.

She pulled me around so I was in front, looped her arms around me and pressed her blue card against the plastic disc. The doors slid open and she shuffled us through.

We spilled out into a grey street. Valentina pulled me past buildings of ugly concrete blocks and a gaggle of young people speaking languages I couldn't understand. Outside a shop with neon lights, and huge buckets full of I ♥ London bags and plastic red buses, she said, —I'm late for work. Riffling through her handbag. —You'll be okay?

She began to walk backwards, waving me away. The people on the street surged and traffic roared and spewed dark clouds into the air. Panic battered me.

—Wait! I don't know how to. Come with me!

—God's sake. Here. She thrust some coins into my hand. —You can catch a bus from by the park.

—I was supposed to get to the river, I said.

—Just get on a bus.

—No, please, don't—

The group of foreign-tongued girls were staring. Valentina strode back and shook me by the shoulders.

—Get on *that* bus. She jabbed the air as a red blur went past. —Find your way to wherever. It's easy. I'm going to work.

She disappeared into one of the concrete blocks. I followed to a flight of steps that stank of cigarettes, and settled down on the bottom step. In the ash at my feet I traced lines with my little finger. I had never counted Valentina before, but now she had dropped into the frame, so I added her into the right section. Now the pattern looked like this:

To the left were the known places. A stick for Freya, Richard and me. I added Valentina to make four. The still lost lived in the middle box: Pet and Egg somewhere together, the others drifting alone. I was tempted to move Toby, but I couldn't yet, until I could be sure. And then two in another box: Kai and Blue, who didn't belong in the known or the unknown places.

There were so many others, but these are the ones my memory keeps and marks down. Other Leavers too far back to count, too lost, or drifters, drop-ins. These marks though, these are the core, the Family.

The neon shop played six songs before a flood of people came out and flopped onto the steps above and around me. One of them, a boy with olive skin and a beard shaved into a strange thin line, sat down next to me and scuffed my pattern away. It didn't matter, I knew it by heart.

—Hello? English?

—Um-hm.

—New student?

I shook my head.

—What level?

I shrugged. He offered me a cigarette and I took it. A bell sounded, and the group trickled away.

I waited for another hour or so, listening to the pop music boom, and watching couples wander into the road, faces stuck in maps, getting yelled at by taxi drivers. When another bell sounded clusters of people climbed over me, giving me puzzled smiles, or some of them, girls with long blonde hair and belts with giant diamond clasps, tutted and tossed their ponytails over their shoulders.

When Valentina came, she had files and papers under her arm.

—Still here then, she said. She pinched the bridge of her nose, eyes closed. —Is it, you know, an emergency? Do you need to find Richard? Because we aren't in touch.

It dawned on me that she thought I'd come for her, that I'd followed her.

—I was supposed to go to the river. I didn't know you'd be on the train too. But now we've …

—You'll be fine, she said. —The bus, I pointed it out, remember?

I shook my head.

Valentina sighed. —I need a drink, she said.

She took me to the end of the road where a pub leaned into the traffic, looking like it was about to fall down. Inside, wood marinated in spirits. Bowls of chips stood on the bar, giant spoons painted with numbers stuck into them. Valentina pointed to a booth with leather seats and I went.

She brought two pints of something.

I twisted in my seat to look around. —There's somewhere like this near where I live. We go sometimes, I lied.

—We? Are you with … others?

—No. The people staying at the hostel. Sometimes they want to go drinking and they come and bang on the doors, and ask me to come.

I sipped. Like milk gone bad.

—And, I said, —I went to a bar sometimes at the school. I snuck out.

—School?

—Until I was sixteen. Until they guessed I was. It was nice. Mountains. They did everything for you. I had to learn new things fast. I can read a little now. I can write a bit, I said.

Valentina wrapped her lips around her glass and took half the pint down in gulps.

—I'm living here in London now, I said. —Foxlowe is all closed down.

She studied brown photographs on the wall. Old pictures of the same street, with horses and carts. Up close like this, I could see the stubble of her eyebrows faint under the thick kohl. —Yeah, I know, she said.

—I hate it here, I said. —But now we've, now I've got you, we can find everyone else. Can you believe we just found each other just like that? Maybe it won't be hard to find the others, maybe we can go somewhere new, if Richard won't let us use … We can go and wait for Freya and then everything will go back to normal.

Her face twitched when I said the old names. I held the tacky edge of the table, to make the little island we'd made safe.

—It doesn't matter that you're a Leaver, I said. —That won't matter now.

—I'm sorry, she said.

—Valentina—

—It's Charlotte, she said.

—Oh.

She shrugged. —I never liked it. Sounds like a pudding. A fat girl name. Charlotte took another gulp. —So, is he … Have you heard from him? Is he okay?

A tiny collapse somewhere in my chest. —I thought he might be with you, I said. —I thought he'd gone to find you.

—Well, maybe he will one day. He must be all grown up now too.

—Richard didn't send him away. It was just me.

—He's older, must have his own life somewhere, she said.

I drained my glass. The sour taste became something sweeter. I'd tried to make moonshine at the school, in the bathroom that smelled of stale sweat. It never worked and when I got caught I was kept inside for three weeks. They'd worked out that I hated to be inside. I'd never snuck away to a bar, that was a lie; I'd heard the older ones talk about it. I remembered the hot wine and the sharp edge of moonshine at home. This wasn't like that. It was like drowning something, pushing it under and holding it. It kicked and struggled but the drink held it there, away from me, so I could breathe.

—Another? I said.

—I should go. I'm skint anyway.

—I have money from Richard. I get it with this.

I dug out the plastic card, and Charlotte grinned.

We had some shots. A few with stupid names, that tasted of cream or mint. Then vodka. Everything was funny and on the edge of the funny was a big hole of fear so we kept drinking and laughing.

—I'm sorry, Valentina-Charlotte said, lots of times.

—It's okay, I said, forgiving her for I didn't know what.

—Thought it would be him, she said. —Lucas. That found me. Is he okay, do you think? He was always okay without me.

Lucas. That must have been Toby's outside name.

His breathing that day, watery gasps. He was crying so hard.

—Yeah, I'm sure he's okay.

Charlotte finished the dregs of something, gin and a mixer.

—He was always okay without me, she said again.

I thought glass tube boy would worry about me, but when I showed up hours later, all the time it took for me to find my way, he was in his room, smoke curling under the door, and I knew not to knock. Later he found me in the TV room and I told him about Valentina. He told me to watch out, in case she was an imposter.

After a while I could do the journey to Bayswater in my sleep. I waited for Valentina on the steps. Sometimes I got the time wrong, and she'd never appear, or the school would be closed. But when she did find me there, she took me along to the same pub and we drank more and harder each time, not saying much, waiting for the laughter to come. She seemed to like having me around, as though she'd made me into a new person in her head. She even called me a new name: Jess. You look like a Jess, she said to me one day, skidding a shot towards me which spilled into my lap, making us both laugh. —Let's call you that. Jess.

At first, when we'd had a few drinks she let me talk about Foxlowe, and then she'd join in and tell me things I was too young to remember. Sometimes we argued over stupid things, like the size of the grandfather clock in the hall, or the colour of the rugs in the ballroom. But after a while, when I tried to blend the memory —

Valentina in her long skirts and her sad face, and the way she pulled Toby onto her lap, or shouted at me for hitting him — with this woman, it was like talking to her about someone she'd met once, and now couldn't remember. At first I called her Charlotte, but in my head she was still Valentina; after a while she became Charlotte, and Valentina was like a nickname she'd lost long ago.

I lost some time. The Mulch. Waking with the warm seep of piss through tights and dresses. Getting angry with strangers, casting around for things to throw. There were burn marks on my legs from falling into hot metal, the side of a train. Sometimes I found my way home, the lights through the hostel windows too bright. Crusted clothes. I slept with glass tube boy, our arms tight around one another, sweat pooling in the small of my back, and sometimes we fucked lazily, never kissing, and other times I listened to him talk, saying things I didn't understand, getting upset, raking his hands through his hair, and he listened while I tried to explain my plans, and how frustrated I was that I kept forgetting them, kept losing time. I got to hate the daytime, and kept a bottle of vodka by the bed to keep things dim. Waited for the end of the day, to meet Charlotte out of work.

One night we lurched to Soho, Charlotte and me, tripping in front of cycle rickshaw drivers and snatching fliers we screwed into balls and chucked at each other. The crowds parted around us. I shook hands with and hugged all the strangers with their outside lives and their happy, open, affectionate faces. In the bar-shine, Valentina's red-lipped grin was hypnotic, her orange hair aglow. The drowning, kicking thing was buried deep and I threw my arms out and spun in the street, stupidly happy.

In a queue, our arms around the men at the door, kissing cheeks. A lurch down into dark spaces and a mirror that caught me and showed how my top became see-through, bra-less, so funny, I yelled at Charlotte to come look but she was gone, towards the bar. We hung from the cool metal edge as I tried to make my feet stay still, sliding as though on ice. Charlotte's face against mine, leaning her head on my shoulder, then pitching her lips onto mine, tongue against my teeth, then laughing, we fell, broken glass, someone's strong hands under my armpits, Charlotte's face, still laughing, the red-lip gash, but spilling, too much red, and something missing. We tried to look for it, tugging at the people around us, *Help us look, it was here*, laugh, drown it, keep it down, laugh, *The tooth, where is it*?, then pulling harder, outside air, doors slamming.

When I woke again Charlotte was gone and dawn light was threatening in, through the glass double doors, showing the room, people asleep, stretched out on plastic chairs. Phones trilling. Low voices.

I shuffled towards a woman sitting behind a desk. She spent a long time typing and flicking through papers. She could see I was standing right there. I flicked her under the chin. She batted me away and sighed, kept typing. But I could see I'd got to her by the little flush around her cheeks.

—Oi. Oi. Hello. Where's my friend? I said.

—Sit down, please.

I went through some doors that appeared to loom up out of nowhere. My top was sticky; maybe I should find the bathroom, I thought. Behind me, faint moans of protest from the desk girl, *You can't go in there.* Charlotte was right in front of me, on a narrow bed. Her lip was stitched up with ugly black lines.

Someone pulled at my arm and spoke gently. —You shouldn't be in here, love. Let's go back, shall we?

—That's my friend, I said, my voice sober. At my side was a man dressed all in white. He looked so tired that I wanted to hug him.

—Okay, you can sit here, all right? Nice and quiet, he said.

He settled me into a chair. Around us, beeps and shouts and the drawling, spit-filled voices of the drunks. I had a sudden urge to call Freya, or to write to her. Summon her here. I imagined her picking me up and carrying me, tucked into her shoulder, out of the hospital. Glaring at the nurses. Throwing a bucket of hot suds over me, then wrapping me in the rough wool rug from the ballroom. She'd let me sit by the aga until I got warm again.

Charlotte opened her eyes and moaned. She tried to touch her lips but I stopped her. When she spoke, she winced with every word.

—Ugh. You look a right state, Jess.

—Yeah.

I paused. Stroked her hair where it was clean. —We keep losing time, I said.

—Hmm?

—The Mulch, I said, remembering. —The lost time. We're still in it.

—Will you call work for me?

—We're wasting time, I said. —We should be finding the others, going back.

Charlotte spoke in a strange clipped way, because she couldn't open her mouth very far. It changed her voice, made it harsher.

—Come on. It's not going to happen. You don't even really want to.

—I do! We just need to find everyone first—

—Nothing stopping you getting on a train back right now. Freya will be out soon. That's where she'll go, if Richard lets her.

—But—

—So why don't you?

I stared at the stitches. Imagined the needle puncturing the lips.

—I'll tell you why, Charlotte said. —You *do* remember what Freya was really like. Keeping yourself safe.

—No, I miss her.

The man in white came back.

—All right there petal, if you're sobered up we can let you go, okay my love?

He wiped around her mouth, pressed down on the stitches.

—Keep them clean, okay? he said.

She grimaced, and I saw that her front teeth were missing. She spat some blood and the man in white wiped her face again, so gently I wanted to cry. He pulled her up. —Okay? I'll sign you out.

Charlotte stood over me now. —So you miss her. Easy to miss someone and love them and know they're an evil bitch all the same, she said.

We took a night bus back to the hostel. She didn't want to but I said I had a kettle there and she could have the bed. Sat in the front at the top, her favourite place, like a ride, she said. We drew in the condensation, stick figures and flowers and smiling faces. Then she touched her lip, and sat back in the seat, grim faced. The city shone through the lines she'd made; flashing lights, bus stops, shouts of joy and of rage.

—Ever tell you why I went up there? she said.

—No.

—'Cause of him. 'Cause of Lucas. Toby, I mean.

She curled her tongue, probing the stitches. Her eyes watered. She mumbled, and sometimes spit gathered at the corners of her mouth and she had to stop, and I stroked her arm and said, *All right, don't talk now*, but she carried on, and got it out in pieces, like spitting out rocks from a badly rolled joint.

—It was on a train. I had him for the day, usually my mum looked after him, but I wanted us to spend some time together, so I took him to Hampton Court Palace, out west. I couldn't pay to go inside, but it was hot, it didn't matter. He played in the maze and in the gardens. I bought him an ice cream. I have a photo somewhere of us standing at the gates. He's clinging to one of the lion figures, balancing. I'm standing with my hand over my eyes, keeping out the sun. I think it's the only one I have of us together. He got tired. But he was such a strange kid. When he got tired he wouldn't sleep or go quiet. He'd get more hyper. On the bridge back to Hampton Court station he kept running into the traffic. I was tired too. Like, you can't imagine that kind of tired, Jess. It's not like you need to sleep. It's in the bone. You can't shake it out. I was only fifteen when I had him, Jess.

—As soon as we got on the train I knew it would be a nightmare. He leaped on like a frog, fell on his knees. People looked. I dragged myself after him and asked him to sit down. He just laughed. I was annoyed then, so I looked out of the window and left him to it.

—There was this girl with her boyfriend on the seat opposite. She kept glaring and putting her head on her boyfriend's shoulder, and I kept thinking, Fuck you, you take care of him then, you stop him jumping all over the place. But I just stared out of the window. Lucas was swinging from one of the plastic bars, I could see from the corner of my eye. Then someone swept him up and yelled in his ear and he was laughing and I saw the girl and her boyfriend look up and stare.

—The guy was wearing a long leather coat. I had a boyfriend who had one of those, and remembering that, I smiled and the guy held his can up to me, like a toast. Everyone was watching. He still had Lucas in the crook of his arm, and Lucas was giggling and wriggling and he looked fine. I said something like, Come on, sit down, but I was already closing my eyes again. The girl opposite me shifted so her leg hit mine, and caught my eye. She had her eyebrows raised like she was asking me a question. I realised the carriage was quiet now.

—Weeeeee! The guy yelled, and spun them around in a circle. He sat with Lucas on a seat near us. He pointed a finger at him, in his face. Youbeinalilshit, he mumbled. Whesyoumum, eh?

—Don't, I thought. Don't point me out. For fuck's sake, just stay quiet. Lucas yelled, There! I looked at the man. He was smacking his lips together. Lucas wriggled away, clambering on the free seats. The man stood up and swayed over him. He was between us now, so his leather coat was all I could see.

—Maybe he'll fall asleep, I thought, he's that drunk. Or move on, get bored. Swear to God that whole carriage was watching. I knew he'd be all right. I looked out of the window again. I took a chocolate bar out of my bag, and saw my hands were shaking. I held it out to Lucas like I was calling a dog. Come on, I whispered. Come on. He shouted back. No don'twantyou!

—Don'twanyou, donwanyou. The drunk man sang, and danced with him. His hands were under my boy's jumper.

—Every station I thought, he'll get off now, but he never did. The girl stared and stared. Her boyfriend had his face hidden in a magazine, but his face was red. The man and Lucas kept dancing, twirling, singing, out-shouting each other. When he could get Lucas to sit down, the man squished his face so Lucas's tongue came out, and that made them both laugh and laugh.

—I could, I thought. I could get off real quick, and walk quick, and no one would stop me. But I stayed. I ate the chocolate. I stared back at the girl, who dropped her eyes and watched Lucas instead. She crossed and uncrossed her legs, arched her back, ran her fingers hard along her scalp and through her hair.

—After a million years we got to Waterloo. The man shuffled off down the carriage. Sorry, sorryyeah, sorry-Mum, he yelled, holding out his hands. The carriage stared him down, and I grabbed Lucas by the waistband of his dungarees, dragged him to me. He pulled away, back towards the man. The girl opposite leaned forward, into my face. She called me a stupid idiotic irresponsible woman. Right in my face, she said that! Her boyfriend was pulling at her shoulder. She said she felt sorry for my son.

—Then she was gone. Her boyfriend ruffled Lucas's hair as he went past. I held fast on to him as the rest of the carriage trundled out. Some people smiled at Lucas. No one looked at me at all.

—I asked my mum that night, Can you take him? She said she couldn't, not all the time. So I went up to the Midlands because this girl at my college had told me about a girl she knew who'd heard of Foxlowe. Commune, she said. And all I knew about those places was the childcare was shared. I thought, I'll take him, and he'll attach to someone else, and then I'll just leave him there.

I stayed in glass tube boy's room, whispered Charlotte's story to him so it wouldn't be lost. Charlotte stayed in my bed, and when I went to wake her up she'd gone, the blankets rolled up neat and placed over the pillow.

I lost a few weeks. Eventually I went back to the concrete steps. I had plenty of vodka at the hostel, but I suppose I'd got bored of drinking alone, while glass tube boy was smoking. He offered the smoke to me a few times, but even though I liked glass tube boy I didn't want my face to look like that, or to shake so much I couldn't make a cup of tea.

The students were already milling around the steps. I saw the boy who had scuffed my pattern months before. He nodded at me, so I went over.

—See you all time. Not so much last weeks.

—No.

—But no in classes.

—No.

—Sorry, today no cigarette.

—That's okay, I said.

The need for a drink swelled in my throat.

—Why always here?

—Friend of mine works here.

—Teacher?

—Yeah, Charlotte.

—Oh! Teacher Charlotte!

He spoke in a rapid, beautiful sounding language to a man sitting behind me. It curled somehow; I thought if it were written down, it would be in circles.

—She's a Leaver, he said.

20

With the curtains drawn and the bulb alight under the pink lampshade, the bedroom walls take on a red tinge, like a sunset, or a peep-show room. I could turn myself on, feel something else. Idly I rub between my legs under the covers. It's no good, I'm hot, too hot, can't breathe. I nudge a hand under the curtains to chill my skin. A long padded snake lies across the windowpane, absorbing the draught. Its eyes are coloured buttons. I could pick them off, pull at the threads like nerves. I drift dreamless on hot radiator air, kicking myself awake when I sail too far.

My suitcase, the one I brought with me when I came here to Mel's house, is stuffed into the gap between the wardrobe and the ceiling. Inside, in the back pocket folded into a plastic wallet, is Freya's photograph. I imagine it making the suitcase thrum. A beating paper heart. Through the woolly air I heave the suitcase down. Back in bed, I curl up with the wallet in my hands.

Freya peers at me. I feel my stomach drop and clench, as though I've missed a step on the stairs. In the picture Freya is crouching, her hands still in the soil off-camera. Her tall, graceless figure is coiled, one of her legs sticking out at a strange angle. She looks interrupted, twisting her head round to squint into the lens. The sun has bleached her features and softened them. Again I search the rest of the picture, the black and white pixels. All I can see is a low wall rising above the vegetable patch, and grass behind Freya's figure. It could be anywhere. I wonder what she said to Ellen just after the click of the camera captured her unawares. *Oh, help yourself to my image, picture-snatcher. My soul will come out of your camera and strangle you in the middle of the night.* This photo was pinned up in the ballroom along with the others. Freya must have snatched it when we all became Leavers. Or perhaps Ellen sent it to her, where she was locked away. In the white space underneath her image is her handwriting, *Freya Marsh, Foxlowe 1989*.

Freya sent it to me at the school, a year after I was taken away from Foxlowe. In the dorm that day I stared at the sloped handwriting on the envelope. One of the girls came in, and I threw a clock at her. It smashed against her side as she fled.

Perhaps Freya was asking for help. But what could I do? Or perhaps that wasn't her message at all. *I miss you. Come home.* But I knew Freya couldn't be there. She had been locked away, Richard told me, somewhere I couldn't visit and far away from home. I'd thought about Blue behind the locked attic door and nodded. Life had to be in balance. *Don't forget*. I missed Foxlowe in a sharper way back then. I threw things, like the smashed clock, all the time.

I'd hidden the polaroid under my mattress with the weed and sleeping pills. They never found it. Freya must have sent other things while I was away — sketches, maybe even letters, she might have guessed I was learning how to read. But I never held them. I think Richard had told the school to monitor my mail. The photo was still with me at the hospital when Mel found me.

The carpet rustles like grass.

—I brought you pudding, Mel sings.

I shove Freya's image under the duvet, but I'm slow, frightened to crush it, and Mel snags her eye on it. She sets a bowl of cake and custard next to the bed, spiralling steam into the room, then crouches to the suitcase lying open on the carpet, clicks the handles shut, and lifts it back into place. When she turns back to me she glances at the top of the duvet and I know she will take the photograph. She's gentle as she peels back the bedcover and lifts the photo away. It rotates in her hands and Mel twists her head. She's very quiet. I won't apologise. It's mine.

—I'm going to take it with me when I go back to Foxlowe, I say.

—Where have you been hiding this?

That's all she has to say. In her cell house, with a piece of Foxlowe in her hands, a piece of Freya. The precious edges are dimpled under her grip. She could tear it up in my face. I hold out my hand. —Give it back, please.

—So this is her, Mel says. She stares at Freya, then turns the photograph over. —Do you have any others? Do you have one of you when you were little? I'd love to see that. So would Richard, she says.

—No, I say. —I don't remember anyone taking a photo of me.

—What about the beautiful one? Mel asks.

—Libby?

—Oh yes, that's her name.

—Richard told you about her?

—He talked about her just the once. He was drinking. It was a long time ago.

Something like bubbles rising in my chest. Foxlowe names here. Mel has never even spoken about it before, and here are all the ghosts perched on the end of my bed, and Mel asking questions about Leavers.

—Libby became a Leaver years before the rest of us left, I say. —I don't have a photograph of her, but I can tell you—

—Oh, never mind. Being silly, Mel says.

She transfers the photograph into the hand furthest from me. She sits, pats the duvet with her other hand, three small flutters, as though a summons, but I'm already next to her. I don't know what to do. Sometimes I can't tell what people mean, when I've had a bad day, and this one has been awful. I shift closer, and Mel smooths my hair. I could snatch the photo back, but it might rip.

—What would make you feel better, my darling? Mel says. —Want to do some shopping online? Buy something nice?

Something nice. It's too much, nice. I have to be nice to her, I have to be nice.

—Give it back! Give it back to me right now, you bitch! It's mine, I told you it was mine! Why are you still holding it? Give it to me!

Mel takes my wrists and crosses my arms over each other, shushes me. Freya falls into my lap. I could scratch Mel's eyes out, but she loves me, her hands on mine like a mother's would be, as Freya's were, many times. I can't fight. Her hot breath cloys to my forehead. —All right, she says. —All right.

My wrists hurt.

She releases me and then lies down next to me on the bed. She picks up the bowl, begins to eat. Her lips curl around the spoon and stick for a moment, before peeling off. I wish I could open a window.

—Sorry, I say.

Mel nods. She watches as I pick up Freya's photograph again.

—You know you can't go, sweetheart, she says.

Making silent promises to Freya's face, I take a bite of the pudding, sponge and jam, burning my tongue. Mel wipes my lip and chin where the custard has dripped.

—You tried before, remember? Mel says.

* * *

It was in the Mulch Time, after I'd lost Charlotte. Freya was beginning to fade. But then as we passed the huge wooden honeycomb in the hallway, glass tube boy had picked the letter up. —It's for you, he'd said, surprised, curious, and there was her handwriting, cramped and beautiful, with low-looped 'y's and a blooming capital at the beginning of each line.

—Is it from your mum? he said. —Mine writes too. I open them sometimes.

I thumbed along the seal at the back, where Freya's own fingers had pressed. Her name was written in the corner, and a tiny drawing underneath it of the house, of home. I slipped a nail under Freya's seal, made a tiny rip, then stopped; I wasn't ready to face whatever words were waiting inside. Instead I looked at the little Foxlowe again, its driveway stretching towards me. An invitation.

—I have to get a train, I said.

He showed me the station with its squeaking floors and crowds around television screens with no pictures, just writing, and spoke to a man in a uniform who looked us up and down like we couldn't be real and spoke over our heads, until glass tube boy said, —Look, we have the money, wouldn't be asking about tickets if we were dodgy would we, I mean we want to *buy the tickets* for fuck's sake, and then later, walking back to our streets, the streets that I knew, he told me the cheapest one was the next morning at five, and did I think I'd be coming back, only he'd miss me.

In the orange-tinged dark, the streets dulled with the quiet of millions asleep, so everything was louder — night buses heaving around corners, the scream of a fox or a cat or a woman — and the insomniacs making ghostly figures behind their curtains, smoking, rocking babies, pacing, the shuttered shops like blank faces, and the occasional car, late-night taxis, too late for the clubs but for the later pick-ups, people wishing for their own beds after all; in that dark which is not dark at all, I found my way back to that station — more shutters, yawning men in uniforms, other travellers in thick coats with their suitcases piled before them, steaming polystyrene cups, and the other ones, the dregs of last night, pissing against the outside concrete walls, weaving their steps, dropping and crushing soggy chips into the shining floors. I belonged with them; this is the time we lived in, glass tube boy and me, but then I was sober, my ticket to Freya gripped between my lips as I zipped and rezipped my bag, to check for I didn't know what, to keep moving.

The night world sparkled outside the train windows, then the dawn came, and I watched like I had when we were small, Blue and me, in the days when she fitted into my arms and I would rock her to stop her cries, at the attic windows looking over the moor, the light spilling into the darker blue like mixing paints. On the train it was a mottled sky, the stars still out for a while, until early mist rolled out, coating the fields and towns in white so it seemed we all of us floated amongst clouds. I opened her letter then.

I hate you. Blue's here with me, she never left me.

It took me a few minutes. The first line, like a circle coming back to *I hate you*, easy enough, subject, simple verb, object. At the school, my teacher, a blonde pretty woman who always wore red shoes, cried when I got it for the first time. I was her greatest achievement, she said. I folded the letter back into its envelope.

It was the first time I'd heard from her since the school. Perhaps she thought I could never read it, that I'd keep it, thinking it said other things, frame it; that was her kind of joke. The landscape outside disappeared into a platform with lights around a café and a shop. Shufflers off and on. The doors beeped urgently. I got off the train.

The train hissed and settled into the tracks like a fat old woman. The station was small, frosted flower baskets hanging outside a closed newsagent's, fields beyond, sunk under the mist, where the brown shapes of cows stumbled awake, and in the distance, a cathedral spire, not like the one in London I knew, on the river, but tall and thin, puncturing the mist. Birds flew from wire to wire across the tracks, training for the winter journey, just like Foxlowe birds, and I wondered if the mist had confused them, made them mistake us for higher sky.

A voice shuddered around the concrete walls and made people unbury their faces from scarves and pause their stamping feet. A London train was coming. Back at the hostel, the clothes would have to be unpacked, and Freya's photograph, and the photographs I'd packed for her to see: school, the hostel, Charlotte and me, London. Glass tube boy would ask questions about the letter and read it and then say things about Freya, call her names. We'd get drunk and high and fuck each other before falling into sleep and I'd wake from a nightmare in which Freya was waiting for me in the kitchen, weeping, or gripping me by the wrists.

The London train came and went, and behind me the shutters of the shop snapped up, lights flickered on, warmth against my legs. The man behind the counter, wearing a baseball cap and with a dark beard over coffee coloured skin, raised his eyebrows. —We have latte, hot chocolate, he said. —Tea. You want tea instead? But when I asked a second time, he sold me the bottles.

I liked drinking outside, where my breath smoked and the burn felt good. The vodka slipped across my tongue and around my teeth, warmed my throat, made a glow in my stomach, and better, eased Freya away, took her grip from my arms, faded the pain of her knee in my back. The mist rolled back to show the town and the cathedral grey against the bright sky, and I wondered where to go. Not the hostel just now, and I wasn't, I knew, strong enough to face Freya, and walk through those rooms, and remember. When I returned to the newsagent, he frowned and said, —How about I call someone for you? And I said, —I'll have that tea, and he smiled, like I'd said the right thing at last, and went into the back, to the hiss and steam of the machine. I felt sorry to steal the bottles this time, but there was the train at the platform, and I walked fast to let the doors seal behind me with their frantic beeping, the cold glass of the bottles against the inside of my coat. Through the doors I saw him watching me sadly, sipping the tea himself.

On the train, a woman with a whippet dog and a dirty fur coat was asleep outside the toilets, and I stroked the muzzle of the dog, drank, found Libby in my breathing, perhaps fell asleep myself. I remember trying to find my ticket, and my teeth shuddering together, setting off the nerves, and the sudden cold of the outside again and the world no longer rocking and shuddering, some lost time, asking for a phone, to call the hostel, to ask glass tube boy to please come and get me. A long blackness became faces around me as though staring from a great height, strong hands under my armpits, then gentler arms, the slam of doors, sirens.

I thought Mel was a nurse at first.

They didn't wear the uniforms all the time; sometimes, hair loose, their features coated in powder, they dipped into the plate of cakes at reception, licking chocolate icing from their fingers. Their voices changed, became harsher, higher, more ready to laugh. They bargained over hours, selling afternoons for late shifts, and leaned so the weight was off their feet, twisting ankles in heels, ready to go out. If you came to them then, asked for a glass of water, they stepped back, and I loved the seconds in which their shoulders rolled, their voices dropped, and they struggled with their irritation. But they always replied, even if only to refer you, so professional, to the colleague behind the desk. *I've just finished my shift. Here, Rachel will look after you.* All those hours, all those gently pressing fingers, soft words, frowns, all evaporated when the glass doors sealed shut. They were only doing their job.

So I thought she was one of them. She strode in like that, purposeful, like she worked there. Clearing her throat, about to ask, prod, double check. Then she perched on the visitors' chair by the bed. She wore a dress and boots, painted lips, earrings that stretched the lobe. Her dark hair fell to her shoulders, so straight you could see the line of the scissors. I looked away, out of the window. My room at the hostel back then had a view of a brick wall and some black bin liners that foxes split open every night, leaving a plastic river in the morning. Here in the hospital I looked out over Waterloo Bridge. I wanted to watch the dark fall over the Thames and the lights of Westminster flicker on. I wouldn't be able to stay for long.

—Hello, she said.

I closed my eyes.

—They told me you'd be asleep. I thought I'd come and sit, so I'd be here when you woke up.

So, from some volunteer charity. Maybe she'd take me to a soup kitchen. Maybe she'd start reading from the Bible. If she starts reading from the Bible, I thought, I'll throw up so she has to grab the polystyrene dish from the bedside table and some of the vomit will seep onto her hands.

My throat was raw. Not from the drink, or the retching even, it was just from being outside in the cold so long, they said. It was freezing when they found me. Exposure, they said.

—I don't know you. Piss off.

She came over to the bed, folded the top of the covers down, under my chin. The sheets tightened as she tucked them further under the mattress, pinning my legs down.

—There. Snug as a bug in a rug, she said.

I stared at her. It struck me that she might not be a volunteer at all, but a wandering psych patient.

—Thanks. Go away now.

—You *don't* know me. But all that's going to change now, she said. She stroked my hair. —It's all going to be okay now.

This was why I loved the hospital. It had been a very long time since anyone had touched me with gentleness like that, or whispered to me. She took a breath.

—I'm Richard's wife, she said. —I'm your stepmum.

I snorted, sending ripples of pain into my throat.

—So leave me whatever money he sent. Say thanks and everything. Oh, tell him well done on getting someone to marry him, and a big thank you for the wedding invite and all that, and also, tell him to go fuck himself. Bye.

She smiled at me, nodding. —I'm *so* cross with him too. I only just found out about you. We got married two years ago. Look, I brought some photos for you, if you like … She brought out an envelope, and when I didn't take it she said, —Maybe another time, and put it back into her handbag.

—Okay. Bye then.

I'll stay while you fall asleep. What a lovely view!

She settled into the chair again and gazed at the darkening bridge. She's young, I thought. She caught me looking.

—If I'd known about you … I'm *so* cross with him. I'm not explaining anything very well. See, the hostel has his number, in case anything happens. I picked up when they called.

She chewed the inside of her cheek. I wondered if she tasted blood, or just worried at old scars. I shifted under the blankets, ran my hands over the paths and ridges on my arms.

—I, she says. —*We*. We want to start again. What you've been through. You're troubled, clearly. You're unhappy, and we're family, I would like us to be family, and when you're ready, if you like, you can come and live with us. I mean, you're our *daughter*, it's just—

—It's not like that. Me and Richard, we're not like that. It's fine how it is.

She rolled her thin lips in and out.

—I'd like to know you. I feel that you are my … That I can help you, look after you. You see? We can help each other. You should live in our house, with us.

Was this Richard's life now? I stared at her, neat, sharp-boned, existing in the world of *It should, This is right, This is the way.*

—I'll stay. Go to sleep now, she said.

—What's your name?

—Oh! I didn't say. Sorry, it's Mel.

Mel. *Mellus, mellifluous*. That's a favourite word of mine. Something to do with soft, or is it honey? What a wrong name for her, despite the voice. All angles and sharp edges, the jagged snip of the hair.

—*Mel.* I'm going to sleep now, so get out.

She did that nodding smile again, settled further into her chair, so I hissed *Getoutgetoutgetout*, my eyes shut so tight I saw blooms of colour under my eyelids, until I heard her heels clacking in the corridor outside.

Later, the tug of blankets folded down, clicking lights, the efficient snap of sheets. The lino froze my toes when I swung my legs over the thin mattress. In the early light my skin looked old, the colour of rain-bloated worms. Perhaps I could stay. The doctor pressed my stomach hard, nodded when I winced. He signed my notes with a hard flick of the pen.

The clothes they'd brought me in with were in a bin liner in the corner. I peeled the plastic away from the sticky jeans, and sniffed at the t-shirt, sharp in the armpits, stained. Some of that day came back. Cold, acid in the stomach, wet skin. There was mud on the t-shirt and I wondered if I'd been on the ground for long. My coat was gone.

A nurse came in, hair in a pixie cut, a tiny tattoo of a star on her wrist. She'd brought me water through the night, after Mel left, and acted as though there was lots of time, which there wasn't. I liked her. I gestured pathetically at my clothes.

She grimaced. —Can anyone bring you a change of clothes in?

—No.

—Here.

She scooped up the rags, hooking the jeans under her chin, and bundled them into the tiny cubicle. At the sink she used a flannel to sponge off the denim, while I watched from the doorway, chewing on a hangnail. A gold chain glinted at the back of her neck. On her hand, below the star, there was a nightclub stamp, turning green. We could be friends, laughing and leaning in at lunch, around a kitchen table. Laughing over how we met.

She glanced at me in the mirror. —We need this room in five minutes. Can you get your stuff together?

Weaving down the corridor, I realised I was hungry. In my room at the hostel there was dried pasta and some tinned tomatoes I'd left. I'd meant to take them downstairs to glass tube boy. But in the rush, throwing clothes into bags, the letter from Freya unopened in the pocket of my jeans, I'd left them in the cupboard above the microwave.

Bus journey. My bare arms cold in the queue before I could get on. The thigh-aching tramp up the stairs and the door catching on the brown carpet; it all weighed on me as I went to the front desk. The nurse with short hair handed me a form to sign, and with it a note.

—From the lady who visited. She left it for you.

A phone number, a name, an address. Later, glass tube boy would explain to me how close I lived to Mel's house, that if you kept walking past the shop with the kind man, crested that hill, the other world was waiting. I crumpled the paper into the still-soggy jeans pocket, next to Freya's letter.

21

That night, Mel's heart of pills sticking in my chest, I wake to Jimmy snuffling around my bed. I get up and pull him across my knees where he collapses with a sigh, nuzzling my stomach. I scratch behind his ears and we settle there, sinking into the carpet, and I begin to whisper my fears, and about how things have changed, how my old life is reappearing, how I'll take him with me, and show him the world I knew. It helps for a while, but my mouth is still dry, and I feel untethered, as though I could fly apart. I need to be weighted down.

On the wall next to the step that creaks there's a map of England. Richard and Mel brought it back from a car boot sale one Saturday. Dusty glass in a flaking pine frame. In the streetlamp glow I trace a line up from London until I hit the black dot I always look for. The moor is there: a tiny green puddle, spilling out into places I don't know. My little finger blots it out.

Jimmy clicks around Mel's paved garden like a smaller creature; quick, nervous steps, sniffing the air. I watch him from the kitchen, where I find a packet of biscuits, oatmeal with chunks of chocolate, and devour them, hardly chewing, coughing when crumbs dust the back of my throat. They sink into my stomach and I lick my teeth, then the wrapper.

Behind the bin, stuffed into an empty laundry-powder box. It's still there. I'm surprised. A tiny bag of weed and a few rizlas, along with a bottle of vodka. I put it here a long time ago, for emergencies. Since Freya began to tug at me, since the Sunday on the study floor, I've taken out the bottle and held it, turning it, watching the liquid slosh and flow, but not opened it. I twist the top in my teeth and it cracks satisfyingly in my mouth.

I sniff the vodka: the hairspray kind. It's been a while, so I sip a tiny bit and don't swallow, but bubble it around my teeth and hold it in my mouth. I return to the back step and scratch Jimmy behind the ears.

The rizla paper is greasy and familiar under my fingers, the hash stale and full of rocks, and I've got no lighter, but I make a roll up anyway, for the calming motion of the roll and lick and the old smell drifting up along with the night air to calm me. I take it between my teeth and roll it between my lips, then balance it between my fingers. The vodka I ration, imagining each drop from the lip where it sits on the dry skin and across the bubbly plateau of my tongue, to the back of the throat, down into the stomach, where it joins the others in drips.

Jimmy ambles over, edges down to lie on the gravel. In the glow of the garden lamps his eyes have a splash of green in them. I feel his nose, dry. I wet it with some vodka on my fingers, and he licks it clean, making me laugh.

—Let's get drunk, I say. Me and you.

The whirr and click of a lighter sparking. Richard, in the kitchen, I see him through the glass smoking and dropping ash into the sink. He's in a silk bathrobe, must be Mel's. His little belly pokes out. White hair around his navel, a trace of old man coming for him. He can't see me, where I'm crouched on the back step, but I see the outside lights catch his eye, and Jimmy whines, he must sense him there. I smile into my vodka bottle, giggle like a child, hiding, Blue and me, thrusting our hands over each other's mouths, breath hot on skin.

I hear him step towards us, and when he jumps it's even better than I expected, a hand on heart stumble back, a windmill arm reel. I don't laugh, just watch him, cold. Freya is cackling somewhere.

Richard breathes out a snort, like a horse. —What the fuck?

—Can't sleep either?

—Are you *drinking*?

I make a wide-mouthed face. —Are you *smoking*?

—How long has this been going on? We agreed—

I stick the roll up between my teeth and make a silent snarl at him. Richard makes a weary gesture with his cigarette.

—What's that?

—A dildo.

—You shouldn't have that stuff here.

—Do you sneak down here every night to have a crafty fag?

He smiles, so now we're baring our teeth at each other.

—No, he says. —Only when Mel's being ... She's so stressed, you know, by all this.

I wonder what I've missed, being down here with Jimmy. What hissing angry sounds, what slammed doors. Richard takes a long drag on his cigarette and looks at the thing in his hand, studying it as though it's interesting.

He holds out his cigarette. —Go on. I won't tell if you don't, he adds, with a low, joyless laugh.

I keep the roll up unlit for a moment. Perhaps I shouldn't smoke it now. That bag was my last.

—It's my last stash, I say.

He doesn't answer.

—Could buy more, I say.

—No.

I wonder when Richard's life became sanitised, like a white rail in a hospital, like a plastic glove. Was it immediately after we left Foxlowe, or did he find Mel and think, *That's it, I can hide in her disinfectant, in her floral curtains. No one and nothing will find me there*?

—When did you get so boring?

He smiles into his cigarette. —I was always boring, he says.

I suck on the end of my roll up with Richard's cigarette against the tip to light it. I wave the smell in his direction, to see if it will drift through his screens unnoticed, if tonight he will dream about soil smells and grass under his bare feet and the cold in the kitchen and where we are going, if a smell could do all that. But he just takes his cigarette back and holds it out like a glass, so I bump it with mine.

—You say Cheers, he says.

—Oh.

—Didn't we teach you that?

—I think Kai used to say Sally.

He laughs. —It's *Salut*. It's French.

—Oh.

—I saw empty packets in there, he says.

—Yes.

—You don't have to binge like that, you know. We won't run out of food. You'll never be hungry here.

—I know, I say.

—I'm sorry you feel you have to do that.

Richard is expert at *I'm sorry you feel.*

I've always thought there's something strange that happens if you're up late at night, and talking to someone. It might be someone really close, like me and Blue, or Toby, and then it's like your day conversations, only boiled down to the real things that you want to say, without all the noise surrounding them. Or if it's someone you don't talk to a lot, like Richard, it's like the dark and the strangeness of the air and the silence all around is a blanket you can hide under while you say things you would never say in front of the TV, or in the car. I try for something real, anyway.

—Don't you think, I said, watching the smoke rise, —don't you think you'll get there, and want to stay, want to go back forever? That's what I think. Start again, see if the others will come.

And I'm right about the night, because Richard doesn't change the subject or ignore me at all.

—No. I don't want to go back there. You don't remember things properly, he said, twisting a loose thread on the silk gown. —If you did, you wouldn't be pushing to go back, be pushing to say goodbye to her, like she was someone good.

—I know she wasn't *good*, I say. —What are you talking about? I know *that*. Richard looks at me then. —I *know*, I say again. —What's that got to do with anything?

The smoke we make curls into the air and over Jimmy.

—Can we take him with us, to Foxlowe? I ask.

Richard flicks ash over the gravel.

—What for?

—Just to have him there.

Richard looks at me. I shrink a little, but inside; outside I keep drawing the woody smoke into my lungs, holding it there, where it burns, and pushing it out again.

—Is it cruel? Are we being unfair to stop you going?

He asks this as though he is simply curious: *Would it hurt if I pulled the wings off this fly?*

—It means so much to Mel that you stay, he says.

—I'll come back.

—Maybe, maybe not. It's more, she likes to keep you close, she worries about you. She just wants to look after you, and you seemed to need that too. I think it's hard for her that since, you know, the news, you've been a bit different with her, he says.

Is this a rehearsed speech? Did they plan this, under the duck feather duvet upstairs, in a tent they made from the sheets? *What shall we say? How will we make her? You do it, she won't suspect, pretend to sneak down for a cigarette.*

—No, I say. And it wells up, and I say no, again and again, and when I open my eyes Richard is standing in his ridiculous silk robe and crushing his cigarette against the open door, where it squirms and is crushed, and there's panic in his face, controlled, quiet panic, so I start smoking again, to show him I'm functioning.

He steps back into the house and ties the dressing gown tighter.

—I won't drive you, he says.

—I'll get the train. I'll meet you there.

—I won't give you the money.

—You really don't give a fuck about me at all, do you? I say.

—I'm trying to protect you from—

—Well done, big protector man, excellent job, you did really well.

He's gone when I turn around. Jimmy rolls onto his back as I draw the smoke into my lungs. Across the garden, the Bad drifts in the trees and the rose arches, skulks across the grass.

A sudden crash of the door, and Richard is back, his face screwed up with rage.

—Yeah, all my fault. Freya's totally blameless, right? Won't hear a word against Freya, will you?

—Freya loved me, I say. —She loved me and Blue, she took care of us.

—You have no idea what you're talking about, Richard spits. —You have absolutely no idea. She loved Blue? How can you say that to me?

—I remember, I say. —You can't tell me how it was, you weren't even there when—

—Don't tell me what you *think* happened. You have no idea. Don't you dare try to talk to me about Blue, for fuck's sake! I'm done listening to you talk about Freya. The woman was fucking sick. Don't you mention her to me ever again.

He slams the door, making Jimmy jump. When I follow, I see Mel coming down the stairs, pulling a jumper over her nightdress. —What? she says to him, sleep still crusting at the corners of her eyes. Richard pinches the bridge of his nose, speaks softly. —Sorry, he breathes. —Go back to bed.

—You treated Freya like shit, I shout at him. —You broke her heart so many times—

—Shut up.

—Richard, leave her be, Mel says, pushing past him to put her arm around me.

—She was everything, I say, feeling the loss of her open up before me like a cliff edge.

—Get out.

Just tired, that's how it sounds, at first, so tired that it's hard to hear the anger underneath.

Mel twists the skin on her wrist.

—It's not her fault, she says. —She's had a …

—Don't talk about me like I'm not here, I say.

It's not what I mean. I really want to hear. I want to know what they think of me, I want them to forget I'm in the room.

—We've tried, Richard says to Mel.

—Can't just give up on her, she says. —She's our daughter.

—Except she isn't, he says. —Ours, I mean. I'll still give her money, Richard mumbles. —Can't keep her here any more. Making you ill, he says.

He makes towards her, a look of tenderness on his face, but stops. Mel and I are holding hands, and perhaps he can't touch her when I am there, the witch, the remnants of Freya in my head.

—Get out, he says again.

—I don't … have anywhere to go—

—I'll give you the money.

—But where can I—

—Go back.

Mel lets go of my hand.

—Go back, he says again. —We're not stopping you.

—But it's the middle of the night. What am I supposed to do? Where will I go after the funeral?

—Stop asking questions. You're an adult. You'll figure it out. We've tried, but this is not going to work, you living here.

—But, I say.

—It's only what you wanted, he says.

—Richard, Mel says, but he holds up a hand, and she is silenced.

As I go for my things I have time to think, *You hated it here; this is what you wanted. Apart from Jimmy, what is there to stay for?* I answer myself as I walk up the stairs, not even straining to hear the sobbing that's coming from below, and the low murmurs Richard is making in return. The warmth, the soft sheets, the heavy thud-click of the windows at night, the hot fresh coffee and the walls around me and the key she gave me, on a key ring in the shape of a house with a heart on it. I pass the map and trace my line home, feeling afraid, the cliff drop of Freya widens further, and no one is there to pull me back from the edge.

22

The taxi reeks of chemical flowers and old beer; stains bloom over the seats. The driver is aggressively friendly, big smile and questions with an aftertaste of *fuck you*; how we used to speak to outsiders, sometimes, when we felt brave enough. When I ask him to turn the radio down so I can think, he clicks the dial, winks. He is small, except for biceps like balloons under his t-shirt. He sees me looking at these, smiles wider, settles back in his seat.

On the train, I'd sketched out as much as I could remember: the route behind the Cloud, how many turnings until the Foxlowe road. It was cold on the train, air conditioning sucking out pores, cramping up my feet. I shivered and forgot about walking, out in the grey air. Mel's house has softened me up like butter left on a summer sill. When I got to the station and followed the signs to the exit and found the cars there with the lights on their heads, the first man I asked said I was still far from home, I needed a bus. I fumbled in my bag for notes, Richard's money. He waved me into the back. —At the end, babe, he said.

The red numbers above his head flash. I stick my nose against the window, ignoring the drips that fall into my eyes. Green and brown blur past, stone walls snake across fields. Mel's house pulls at me; its pink walls, the fug of thick drawn curtains and hot food, and Jimmy's warm muzzle nudging at my shins.

We turn, and the road changes, a thinner, steeper track, cresting and dropping past signs to the moor, black and white arrows looming up in the rain. I settle back. We fall into the villages, and the driver asks me if I recognise anything, but I can't be sure. Clicking his tongue as though calling a dog, he keeps one hand on the wheel and pulls out a map from the passenger seat pocket. —The old Langley place, is it? he says. —What's it called? —Foxlowe, I say again, and try to describe it, how it sits on the edge of the moor, how you can see the Cloud from the oaks, but he waves his hand to silence me. Perhaps I should abandon the car, and find my way walking; the moor is there, behind that village, I see it cresting with rocky outcrops, and I know I can feel it out from there.

Then we swing onto a new road and I see the double peak of the Cloud on the horizon. Of course, there's the road we'd take when the farmers got angry and we had to walk like outsiders. The Foxlowe road is long, I think, so I have time to prepare, time to steady my shaking hands, but then it's there: home, old home, red brick and a hundred window eyes. All the herbs and the fruit trees from the front lawns are gone. The gravel is patchy, brown weeds hunch in the bald spots. Vague shapes lie in front of the house, but I focus instead on the car in the driveway. Not our old Ford, a shiny thing that doesn't belong.

I hold out my hand full of money for the driver to take what he needs. He picks out the right notes, and smiles. I could've done it myself, but I'm too tired to remember the right colours, and whether the face on the back should have a moustache, or not. The driver pats his stomach, like he's going to eat the money. He's not so bad, I think as I scramble out, hauling the suitcase. Then I see him sneer at me as he drives away, shaking his head; I hold my finger up, the way Charlotte showed me once.

So I stand on Foxlowe ground again. I dig my feet deep into the gravel, imagine roots flowing from my toes and down into the ground, holding me in place while I sway. It's so quiet. I hum to make it better. The shapes on the lawn are furniture. Some of it I recognise: the old red rug, rolled into a snake and stinking of damp; the grandfather clock, on its side, the wooden back panel kicked in. Cushions — that pattern, I'd forgotten, I used to run my fingernail along it, following the swirl, during Meeting. All damp and rotting now.

The front door is open. It's been painted since I left. Flaking off at the bottom. It's heavier than I remember, and then I stand, just like that, back at the foot of the stairs. The blue light from the stained glass is dull in the damp day, but Foxlowe gathers me in, and I could glide around from room to room like falling into a dance, the old movements coming back to me, this way ballroom, kitchen down here, the dip in the third step—

I scuttle back like a kicked dog, all the air sucked out of me. It takes a few seconds for me to find the rhythm of breath, and to feel stupid for jumping at a reflection. Our mirror, the yellow room mirror, is propped up against the end of the banister. I stroke the spotted glass and let myself sink into my own face. There are Freya's eyes, and I'm tall now, like she was, but otherwise I'm an idiot; I could never be her. Look how I'm hunched over like Jimmy when voices are raised, look how my shoulders slump, and my belly and arms sag with fat. Somewhere in that glass, Toby and I stand in sunlight, bare bodies skinny and young, blood racing in our heads.

—Hello?

A man's voice, strong, with a hurried, annoyed undertone, like a doctor. I clear my throat, but no words come out.

I see him in the mirror first, and it feels right like that; we stand side by side, in the old way. He wears the uniform of the outside: suit and tie, shiny shoes that look too small. Thick rimmed glasses which he pushes up with his middle finger, smiling as he lets me examine his reflection. The same brown eyes with flecks of orange that I recognise more from Charlotte, now, than him. His hair is brutally short. His nose is different: thinner, longer. He turns to look at me.

—Thought you'd come, Toby says.

I stay a while longer, pretending, but in the end I have to turn to face him.

—Hi, he says, leaning down like he's talking to a child, even though I'm slightly taller than him; the effect is like a little bow.

I nod, and turn to inspect some imaginary thing behind me.

—You moved all her things. You shouldn't be touching Freya's things.

—That wasn't me. Did your dad come with you?

—My *dad*?

He blushes. —Sorry, I … I heard that you two were … He called us, to tell us she'd died. Thought we might want to know. He seems … rehabilitated.

He looks pleased with the word, rocks back on his heels, making the shoes squeak. I remember that day, Richard on the phone all the time.

Toby looks up to the rafters and around the hall.

—I couldn't come before. But now … just thought I'd see. See if I remembered right, he says.

—And you thought Valentina might come, I say.

The red goes to his ears, and it is this, more than our little mirror dumb show, more than his careful smile, it is this old thing, the way his blood still remembers how it flows, the same way my legs feel the old routes through the rooms, that makes me go to hug him at last. He smells of hair gel and shaving cream. He shakes his head into my shoulder. —Nah, he says. —She won't come.

I go to sit on the middle landing, as this is one of the things I have promised myself. He comes to sit next to me. —So, he says.

He's wearing a wedding ring. I grasp it, and twist it around.

—Yeah, he says.

—That's nice.

—Yeah. Gwen. She was going to come, but … I didn't want her to.

—Why not?

I know perfectly well why not, but I need to keep the conversation ticking.

He shrugs. —I didn't want any … outside things.

He looks at me when he uses the old words, and I nod to show that I understand.

—You? he says.

—Me?

—Do you have someone?

—Of course not.

He laughs. —Why of course not?

I stare at him. —I'm not well, I say, wondering if it's true.

—You look fine. Do you need a doctor?

He whips out a silver phone, and I catch a glimpse of a woman's photograph on the screen. I jump up. —Let's look around, I say. —Is anyone else here?

He shakes his head.

—No one? I say.

—Want to see the ballroom? he asks.

It's empty: stripped of all its cushions and hangings and our paintings on the walls, cold and echoing. I pace from the windows to the wall; only ten, I thought it was more. My memories contract a little, to account for it.

—I always come here first, I say. —When I think of home.

—Oh?

—Yeah, I always think about the winter Blue came. We sat here, I say, pointing. —Me and Libby. Then you came and we chased each other.

—Always running, he says, smiling, hands in his pockets.

—Do you remember?

—Sure.

—Why's it empty?

—I think she never used this room. She boarded it up. He points to cardboard lying torn behind the door. —She just slept in the attic and used the kitchen, I think.

I try to imagine Freya cramped into those small spaces.

We take the Spike Walk. The nails are still up, but now we are grown they catch at our hips, and Toby swears when one catches on his jacket. The yellow room is bare of most of its furniture. The wallpaper is still up, huge damp patches eating it away. A piss-soiled mattress lies in the middle of the room.

—Are the dogs still here?

—No.

I don't want to be in this room for long, so I turn to go back to the ballroom, but Toby opens another door.

—Was that door always there? I ask.

Toby smiles, a faint smile, worried or tired of me, I can't tell.

—Yeah, he says.

—I'd forgotten it.

—I'm amazed you remember much at all. It was years ago.

—I remember everything, I say.

He gestures towards the door, half a smile, as though he is about to tease me, before silence floods in.

The new door takes us through the studios, broken canvases and some half-finished pieces, and the windows onto the back lawns. I take the gardens in in glimpses; it's another thing I have promised myself, to go through the kitchen door and follow them down to the moor. Painted white, the studios always felt like the cleanest place. Now we wade through rubbish: papers and notepads and compost, rotting potato peelings, bits of carpet, clothes. I see the culprits responsible for the urine in the yellow room — foxes under a broken window. Toby claps his hands, and they stare back insolently. I see tapes I recognise, and bend to salvage them. I'd like to have that music, but Toby pulls me up.

—Urgh, don't, it's disgusting, he says, kicking his shoes against each other. —Sorry, I haven't been back here yet. She must've been using it as a rubbish dump.

I take the tapes anyway, rattling in my coat pocket.

Then it's the kitchen. I brace myself for change, for everything to be cleared out, for rubbish on the floor, even a new fitted version, like Mel's, with shining gold taps and cupboards that glide shut without making a sound. Toby holds the door for me and I step into the past, or one of my dreams. The table is more marked, less cluttered, but it's the same thick oak with the flowered feet. The flagstones still dip in the spot next to the sink. Dusty herbs hang in their proper places, the alcoves are unmoved; I trip over the drain, where we were stripped and washed in winter. It feels impossible that Freya will not sweep in, throw me an apple, that Blue will not come through the back door, and chuck her shoes out into the garden, that the others are not simply elsewhere in the house.

I spot new things: a radio, postcards with writing I can't read.

—Have you been up to the attic? I ask.

We sit at the table. Toby closes a notebook hurriedly.

—No. No, I haven't been up there, he says.

I gesture at the notebook.

—Is it Freya's? Does she say anything about me?

—No, it's mine.

—Yours? When did you learn … that well?

—Oh, straight after I left. I'm writing … just some thoughts, about my childhood. It's part of, a thing, it's … He blinks around the kitchen. —I talk to someone, about things. I've always done it, since I left. It's good to order my thoughts. You should, he says.

—I can't write very well, I say. —I wish I could've come with you, where you went.

—I don't know, he says.

—I hated being on my own.

—Yeah, it was hard at first, he says.

A wish that Toby wasn't here at all rushes through me. I wanted to see them all, but I realise I don't want this man, flaunting his suit and his ring and his *Just thought I'd see* at me, like he's never even thought of it until now; I want *my* Toby, in his stained and ripped t-shirt, with his hair wild and matted, and his hand swinging next to mine, easy to take.

—Where were you? I know you didn't try to find Valentina, I say.

—No, he says. He doesn't ask how I know. —I went to live with my gran on my dad's side. When it happened, the police looked me up and there were queries from my gran about me, so I went to stay with her. She was great to me, he says. —She was really great. We figured if Valentina wanted to she knew how to get in touch, but she never did.

—When it happened, I repeat.

It is dangerous, this.

—Yes, he says. —You remember.

I stand up, and the table shrieks against the flagstones, making Toby jump. He holds his hands up. —All right, he says, but there's a glint of satisfaction in his face, that makes me push the table again. —All right, he says again and again, until I sit down.

—It's good to come back here, he says.

I nod, eager to turn this way.

—Look, he says. —I'm standing in the kitchen, by the sink, in Freya's kitchen, and she's fucking dead. She can't hit me, she can't kick me, she's mute and cold and still somewhere, and Foxlowe is safe now.

23

Freya strokes me awake, her rough skin tickling my cheek. *Wake up, sleepy head*, she whispers, and Blue shifts next to me, pointing her toes in a stretch. She'll roll over and the mattress springs will creak and that is what will make me open my eyes at last. Still I keep them closed, keep them with me for a few more seconds.

I roll over to lie like a starfish. There's the attic Solstice beam, the whorls in the wood making their faces. *Look, Blue*. Neck cricked, I roll off the mattress, sending dust up into the air. Freya might have died in this bed. A terrified mouse shoots across the floor. *Get him, Jimmy*, I whisper.

Down the stairs, in time for breakfast, then we'll go outside, check on the goats, no, the goats are gone. Check on the trees, then.

In the kitchen, Toby is asleep in Kai's chair, his note-book open on the table. I go to read it, but I can't make much out, except my name.

—Hi, he says. He's still a light sleeper.

—Thought you'd gone.

—I was going to stay at a hotel, then I thought … so I slept in the car for a bit, but I got cold. It still works, he says, tapping the aga.

I'm not sure what to do with my body, so I sit at the table, to hide half of it.

—Look, I'm sorry, he says. —I don't want you to be upset.

It's so like the way Richard and Mel speak to me, stroking words, shushing words, that I claw my feet inside my trainers.

—I don't, he says.

He's struggling. I notice his hands are in his pockets and wonder if it's to hide trembling fingers. He takes a breath. —I don't blame you. You were only a child. We were all just children. It wasn't your fault.

He nods, pleased with himself. I picture him practising this with his *talking about things* someone, rehearsing the words into mirrors. I realise that he knew I would come here, that he came to say these things and be free of me.

—I met Valentina in London, I say. —She's called Charlotte now.

He leans forward in his chair, eyebrows raised. —Oh, you did? Oh.

He stands up, goes to the tap, which bursts a stream of brown, and he leaves it running.

—Oh, so. How is she? I knew that was her real name, my gran said. Did you, um. That's strange because Richard didn't say, on the phone.

—It was before.

—Before?

—I didn't live with Richard till a few years ago. I was on my own till then, I say.

He stops the tap, and dries his hands with a cobwebbed towel.

She told me she came here because of you, Toby. Because a man on a train nearly took you or hurt you, and she nearly let him, because a woman there told her she was a shit person, and because she planned to leave you here all along, that was always how it was going to be.

His hair, at the back, still sticks up fluffy, like Jimmy's around the neck. He's still drying his hands, rubbing the dirty towel on them like he's scrubbing them clean.

—She said she was sorry, that she missed you. She knew you were with your grandmother, so she knew you were okay, I say.

He turns, twists the towel into a long snake, then releases it, and it flops onto the side of the sink. He smiles.

—Sure that's a load of crap. But thanks.

I wait for him to do the same for me, an exchange of kind lies, to admit he used the wrong words last night, to say that he knew it wasn't really like that. Instead he rubs the back of his neck, looking around the room.

He writes silently at the table for a while, as I open cupboards, sift through Freya's life. I'm surprised to find childish treats: popcorn, a jar of chocolate spread, packets of crisps, things she never would have allowed when the Family lived here. Rain begins to dust the windows, and this with the rustle of Toby's pages and the simple fact of being home, of at least the two of us in this kitchen again, the warmth of the aga, lifts the weight of Freya and Blue hanging from my back.

After an hour or so, Toby looks up from his notebook. —We haven't been outside yet, he says. —Want to go to the goat shed? he asks, and I laugh for the first time since I left Mel's house.

The goats are long gone, the straw is dank and brown, but the light is the same, softened by the newspaper still stuck over the one window. We lie in the old place, not touching. Toby puts his coat down first, but I can feel the straw tickling the small of my back, something I'd forgotten.

—Let's talk about it, he says.

It is so easy, here, to sink into our old selves, talk as we used to, and I realise how alone I have felt, without him.

—You go first, I say.

—I just wish we'd gone, Toby says. —I wish we'd gone and taken Blue. We were so close to leaving. I think that would've been our last Solstice anyway.

I find the tip of his fingers. — I'm sorry, I say.

—I remember Dylan and Pet were screaming at Freya that day. They knew, though. We'd all seen it. Freya was crouching with you in her arms, and you were both just staring.

—I wanted it to just be us, I say.

—What?

—I wanted it to just be us, just us to leave together. But then I wanted us to all stay, for everything to be the same. I don't know, I say.

—Green, it was all ending anyway. We all would've left, once we got older. And the three of us would've stayed friends our whole lives, he says.

We lie for a while in silence.

—I miss you, Toby, I say. —Are you okay now?

He shifts on the straw. —No one's called me that for a long time, he says. —My name's Lucas now. I won't be named by Freya.

—No one calls me Green now either, I say.

—What should I call you now?

—I don't know, I say, and we laugh.

—Are you okay now? I ask again.

—I'm fine, he says. —I'm happy.

I count five breaths before he says, —But you're not okay now, are you? Under his breath he adds, —How could you be?

—It's better than it was, I say.

He turns to face me. Close up, his eyes are so unchanged. —You shouldn't rely on Richard, he says. —You never could.

—We're the grown now, I say, and he nods and kisses me, once.

—Come on, he says, and pulls me up to explore the back lawns.

The fountain is there, cracked and mossy, but the

shoal is gone, and the shrubs and rockeries have been swept away. The grass is matted as we go further from the house, towards the copse. I glance back to the house, winking in the winter sun. I pick a snowdrop, tuck it behind my ear, where it drips soily water. We pick at the grasses and weed flowers, and practise calling me by each one, to see what clings. When we find my name, it fits so perfectly, and I ask Toby to chant it with me, but he tells me he doesn't like to do ritual things now. I whisper the name to myself until it seeps under the skin. I'll carry this name until the end.

Before Toby drives away in the shining car, I tell him the name of the school where Charlotte was, in case he wants to find her. He writes it down in his notebook. I ask him to stay for the funeral; he's shaking his head before I finish asking. *Good to see you*, he says, but he bites his lip, and when we hug goodbye, we say we love each other, and he holds me a few seconds too long, until I whisper to him, —I will, I'll try to get better.

24

Now it is me and Foxlowe alone for the first time ever. I used to wish it like this, when I couldn't find an empty room, when I wanted to sit and be still but the party was raging and spilt upstairs, and my eyes itched for sleep.

Hunger builds, and I welcome it like an old friend, it helps me recall things. So I go back to the rubbish in the studios, and find a jumper I know, with thick knitted crosses, that I wore sometimes, sharing with Libby. I find a blue bowl that I drank goats' milk from. In the corner, near the foxes' den, there's a pile of Freya's paintings. There is one small sketch of a female shape, standing squat and fat, her bare arse flabby and wide. Underneath, in pencil, she's written *Self Portrait, Pregnant?* It's the same size as my photograph of her, and I take it back to my bag, still in the front hall, and slide it next to its sister.

As I'm leaning down I catch them in the mirror. He's brought her, holding her arms around herself, wrinkling her nose. She sees me before I can speak and gathers me up, her fingers pulling my hair. Richard stands to one side, looking at the floor.

—Love, my love, Mel says. —I'm so sorry. I made him drive us up.

She holds me at arms' length. —You look awful, you're all wet, you're hungry, are you hungry? Urgh, she says, —It *stinks* in here. She strokes my hair. —Let's forgive each other, she says.

I watch Richard over her shoulder. He's lifted his head and is drinking it in, slow and steady. He takes a few steps on the staircase. His hands in his pockets, so he doesn't have to touch anything.

—Thought you'd kicked me out, I say.

—No, no, just a row, says Mel. —Just a silly row. I was thinking, she says, as she puts her arm around me, —we could get another dog, if you like, company for Jimmy, maybe a puppy, we can go by Battersea on the way home —

—No, I say. —I'm staying, for a while. Until the funeral, anyway. The others might come.

—Okay. Come back to our hotel.

—No.

Mel reaches for my hair, to smooth it down, but I step back.

—Come and look around, I say.

—Oh, it's awful, she says. —It smells.

—Right here on the stairs, the middle landing, is my favourite place, I say. —And Freya's kitchen is down there. The gardens and the moor are that way. Let me show you.

Mel calls up the stairs to Richard. —Let's take her back. I can see she's struggling. Your pills are in the car, she says to me. Let's go back to the hotel, have a bath, watch a DVD.

—No.

—Okay, then we'll just go home, Jess.

She's steering me out of the door, where the ivy still clings. I'm twisting, but it's my words that untangle me.

—Don't call me that, I say. —Don't, it's not my name.

Later, we sit in the kitchen. Mel is wrapped in one of Freya's shawls, in the same chair Toby slept in. She rubs her hands together and blows into them.

—How can you stand it? she says. —It's freezing, you must've all caught your death.

—Yeah, god, it was always cold, Richard says.

Mel sniffs. We've both been crying, during our long, circling conversation about how I will move out.

Richard begins wandering around, touching Freya's things, opening cupboards and old boxes, just as Toby and I did. He calls out to Mel when he finds a shattered vase, blue and gold, taped up with sellotape, broken seams running like rain on glass, but she's dozing now, curled up by the aga. He holds the vase out to me.

—Do you remember? he asks, softly, to let Mel sleep.

I shake my head.

—I wanted you to have it, he says. —It's a ... Well, it was my mother's, a beautiful piece. I gave it to Freya to give to you and she smashed it. She was angry about something — can't remember what — and I taped it all back up for you, took me ages. Do you remember?

I shake my head again, bored. Instead I remember the last time we were together in this kitchen, so I risk a *Do you remember* of my own.

—When was the last time we were both here? I ask.

He stands up, puts the vase carefully on the windowsill. —Maybe a specialist could fix it properly, he says.

—Must have been before you left, to go after Libby?

—No, he says.

He'd looked terrible, that last time. An outsider sat beside him at the oak kitchen table, yellowing papers spread out. I'd come from the back of an unfamiliar car, been given tea that burned my mouth, and I probed the flabby wound behind my teeth all night. So even though it was Richard and not one of my closer ones, it was still one of the Family and he was back and the only thing not completely strange that day, so I went to him when he held out his arms. His whole face was swollen, red and sore, but his body looked shrunken, suddenly old. He knelt beside me, said my name, said Blue's name, pressed my head to his shoulder. I'd never been so close to him before, smelled the soap and mint and the must of the old clothes he liked to wear, the tweed. —Sorry, I'm so sorry, he'd said, getting stuck and stuttering on the word.

—Where's Freya? the ungrown me had asked.

—Gone, he said.

I couldn't reply to this.

He nodded at the outsider sitting at our kitchen table.

—We're going to leave too, he said. —All of us.

—Come and look around with me, I say to Richard now, remembering the arms of the younger him encircling the broken and frightened ungrown me.

So we go wandering through the rooms. He touches things like I did, and when he finds a bracelet in the yellow room, left on the floor, he picks it up and puts it on.

—Was it hers? I ask. —I don't remember it.

—Libby's, I think, he says, and he kisses it.

Then in the studios he stands for a long time and I poke around in the alcoves until he turns and his eyes are wet.

—Toby was here, I say quickly.

—Yeah? Good man. How is he?

—He's called Lucas now. He's great. He wears a suit. He's married, he talks to someone about everything, he writes it down, he's fine. He wasn't alone afterwards, I press. —He had a family to go to, and he's fine now.

Richard looks so small, so sad and so cold in the stinking room.

—I hate you, I say.

His eyes flick about in panic, but eventually come to rest on mine.

—I thought it would be, this wonderful thing, this wonderful childhood, we thought you would be so happy, I thought it was the best thing I could do, he says.

—I was happy, I say. —I really was.

—It was a disaster, he says.

—I don't remember it like that, I say, and this time he doesn't argue with me or make me try to remember differently. He just swallows and wipes his cheeks dry and says, —Good. I'm glad you remember it that way, then.

—You should never have kept me away from Freya, I say. —I would have been all right, if you'd just let me see her.

—Look, she agreed not to see you, Richard says. —But you can have Foxlowe now. It's yours.

—Freya agreed … to never see me?

—She agreed, as long as she could live in this house until she died.

—But she wrote to me, I say.

Richard takes Libby's bracelet off, places it gently on the windowsill.

—Well, that's … He struggles. —She did love you, in her way.

A thousand questions come: *Where are they, Where is my family, Why did you leave, Why did you come back, Did you realise I didn't have a fucking clue what was happening, and that I was all alone?* But in the end I summon up the courage to ask something else.

—Where was Freya when they found her?

—I don't know, he says, surprised.

But he looks out of the studio windows, across the gardens to the henhouse.

Finally I go to the attic. It is changed and empty. The bed is different; no, it's the same bed, different covers, the red and blue blankets are gone. Wait, the Cancer box is here, restored and refilled, on the shelf as it should be; the books we couldn't read are stacked on the bottom shelf. The light is old light, I smell burnt bread and unwashed hair and sweet damp and I'm home at last, and I find Blue, her leg tethered to the bedpost like a rotting balloon, and Freya beside me, something in my hand, and then there is a long moment of something peeling away, a page of the book turning, slipping into place.

—I won't take the house, I tell Blue.

—That's good, she replies. —We can all be Leavers.

PART 3

Green

25

Freya's yell was a sound for blood or broken bones. The Family came running, some still holding the chipped cups of wine in their hands. Toby and Blue came too, and everyone looked around at each other. Seeing all the Family was safe, they relaxed, and all turned to Freya for her to explain.

—We've been complacent, Freya said. —The Bad has outwitted us. We've been housing it right under our noses. It's so clever we didn't even see it.

—Freya, Dylan said. —It's all right, we're all all right.

—I sensed it. I've been trying to manage it, but it was so much worse than I thought, Freya said. —It's used infants before, remember? But this time it sank so deep we didn't see it so clear. Now Green has told the truth. Blue was outside the salt line, her first Scattering. The Bad passed right through her. Remember the way she screamed that night?

All the blood drained from Blue's face, and as though it flowed into his skin, Toby went red. Blue took a steadying breath, and took Toby's hand, and I hated her.

—It was years ago, Ellen soothed.

—It's been calling her out on the moor ever since, Freya said. —We've tried to heal her but she keeps being called. She belongs to the Bad. And now it's made her into a Leaver.

Intakes of breath to this. Wine and smoke exhaled sour from everyone. Dylan spoke. —Oh, Blue, don't go, we love you. We're your family. We all forgive you.

—Don't do this, said Pet.

—We can't just let her go, Freya said. —You don't understand.

—Blue's just a child, Ellen said. —We can't let her go. What would we say to Richard?

—We know what to do, Freya said. —We'll start with the Spike Walk, and then—

—No, said Blue. —I'm not doing the Spike Walk.

—We *are* Leaving, Toby said.

—With Green, said Blue. —Green is coming too.

Freya laughed, but her voice was small. —Is that so? she said. She moved down the stairs, into the Family group, who were leaning against the banisters, some swaying.

—No, I said.

Toby and Blue tried to take my hands, and Toby whispered, —Don't be scared. Remember the story, it can be just like that. It will be easy.

Freya caught the whispers, took a step back towards them. They cowered. —The story? What have you been putting in her head? she shouted, and I felt, underneath all the betrayal and hurt, the old pride, that I was Freya's, that she would always look out for me, no one could hurt me, not ever.

I turned to the Family, their glassy-eyed stares.

—It's true, I said. —She's had the Bad from the beginning. It was mine and Toby's fault, but she's been infected all along.

—Shut up, said Toby.

—That Winter Solstice when she came, remember I named her, and I took her out to the salt line, and I—

Freya jerked her head, a warning to lie. What I'd done was enough to turn the Family against me.

—But there was a gap, I said, —so she was outside the salt line, and the Bad got in and took her, and it's been there ever since. It's not Toby, I said. —Please don't hurt Toby, hurt her instead, it's all her.

Blue's face went slack, like pinned hair taken down before sleep. Freya went to Blue and took her face in her hands, shouldering Toby out of the way. Blue reared back but Freya held her fast, pressing a thumb into Blue's throat.

—My girl, she whispered. —We have to save you.

We scrubbed the attic door with vinegar, laced the upper landing with salt. The Crisis was on everyone's lips, and we told it and retold it, each with our own version: some dwelling on the colour and shape of things, others simple, the facts. Lighting candles along the staircase, hanging torches from the beams, we strayed to all the stories of the Bad we knew, to try to find some kernel of knowledge we had forgotten. We listed All The Ways Home Is Better to each other, because we knew what was coming would make us need to remember the list. We played music, as though Solstice had already come. Freya had locked the attic door, with Blue inside, and she howled and flung herself against it, and we heard crashing sounds of the room destroyed, and nodded to each other: This is just how the Bad sounds, it is rage, it is confusion, it is violence.

Toby didn't tell stories or scatter salt or light candles. He crouched outside the attic door, inside the salt, and shouted to us that he must have the Bad too, then, and we should lock him up with Blue, if that's how Foxlowe worked now, if people were not free to be Leavers, and that I, Green, was a liar and a bitch, and the salt line crossing never happened. We ignored him, spoke louder, scrubbed harder.

I named her, I was responsible, so it was me that had to do it, the first night. I wore a garland around my neck to protect me, and our strongest flashlight hung from my waist. She started sobbing as soon as we opened the door. Around her, all our life was wrecked: the Cancer box smashed on the floor, Freya's sketches all torn up, the knitted blanket she'd made for us bitten and torn. I stopped feeling afraid of the Bad, felt only hate, that it had come and destroyed the two people I loved most, apart from Freya, and had poisoned us from the very beginning. This was my chance to undo what I'd done, that freezing night when she was a baby and lay with the night air and the Bad swirling all around her.

The wax burned my own arm like an echo. Burning flesh smells sweet, like the gardens in high summer, or forgotten and rotting fruit. She fought hard but Freya was holding her down.

In the morning, the dawn sun showed up the yellow room's faded wallpaper and the coat of dust on the furniture, with the Blue-cot drawer missing. I eased off the mattress, broken springs digging into my back.

The ballroom was cold and full of snores. The group slept in rings, holding hands, feet on chests, the best way to sleep. Freya was curled into Dylan's arms, too tall, her feet stuck out from under the blanket they shared. I felt a surge of love for home. I took a honey cake abandoned by the window with a half-drunk glass of wine, and tiptoed away.

It was always hotter up here. Now there was something else, like there was too much breath, clogging up the air. I'd always known about the Bad in Blue, had slept next to it almost all her life, but now it was spoken to all of us, and was made real, I was afraid. I touched the attic door for a while, listening for steps following me up. Somewhere down in the house, a door shut.

The keyhole was low, far under the doorknob, so I had to squat to see through it. My knees cracked. I pushed against the door, kneeling in the salt, and looked at the tiny metal bar that kept me out. I'd never seen a locked door before.

The edge of the bed, and the ceiling, but Blue was hidden. I shifted to the side until I could see her. Small, asleep. The blankets bunched up in the wrong places. Her leg was propped up on pillows, bent away out of sight. Her fists were clenched in the sheets.

I sank back, sat against the door, and stroked the wood there. I missed the attic, our place, wished I could open the door, lie where I was used to sleeping, whisper to Blue in the darkness, wake to watch the sunbeam approach the Solstice knot in the beam over our heads.

I turned, and Blue's eye loomed up at the keyhole. I fell back, shocked, and then laughed.

—Oh, Blue, you scared me, I whispered.

A thump as she moved. I looked again, and she was squatting back, her leg sticking out straight, sweat sheen on her face as she cocked it to one side.

—Green?

—It's me, I said.

—Get away! Don't come in!

—Don't be scared, I said. —I'm just here to talk, to see if you're all right.

—Let me out.

—I can't, I said. —I'm so sorry, it's all my fault. I'm sorry. I brought you some honey cake, but I don't know how to get it through the door, I said. —Does it hurt?

—Please, she said. —I don't have the Bad. I just want to—

—It's not all the time, I said. —I know that, but it is there, Blue, Freya's right, and I'm sorry I had to tell them, to tell you. I know it was a shock about when you were a baby—

—I knew, Blue said. —Toby told me.

—Oh, I said. —How could you go behind my back like that? I said, hurt welling up. —How could you make a plan to be Leavers without telling me?

—Knew you'd tell Freya, she said. —We were waiting for you to decide to come too.

—I wouldn't have told, I lied.

—Did she send you up here to find out things?

—No.

—I can't believe you burned me, she said, not angry, but with real shock.

—It's the best way to bring you back, I said. —It's Solstice soon, then everything will be all right.

—Let me out. Please.

—It's all going to be okay, I said.

I moved away from the keyhole just in time as something hit the door there, a piece of old Foxlowe bread, cascading spores of green exploding against the door.

Blue's cries rose in tantrum spirals until her voice was making one long wail. I hid behind the door of the first back room as Freya hurried up, took the key from her apron. I glimpsed her haul Blue up by the arms, a shock of pain draining Blue's voice as her wounded leg dangled, before Freya kicked the door shut behind her.

In the kitchen, Dylan sat on the aga with his legs swinging and gave me a weary salute, which stretched into a yawn.

Freya came in. She'd found some make-up somewhere, so her eyelashes stood out, made her look startled. She'd smudged some yellow stuff under her eyes, but it didn't hide the shadows there.

She stroked my hair, told me to make breakfast.

The eggshells caved without the satisfying crack I liked, wilting, their thin membranes underneath snapping like spit.

—They're old, I said.

In the bowl, red clots clinging to the yolks.

—Don't be a baby, Freya said. —No squeamishness now.

I turned back to the eggs in silence. We ate breakfast together, the three of us. Others drifted in and out, to fill jars with water and drain them at the sink, or hunt for matches, or light stub ends from Dylan's glowing paper. Toby came in once, his face a mask, his old silence returned, and the only way I knew he'd seen me was his ears turning red and his hands clenching, just for a moment, into fists. I'd have to wait a while, until Blue was healed, for him to forgive me, but then he'd betrayed me too, so when we came back together, things would be equal.

No one sat with us, Dylan, Freya and me, or talked very much, so we had a kind of peace, and I thought how much I loved Dylan, his oak trunk bulk, and how Freya was calmer when he touched her waist than she was when Richard was here, when her body was wound up tight, and we never knew if she would laugh and dance, or cry and throw things.

I felt the Bad must be stuck with Blue in the attic. It couldn't get out into the sunlit kitchen and poison the simple good things like the eggs with their flecks of garden parsley and Dylan's gentle touch on Freya's arm.

26

We hurt her every midnight, the darkest hour, when the Bad is strongest. We couldn't risk the Spike Walk, knew we had to contain the Bad in the attic, so Freya prised a nail away from the wall, and we used that. Blue's leg was red and angry with the nightly flames and cuts, and I knew the Bad would be thrashing under her skin, and when Solstice came it would be weak, and forced out. Freya said so, and then we'd have Blue back again, and Toby too, and everything would be righted. Every night I would plan to visit her at dawn, in the weak light before the Family stirred. But every morning I woke to the smell of fresh bread and the sound of the Family clattering about; at night, I lit the candles and drank wine and laughed hard with the others, until the grandfather clock chimed its longest, and we went to her, and then it wasn't Blue we saw, not the one I could talk to through the attic door, but the spitting, writhing, screaming figure of the Bad, finally surfacing.

Afterwards, late into the night, the banisters thrummed with thumps from the attic, and we took to lying on the mattresses in the garden, Freya saying it was too hot to sleep inside, swatting away the gnats. If we had to go inside, to fetch drinks or to nibble on bits of cake left swarming with ants, we held our breath and came back quickly, like it was underwater, and Blue's cries could drown us. I'd remember my plan to visit Blue just as I fell off the ridge of sleep, like a yank by the hair, but it was easier to keep falling, and make a new promise to go in the morning.

We took down curtains to let the sun path through, and colours lit up bright; forgotten corners made sun traps for the lolling dogs. At night, candles flickered in every room, softening sharp edges, holding us all suspended in a glow like we lived in the frame of one of the old paintings upstairs. The garden came inside; just like Blue's first winter, pine on the floors, flowers twisted around the banisters, thick leaves tied around every doorknob. Lavender crushed underfoot. Freya scattered it all down the stairs, and along the corridors, covering the dark spots on the wood. There was even elderflower, from the copse near the moor, swimming in sugar syrup to make a cordial.

Everyone at Foxlowe has two names, two selves. Now I saw the Family's lost selves struggling, in tiny ways. Remember, I had no old self to peel away. The grown peeled at their own skin and bit their lips to bleeding. They chain smoked and drank moonshine at breakfast. The tiniest bickerings, over soap or roll up papers, blew into screaming arguments. Kai was the loudest. He ranted and shouted and once he even pushed Freya. She asked him questions in turn, things he should know; when he couldn't answer, she laughed, and he retreated to the back of the house. Toby had gone into silence again, after that first night, and shrank away from the Family, until it was like he'd become a Leaver after all. I knew the Solstice would heal him too.

Thing is, when you live like we did, it's hard to resist the pull of the shoal. So there were tiny signs: fists bunched in clothes, lower voices, and lines of worry etched on foreheads; but the easiest thing to do is wait it out and see what the group will do, as that is how we've been trained. I see people speaking out all the time in the outside world, though not as much as you'd think. They might intervene in a shop when a kid is getting slapped around, say, or if there's a fight on the bus. But then they can walk home, if they are lucky enough not to get bloodied up. They can go to *their* group, who will agree with them, who will say, *Yes, you were right*. But we were the home, we were the group, and there was nowhere to go if you were on the wrong side of the invisible lines, if you were pushed out of the shoal, except out in the cold and the place where there were jobs and old hated families and whatever terrible things out there had made them come to Foxlowe in the first place. As for me, the outside was a murky dream, and my half wish to become a Leaver was gone. I'd say anything, do anything, to stay where Freya was, to shore up the walls against the outside.

Solstice dawned perfect; the beam in the attic would be glowing. We'd slept in the gardens, and Freya went in to gather up the Jumble. We threw clothes across the grass. I wore Libby's pink sundress, hanging from my hips, plastic sandals we passed around on hot days. I plaited my hair and made a daisy chain for a wreath. Good enough, I hoped. Toby didn't change, keeping on his crumpled t-shirt and ripped jeans.

We had to go inside then for water and breakfast. We went through the back door into the kitchen, bringing fresh roses and sweet pea, to strangle into Solstice wreaths. I saw the Family note the silence, glancing around to place the change, then realising, and looking up, as though the sudden quiet was visible, or Blue's sounds had been lost in the air.

—It's quiet, Pet said.

I went into the hallway. I stared up towards the attic, where Blue's thumps and cries were silenced. The sun through the stained glass bathed the hall and staircase in blue. Freya came to pull me by the hand, back to the kitchen.

—Happy Solstice, my love, she said. —We haven't said that yet today, have we? It will be the best yet. Look at that sun! It means, she said, lowering her voice, —it can't fail to work.

—It's gone quiet, I said.

—You look pretty, she said. —Really, you do.

I fingered the slimy leaves of roses cut from the west wall, stalks putrefying into green mush. I twisted them, tied the stalks. Freya squeezed my shoulder, and I knew that soon me and Blue would be ourselves again, she'd be healed like Kai was, not only her skin but the sickness of pining for the outside, she would be returned to us, and everything would go on as before. This dark time coming to an end, perhaps even Richard and Libby returning soon, suddenly seemed as real as Freya's rough and callused skin against mine. We'd make a story for it, and Blue would tell it herself, when she was grown.

Solstice, before sunset, is all about eating. The garden was timed to deliver at Midsummer, so everything ripened for the right week; or if not, it would be taken into jams and chutneys, or dried out, to eat with honey. There should be fresh-egg cake and bread with goats' cheese, apple wine, beer brewed in the goats' shed that tasted like rainwater.

Freya gave out tasks: measuring, flouring, mixing. The Solstice stores were opened up and we laid out the goods; others were sent into the gardens, to fill baskets with the fresh food we hadn't been allowed to touch. Among it all, Pet and me ended up side by side working on bread, kneading it and passing it between each other. The Bad circled and circled, like a dog trying to lie down. I knew it had no power today, but I couldn't help seizing Pet's hand, and pushing my head next to his, so his hair tickled my cheek.

—It's all right, isn't it? I said. —The Solstice will make it all right, won't it?

He shook me off. —Like Kai, he said.

After we'd gorged on the breads and fruits and stew, licked goats' cheese and sugar syrup from our hands, passed cakes around, and spilt wine down the table, the day swooped into a swooning heat that called us back to the gardens, on our backs on the lawns, swigging from bottles, watching the clouds bloom and shrivel. We liked to be in the fresh air, sunning our skin, that was the reason, we said.

I think we slept, listening to the snuffling of the dogs and flicking bees away, our skin stinging with Solstice sun heat. I wanted to bring Blue out here, lie her in the strong Solstice light. Surely the Bad couldn't stand it. But I knew I couldn't go up to the attic without Freya. My hand was curled into Dylan's, who murmured pieces of story to me, or to himself, and Freya came closer, laid her hand on my head, stroked my hair lazily. Even Kai lay with us, his hands over his eyes. Toby paced amongst the oaks, waiting for the double sunset, but the rest of the Family dozed together, as though everything was simple and happy.

Soon our shadows stretched across the grass and the sun began to sink. We gathered up blankets and smokes and wine, and began to move to the Standing Stones.

Freya watched us, nodding slowly. —So then, she said.

—Are you fetching her? Pet asked.

—I'll … Yes, of course. I'll be right back with her, she said. —Why don't you all go down to the Stones now, and I'll bring her.

But she didn't move, her face set, and I saw how her fingernails were digging into her palms. Panic began to scrabble around inside me, but then she held out her hand for me and we turned, walked slowly into the house. Behind us, the Family was still, until I heard Dylan's voice. —Come on then, and they walked away from us, the sky bruising behind them.

Freya's hand was limp and I tried to make up for it with a strong grip of my own, tried to hurry her along. We came through the kitchen door and were plunged into Blue's silence.

—Green, Freya said. —You know I love you very much.

—Yes, I said.

She leaned on the doorframe as we came into the hallway, looked around at the stained glass and the shining wooden panels, took a deep breath of the Solstice flowers. We took the stairs one at a time, and it was the slow, solemn way of ritual walking, like taking the fruit and flowers to the Stones. The light swam into double sunset colours, the purples, the dark blues, so dark they were almost black. The sun must be sinking behind the first peak of the Cloud. Freya pulled me to the stained glass window, and I stood on tiptoe to witness the sun re-rise.

But you can only see it from the Standing Stones, and we couldn't hear the cheers of the Family as the light came back, between the peaks, suspended for long seconds, its rays bathing the whole moor, and flooding the fields, the oaks, right up to the walls of the house. We only saw the light fade, the sky darken. Freya was holding her breath. —Now, she said. —Now.

I was already crying by the time we came to the attic door, and Freya unlocked it to see what silences were there.

She was curled at the very edge of the bed, like she'd had to share, as before, with Freya and me. She'd kicked off all the layers we'd put her in, to try to sweat the Bad out, and she was naked, her skin pale and bright in the good, Solstice light.

Freya gave me a small push to go to her. Her leg had gone off, like meat left in the sun. I hadn't seen it in full light before, and now I saw how deep were the cuts, the shine of the burns. Around the wounds from the Spike Walk nail, red flared out under the skin, ran in lines down to her ankles and up to her thighs. I followed the lines. —Is it the Bad, under the skin? I asked, and Freya nodded.

I touched Blue's still face. The black eye Freya had given her, that first night I told her the truth, had gone down, leaving a smudge there, as though she'd just gently stroked her face with fingers covered in charcoal. All the burn and slick fever was gone; she was cold. I remembered her first night, the ice of her ear, and how high she'd screamed, from the very beginning.

We buried our fingers in Blue's hair, spoke to her, told her to wake, begged her to, for an endless time. —It's Solstice, we said. —The double sunset has driven the Bad out, now come back, come back, come back.

Freya rocked back on her heels, then stood.

—We were too late, she said.

Her eyes seemed to have sunk into her face, completely black.

—If we'd had time to get her to the Stones, she said.

It was only a tiny second that I hated Freya, wanted to hit her, kill her, tear her skin with my teeth. But that second is a strange thing; like the shock of light when a torch is switched on in dead night. I remember it so clearly. After it passed, I tried to make myself feel that Blue was gone, but it wasn't real.

So I told it to Blue, like a story, and tried to make all the things it meant feel true. We will never talk to each other again, I said. You'll never see another Solstice, we'll have to do winter and next summer without you. And all the Solstices ever after you'll be gone.

Freya spoke to her too. You'll never age, she said. You'll always be ungrown. You'll never be a Leaver.

Epilogue

Foxlowe is warm and full of strangers now. They walk through the rooms, stroking the wooden panels and reading from laminated cards, or taking photographs of the staircase as it twists down from the third floor.

I drive myself this time, in the car I bought with my own money. The lessons were easy and it's one of my favourite things to do now: take the car out past the heath and switch on the radio and drive.

Richard didn't want me to go. —It's all very different now, he said. —And you'll have to pay to see inside. But once I said how it was going to be he didn't push it. And Mel only asked me if I wanted to stay for dinner. I went back to my own place.

There is a car park where the front lawns used to be: clean gravel, chalk-white. The entrance has been moved, plastic panels around our old door, to protect the stonework. The lady at the kiosk hands me an audio guide, and asks me to please keep behind the red ropes.

It is as though my book, *The Secrets of Pompeii*, has been made in reverse: there is the covering, a new film laid over the page, so I can't find the past anywhere. Velvet curtains and new wallpaper, the banisters polished to a gleam. I walk without holding my arms around myself; there are radiators in every room. Some new white doors have been put up, marked *Private*. I listen to the audio guide, all about Richard's family, and mine, I suppose, but I switch it off when it talks about the time I knew, using words like *neglect*. In the ballroom, a thousand Meetings and parties and secrets are buried under a shining chrome refit, the hiss of boiling water, scones and sandwiches, tablecloths and cakes.

In the attic, I stand at our window and look down on the front lawns, where the dogs raced, and the car took Leavers away. The bed has been taken out, and all our things. Instead a playroom has been set up, Victorian, the guide says, lace frilled dolls and a dollhouse. I can't find Blue anywhere. I'm glad for her, that's she's got out.

I have to buy another ticket to get into the gardens. A wheelbarrow with a pair of gardening gloves leans against the red brick wall, where posters advertise concerts and picnics, along with today's event, a special late opening. People meander along new paths cut between flowerbeds and laze on benches placed in the shade of the oaks. The fountain is gone. In its place is a sundial, circles and stars etched into the copper top. I go to feel the hot metal and the strong sun reflects back onto my cheeks. Reaching for a stone, I think I'll carve a mark here, stake my place, but the copper is an even gleam, and I don't want to scratch it.

A woman reading on a bench catches my eye. She's under the tap where Blue and I once bathed in a heat wave. I try to imagine she is one of my lost ones: Libby, or Ellen; but she is too young to be either of them now. I sit next to her. —Hello, I say.

She smiles, says hi without looking up.

—Do you live around here?

She marks a place in her novel. —Yes, she says. She sets the book aside. —I'm so glad they opened the house up.

—Yes, I say. —It's a beautiful place.

—You local?

—I used to live at Ipstones, I lie.

—Oh! I know it. Pretty place. Did you go to the primary there? My mum taught there! Mrs Pastell, maybe not your time?

—Yes, I think so.

We watch the tourists weave around the paths, and I ask the woman if she knows the day.

—It's a Sunday, she says, reaching for her book.

—No, I say. —I mean, it's the Summer Solstice today.

—Oh, she smiles again. —Yes, well, happy Summer Solstice. She laughs. —Are you staying for the talk?

Two girls run over the lawns to her, one barely out of toddling stage, another with two thick plaits and wearing dungarees.

—Been exploring? their mother says. —What did you find?

The younger one scrambles on her lap, hugs her hard, kicking me in the hip.

—Sorry!

I smile and wave the apology away.

—Hello, says the older girl.

—Hi.

Let me tell you a story, but I can't say that, I've learned; stories on the outside are not freely given, and you can wait to be asked but it takes a long time. Mel has listened to some of mine, but in the same way she listens to the radio: background noise. She won't pass them on as you should.

The garden shadows grow wide. A grey-haired man wearing a green tweed jacket, like one of Richard's, and carrying a clipboard, calls over from the sundial.

—Our talk and viewing will begin in fifteen minutes!

We go over to him, the younger girl in her mother's arms, the elder holding her plaits like her own reins.

The man is a local historian, he says, delighted to be able to show us this local phenomenon at last, now that the house and gardens are public. This is the best place to view it, though we may have seen it from other vantage points across the region. As we walk down to the Standing Stones, he tells his own version of the double sunset story, much older than the story I knew and without the Bad anywhere at all, and books written about it, and archaeologists mapping the way the stone circles on the moor seemed to make a line to the house, which Freya could have told them.

—We can assume there used to be rituals around it, perhaps a kind of charm against evil, he says.

Our copse has been cleared away and the stone wall is gone. A new gravel path leads all the way to the Standing Stones. They've been cleaned, smooth mottled grey, and the grass around them is clipped so the moor is almost bald. The two little girls run shrieking between the Stones, until their mother calls them, and they lean together against a stone, her arms around their shoulders. I move near to them, my hand close enough to take the smallest girl's in mine.

The man talks about the mechanics of the optical illusion, the degree angle of the peaks of the Cloud, and the tilt of the earth on Solstice day, the positioning of the Stones. The sun begins to dip behind the first peak. There is the familiar emptiness of my hand, where Blue's hand should be, and I wonder about the Family, where they are living now, with what kind of happiness or unhappiness.

Then, something wrong. The sun doesn't reappear, slips away. Only a few rays stream through the gap between the peaks. A collective good-natured groan goes up.

—Ah, says the man. —Maybe next year.

—Wait, I say. —It has to, it's Solstice. It isn't cloudy. Did you get the dates wrong? I turn on the man, who rubs his grey beard and smiles.

—Well, he says. —It doesn't happen very often, and if it does—

—That's not right, I say. —That's not how I remember it.

He shrugs, and turns to a group of tourists, pencils and spiral-bound notebooks, asking questions, women's hair swaddled in scarves, cameras hanging from wrists.

The woman from the lawns has picked her younger daughter up, and wandered to the edge of the Stones with its view out over the moor. The elder still leans against a stone, sucking her hair.

The draining light washes the lawns in their familiar Solstice glow. Now the Solstice stores should be opened up; there should be wine, and honey cakes, and we should light the candles and play music and throw the windows open to the summer air. The healed should be brought into the ballroom and Blue out from the attic and her burnt and mangled flesh should be made whole and smooth, her arms thrown around our necks, and we all ourselves again. The old scars on Blue's arms would be invisible now, and her eyes returned to their baby selves, changing colour, brown to blue to orange flecks in the light. Gone would be the snag she makes beneath my ribs with every breath. I watch the three ungrown ghosts weaving threads amongst the lost long grass around the Stones.

—Ever seen the double sunset before? I ask the plaited girl.

The girl looks at the ground, shy. —Once Daddy tried to take us to see it from Leek churchyard, but the clouds were too thick.

—Can I tell you a story?

She shrugs. —Okay.

—I have to tell you at the henhouse, though, that's where it happens.

—I didn't see a henhouse.

—You did.

She bites at the skin around her thumb, winces when blood comes.

—Don't you want to hear? I say, gently pushing her away from the Stones, and back along the path.

She shakes her head and I take her chin, tilt it. —Don't lie, I say. —Stories are everything. It's how we know about the Bad. It is everywhere on the outside, so you're soaked in it.

I move my thumb to her throat, press it there. The girl goes limp and pliable, like early summer grass. I begin to pull her back down the path, away from the others.

—This is a story for Blue, I say, and as I lace our fingers together in the old way, Freya's fingers ghost into my grip; her voice finds my tongue and makes it her own.

Acknowledgements

Heartfelt thanks to my agent Ed Wilson, whose encouragement and enthusiasm over many years made a Word document into a book. I'm immensely grateful that *Foxlowe* found a home with the fantastic team at Fourth Estate, and in particular with Anna Kelly, who has made this novel the best it could be with her brilliant insights. Thanks to Robert Lacey for his meticulous copy editing. Thank you to Jo Walker for the beautiful cover.

Thank you to the Arts Council England whose generous grant allowed me some time to research and write this book.

Thank you to my tutors and writing community at UEA, especially Giles Foden, Andrew Cowan, Trezza Azzopardi, and my workshop group, who tackled bonkers early drafts with enthusiasm and patience. Special thanks to those who have kindly continued to read and critique *Foxlowe* long after the course ended: Tom Benn, Safia Bhutta, Armando Celayo, Gordon Collins, Alex Ivey, Richard Lambert, Birgit Larsson and Vicky Rangeley. Thank you for your advice, time and friendship.

Thank you, Lynne Bryan at Words and Women, for giving me an early opportunity to read *Foxlowe* to live audiences and for being a great supporter of the book.

I'm indebted to Robert Milner for being a wonderful Staffordshire Moorland tour guide and storyteller; thank you for showing me the Sharpcliffe Rocks, the real 'Standing Stones', for climbing the Cloud with me on a blazing hot day, and for explaining how the double sunset works.

Thank you to the friends I have probably bored to tears talking about my writing over the years, in particular: Jon Ellison, Samantha Lawrence, Lucy Marx, Rowena Mason, Emma Phillips and Ruth Weyman. Thank you for being full of enthusiasm, even when my own was in short supply.

This is a strange book for me to have written, considering I have the most loving and supportive family imaginable. Mum, Dad, Matt, Juliet, Ben, Verity, Kate, Leander: thank you for rooting for me and for being my cheerleaders. Special thanks to my parents, to whom I owe everything, and who have been admirably sanguine about their youngest child's first novel being in part about terrible parenting. Special thanks too to Kate, who is the most inspiring heroine of a big sister a girl could ask for, and who has rightly not taken the twisted sister relationship at the heart of this book personally.

Finally, all my love and thanks to Armando: for living with this book ever since we met, for urging me on, for letting me use his best ideas, for filling our flat with inspiring books, and for always being ready to drop everything to talk writing.